THE MEDICINE LINE

JOHN HANSEN

*To my granddaughters Kristiana and "Gators" Sias,
in the hope that they will one day develop
a passion for reading.*

CHAPTER ONE

July 25, 1874
Eastern Nebraska

It was a little spit of a creek whose name neither of them knew. It meandered through coulees choked with cottonwood trees and willows. This lushness, this oasis of sorts, gave way to the steep sides of a coulee that did not last long before breaking off to the flat grasslands that stretched on to the next coulee. For a man to look out at this country it was at first monotonous but, by and by, if he listened close and realized he was alone, just him and the wind gently teasing the yellow grass and a meadowlark calling so sparingly as to suggest it knew there would be no response, it became intimidating. It could cause a man's imagination to go to work. It had happened to James Coumerilh. Earlier that morning he had mistaken a herd of buffalo way out there in the yellow infinity for a Sioux war party.

Billy Watkins' bit down on the piece of dried venison that he held in his hand and worked his head side to side until he came away with a mouthful. He began to chew while looking over at James sitting cross-legged on the ground near the edge of the no-name creek. He was, at last, finally able to swallow. "I believe this old deer is gittin' his revenge on me."

James uttered a polite laugh, barely audible, as he tossed the stick that he'd been scratching his initials in the dirt with into the creek. For a moment the stick seemed to hesitate and then it went on its way, not swirling much at all owing to the slow-moving nature of the muddy water. Without looking at Billy, James said, "I've ate worse."

Billy came back in a disbelieving tone, "Ya have?"

James snorted, "In the Army. Had to brush the maggots off some beef they gave us after a long spell of not eatin'."

"I didn't know you was in the army."

A surge of dread, close to anger, pulsed through James. *Like our cuttin' wood for the past three days entitled him to know that.* He said aloud being purposely cryptic, "I was."

Billy was quiet for a respectful time, "You fought in the rebellion?"

James did not look at Billy. Instead, he stared at his stick gently bobbing in the chocolate water getting farther and farther away. "Yeah."

Out of the blue it came wrapped in a southern drawl, "Well, was y'all on the right side?"

James now looked up from the J.C. in the dirt and stared hard at Billy for a few seconds, causing the plumbing in Billy's face to go awry. Before Billy could redeem himself, James cut to it, "We lost so I reckon not."

Billy frowned, "Don't mean it wasn't the right side."

James came back, his dark eyes locked on Billy's, "There's those that say providence has a hand in such matters."

Billy snorted, "You sayin' God sided with the Yanks?"

"Just sayin, that's all."

A smirk came over Billy's face. "Well Sir, I rode with Colonel Forrest and the 1st Kentucky Cavalry. And I'm here to tell ya we turned some Yankees under. If we'd had more leaders like Colonel Forrest, the headquarters of this here country wouldn't be on the Potomac." Billy, now clearly agitated, paused briefly before adding, "No Sir, it wouldn't."

James shook his head slightly, "It's not in me to gloat over the men I've killed."

Billy scoffed, "Are you fool enough to think they would have restrained their jubilation had the tables been turned?"

It was not where James wanted the conversation to go, but the tenor of it coupled with the cocky look in Billy's brown eyes and his black unkept moustache that hid his top lip were like quicksand. James stepped in, "The Yankees nearly put me under. To this day I feel the effects of their savagery. Even now my innards don't feel right."

"So, you was shot?"

"Bayonetted."

Billy grimaced. "All the more reason to hate those blue belly bastards."

"I gave as good as I got. I know I left my mark on some fellas that likely still have a reminder of that day."

"That day?"

Apprehension, regret that Billy had drawn him in took hold of James. He hated lying but it was the lesser of two evils. He came back as he had in the past when questioned about his war experience, "Chickamauga. It put me out of the war."

Billy laughed in the arrogant tone that became him, "You were lucky. Git wounded that early in the war and not git pulled back into it. Yes Sir, mighty lucky. Why I knew men that were wounded that went home for two or three months to mend and then came back only to have their luck run out and get themselves killed."

James looked away from Billy lest his eyes expose his shame. He said in a low voice, "Those were not good times."

Billy laughed as he stood up from beneath the big cottonwood where he'd taken his noon meal. He said louder than necessary, "Not like now. Woodhawkin' for the steamboats and dodging the Sioux." He laughed again, "Yes Sir, high times they are."

James felt relief that Billy appeared to be moving on from the war. His past, his secret, buried for a while longer he hoped.

Billy's demeanor abruptly became serious. "I'm thinkin' the warning they gave us this morning in camp about the Indians is sound advice."

James got to his feet. He frowned as he bit off a chaw of plug tobacco. "If those scoundrels upriver would quit tradin' whiskey and guns to 'em they might not be so cantankerous."

Billy snorted, "Whiskey might stoke their fire a little more but when it comes to killin' white men, I don't think they need any false courage."

James tugged at the brim of his black slouch hat adjusting it against the hot sun and then spit a dark stream of tobacco juice on the ground in front of him. He sighed, "I reckon we just stay vigilant and hope we see them first."

Billy shook his head, "I 'spect those boys who got bushwhacked out here last week were intent on doing that very thing."

James knew he was filling in behind dead men, but it didn't deter him. It was a long way to the Milk River country in Montana and he was broke. He came back with a hint of sarcasm as he reached for his Winchester leaning against a downed tree, "Well, I guess we could pack it in and go to town. Be a store clerk or some such."

Billy looked at James in mock surprise, "Well hells bells, why didn't I think of that?" He then walked off toward the tree he was working on falling, laughing as he went.

CHAPTER TWO

They put the bodies in the very bottom of the steamboat *Destiny* away from the wooden boxes of dry goods, grain, sacks of flour and sugar, tools, canned goods and a host of other things that one might find in a mercantile. It was all destined for delivery at Fort Benton, Montana as were three Holstein dairy cows and a sow and boar hog. There were six of them. Two men, one woman and three kids, none over ten years old. They were wrapped in canvas, new canvas taken from the goods destined for Fort Benton. It'd been the mate who had told the other family members they could use the new canvas but only after they said they'd pay for it. And so, here they were three days dead and ripening beyond the mask of the manure from the cows and pigs. The bodies lay stacked like cordwood in the vacant area next to the remaining hay and grain for the animals. But now there was a seventh body. A middle-aged man that died during the night up on the main deck. Turk, a scruffy looking deckhand with yellow teeth and a flat cap stared down at the dead man lying next to a cabin wall. Flies were crawling over the dead man's lips and open eyes. No one dared touch him for fear of contracting cholera and ending up stacked next to the hay and hogs below. Turk said to the mate, with some disdain in his voice, "This fella was a loner. Got on at a woodyard 'bout three days north of Saint Jo. You remember him, don't ya?"

The mate nodded, "Said he'd work for deck passage."

Turk scowled and turned his head to spit a dollop of tobacco juice onto the already grimy wooden deck before saying contemptuously, "I never saw him work. I tried to git him to help me once. He wouldn't do it. Said he'd been totin' wood and feedin' the firebox."

The mate moved on to the immediate problem, "So, he has no kin, no friends to tend to his body?"

"I reckon not."

"Well, he has got to go below with the others."

Turk shot a hostile look at the mate, "I didn't hire on to handle diseased corpses. Let the damned Irish take care of him. They brought this devil sickness with them."

By now a considerable number of deck passengers had congregated to see how the drama would play out. They were witness to Turk's insubordination but sympathetic to both men. The dead man had to go. He was in the midst of their sleeping and eating quarters, lying there on the open deck. But they were not the only ones waiting for the mate's response. From above them in the pilot's house came a shout, "Throw him overboard, Mr. Sherwood, and be done with it."

Startled, the mate looked up like he had received a command from God. The captain and pilot were standing side by side in the window of the pilot's house. The captain frowned and gestured angrily toward the railing. Sherwood nodded and looked back to the dead man and then Turk, "Help me carry him to the railing."

Turk's eyes were cold and vacant. "You can drag him yourself that far."

Sherwood thought to threaten Turk with his job but in the next instant he was already sensing the humiliation that he would likely be feeling when Turk defied him. He glared hatefully at Turk and then went quickly to the dead man like he'd finally worked up the courage to jump off a cliff into the river. He took hold of his feet and began dragging the corpse towards the railing. People gave him a wide berth. The man had soiled himself. The stench was overpowering. A woman looking on began to gag and turned away. The dead man's arms flailed out to his sides like a rag doll. His head and the backs of his hands danced over the rough wooden deck and through Turk's tobacco spit. His green eyes seemed to be calling out for mercy like he was aware of what was about to happen. At last, he and Sherwood were at the railing. There were three white pipe rails bordering the edge of the deck. The bottom one was just high enough for the dead man to squeeze under. Sherwood put his boot in the man's side and began to push when a deck passenger shouted, "This ain't right. You gotta at least say words over him."

Sherwood paused and looked back at the man. His clothing was dirty and disheveled, unlike the cabin passengers who were clean and neatly dressed. Sherwood's first impulse was to ignore him, but shame suddenly took hold of his tongue. He glanced down at the dead man and then looked at the crowd of deck passengers trying to not make eye contact with anyone in particular. His focus went beyond them to the stern where a negro woman was emptying a white chamber pot from one of the staterooms over the side. He began, "Lord, today we are sending this unfortunate soul back to you. His existence among us was painful. May you have mercy on his soul and grant him better days. Amen."

Sherwood allowed the collective Amen from the crowd to settle away for a few seconds before he gripped the top rail and pushed the dead man under the bottom one with his boot. Several young boys watched the body splash. They tracked its progress, pointing and shouting until their mother pulled them away. For a time, it floated and then it went under in the muddy water. In the crowd the father of one of the children stacked by the pig pen whispered to his wife, "They'll play hell doing that to our boy."

The woman winced as if she was about to cry, "We've got to get off this boat. Take Timmy with us and give him a proper burial."

The man nodded, "Next stop for wood and we'll do just that. I don't care where it is. This boat is cursed."

And on the other side of the boat, screened from view of the dead man's departure by the configuration of the accommodations for those passengers of means as well as the internal workings that powered the Destiny, were more deck passengers. A woman in a tattered blue gingham dress stood at the rail pulling on a rope. Hand over hand until at last a two- gallon tin pail of water came into view. She untied the pail but left the other end of the rope attached to the rail for the next person to use. And so began her preparation for supper.

CHAPTER THREE

As western army posts went, Fort Benton, Montana wasn't bad duty. It was recognized as the endpoint of water navigable by steamboat on the Missouri River. The town of Fort Benton was co-located with the military. As so often is the case where concentrations of mostly single men reside, entrepreneurs of vice; drinking, gambling and prostitution sprang up. Today, however, it was C Company's misfortune to be separated from this utopia while on patrol up near the Milk River. A rancher, his wife and two of their three kids had been murdered by Lakota Sioux. At least this was who the young ranch hand that discovered the atrocity believed it to be. It was Company C under the command of Captain Joseph Hettrick who now accompanied the surviving cowboy back to the burned ranch buildings and scavenged bodies of the rancher and his family. The cowboy, whose name was Otto Weiss, rode at the head of the column across from the captain. He pointed and shouted to be heard over the canter and occasional snorting of the horses, "It's just the other side of that ridge."

Captain Hettrick made eye contact and nodded but said nothing. He was not optimistic that this patrol would be any different than others in the past. But this time it had to be. This time it wasn't about a few butchered cows or some stolen horses or trading guns and whiskey to the

Indians. It was murder and kidnapping. This was a serious crime, beyond the ability of the U.S. Marshal in Helena to deal with as it had the potential to result in a lively gunfight, assuming the culprits were ever found. The breathing of the horses was forceful, stabbing at the air as they struggled to maintain their pace climbing the ridge. And then they sky-lined themselves, the captain figuring, and rightly so, that the Indians were long gone and that he would not be remiss in surrendering the element of surprise. Hettrick reined his horse to a stop and began to study the burned buildings some quarter mile below him in what would have been a bucolic setting had it not been for the death that hung over it. A slender string of aspen and willows defined the trickle of a spring that began on the hill above the house and corrals. The trees ran by the house, no doubt providing water to it and the livestock. Grass, green and abundant, filled the little basin. Hettrick was about to comment on the tranquility of the location when several ravens landed near the burned-out ruins and began walking around and pecking at the ground. For a moment it did not register with him but then his eyes teared a little and his vision sharpened. He could see something white, almost shiny in the grass that was short stubble. It suddenly occurred to him what he was looking at. A spontaneous frown came to his face. He made no attempt to suppress it as he looked at the cowboy, "You left these people to vermin?"

Even as he had loaded the words on his tongue Hettrick had envisioned the cowboy embracing his shame, but he did not. Instead, he came back defiant in his manner, "I dare say, Captain, had you been here that day all by your lonesome not knowin' if them murdering savages was gonna come ridin' over that ridge whilst you was waist deep in a hole with noth-ing but a shovel in your hands, you wudda skedaddled too."

Hettrick was taken aback by the cowboy's anger. Nonetheless, he parried, "It would have been the Christian thing to do."

Weiss shook his head in disbelief before launching a stream of tobacco juice into the space between his and the captain's horse. He then locked eyes with Hettrick, "Sir, I do not intend to surrender my life due to ignorance." And with that he nudged his horse down the slope towards the gruesome remains of a one-time dream.

The captain and his men followed in silence. They were an impressive sight riding in a column of twos, twenty horses deep. Their dark blue blouses, yellow striped pants and dark blue forage caps set them apart from the civilian packers that trailed behind them with a dozen heavily loaded pack mules. They rode more slowly now letting the horses pick their way down the steep slope. Apprehension showed in the faces of some. The new recruits mostly. And then they were there. The first sergeant hollering out "company halt." A soft breeze fluttered their guidon flag. With it came the smell of death. The captain could now see clearly what he had struggled to make out from up on the ridge, ivory-colored bones. Ribs, leg and arm bones and skulls. Save for a few tattered pieces of clothing, they were picked and licked and chewed clean. It was a macabre scene as none of the skeletons were intact. Bones were scattered for a good way in front of the house. *Must have got them at mealtime,* thought Hettrick. And then Weiss challenged the audacity of the ravens who had not flown away, he shouted from his saddle, "Go on you filthy sons-a-bitches. Git." The ravens did not leave. Angered, Weiss pulled his revolver and was in the process of thumbing back the hammer as he aimed at one of the big black birds when Hettrick, now concerned with maintaining the element of surprise, shouted, "Hold your fire Mr. Weiss. If there are Indians about there's no sense letting them know we're here."

For a long moment Weiss held his pistol out as if he still intended to shoot. Finally, in deference to the collective silence of 47 men he lowered his gun and jumped down from his horse. He did not look at Hettrick but walked quickly towards the ravens, shouting, "Go on, git."

Hettrick ordered a division of labor. There would be those who would gather the bones strewn about by the wolves and coyotes, and those who would dig the graves, and others that would make the wooden crosses. And then there were the lucky ones that got to help the packers unload the mules. With the exception of the cross makers, and those setting up camp, it was hard to say who had the better duty between the bone gatherers and the grave diggers. In spite of its pastoral appearance, the soil beneath the lush grass was cobbly causing no end of curses to be leveled at it by the troopers as they dug the requisite six feet.

The sun was no longer visible from the little basin when the graves were ready for the bones. They'd dug them next to existing graves out beyond the house and garden. Weiss had shown them where to dig. He'd said, *Their little girl, Ruth Ann, took sick a couple years back and died.* And then he nodded to a wooden cross no less plain than the girl's, *and that's their dog Bosco. Damned wolfers poisoned him last winter.* They made their best guess as to which bones belonged together and then, when Hettrick and Weiss were satisfied that they could do no better, they put them in the graves and began shoveling dirt on them. Their markers were crude, made from partially burned boards. Troopers, absent the emotion of kin, used their sheath knives to scratch the names of the deceased, their age according to Weiss, and the date they'd been killed. When the last of the dirt was shoveled over the bones Hettrick excused the remaining troopers. For some time, smoke from the cooking fires below had been teasing them with what awaited back at camp. Now they strode off bantering amongst themselves as to those possibilities. It left just the Captain and Weiss at the graves. The sun was nearly finished for the day. Shadow engulfed them. It extended clear across the basin to the far rim where a sliver of light hugged the horizon. In a way it was peaceful, serene almost. There was a smell of wood smoke and fresh dirt. The chatter and occasional shouts of laughter from the men below were mostly immune to the sorrow caused by the deaths of Amos Bellows and his family.

Weiss said, his voice soft and respectful of his adopted family's long sleep, "We ought to say some words over 'em, don't ya reckon?"

The captain looked down at the markers, all in a row, before him and Weiss. When he was on post, he and his wife, their two kids and their colored housekeeper, never missed a Sunday service. Nonetheless, he deferred, "You should Mr. Weiss. It should come from you."

Weiss shook his head, "I ain't much for words."

"Just talk to God. He doesn't need a flowery speech."

For a few seconds, the cowboy studied the captain's eyes. The matter was settled. He removed his hat as did the captain. His thick blonde hair rippled gently in the wind as he looked down at the graves and began, "Lord, these is good folks. They didn't deserve what happened to 'em. So, I hope you'll treat 'em right." Weiss paused like he was done but then he added, "And lord, I aim to git their daughter Sarah back and make this place whole again for her if she wants it, but I'm gonna need your help. Lots of it, I reckon. Well, I guess that's all I got to say. Thank you, Lord."

Hettrick, still holding his hat near his waist, said, "That was a fine prayer, Mr. Weiss."

Weiss nodded and then put his black wide brimmed hat on as they began to walk down the slope towards camp. He came back, "You should know, Captain, I'm intent on getting Miss Sarah back."

The implication of Weiss' words was not lost on Hettrick. He noted the anguish in his eyes. "You know the Indians have kidnapped a good number of white women, don't you? It's no easy task getting them back."

Weiss shot the captain an irritated look, "I'm no fool."

"I don't believe you are, Mr. Weiss, but reality is often a difficult pill to swallow."

"I'll grant you that, but I cannot abide Miss Sarah in the hands of those savages."

"It sounds like you are sweet on this young lady."

"I may be but my wanting to rescue her goes beyond that, Captain. It's just the right thing to do."

Hettrick felt slightly embarrassed. He came back conciliatory in his tone, "Without doubt, Mr. Weiss, it is. However, my cautionary approach in this matter stems from past experience."

Weiss stopped and looked at Hettrick, "You will help me, won't you?"

Hettrick nodded, "I will, but just know that I have other duties as well."

Still standing before the captain who was a head taller and twenty pounds heavier, Wiess angrily poked his finger towards him several times, he said emphatically, "If you'll pretend, Captain, that you're trying to get your wife back I believe your priorities will git in the proper order."

Hettrick's scowl was partially hidden by his thick black moustache and goatee. The words, *civilian upstart*, danced on his tongue but they went no farther.

CHAPTER FOUR

They'd slept under the night sky using their McClellan saddles and saddle blankets for pillows. The stars were in retreat, but not all of them by any means, when the sergeants roused the men. There was work to be done. Horses and mules were led to the trees to water at the little rivulet that was no wider than a tall man's step. But it was clear and icy cold. Back before Amos Bellows had built a storage cellar with blocks of winter ice bedded in sawdust lining its interior walls, his wife, Harriet, kept a five gallon can of milk in a depression that he had dug in the little creek. And nestled next to it was a tin pail with butter she'd churned. And in a gallon crockery jug there was tea. But those memories, like the people who had created them, were now ghosts to Otto Weiss.

By and by the cold fires from last night were rekindled. Soon the smells of coffee and frying bacon permeated the air. A gallon sized coffee pot suspended from a wrought iron tripod above the fire next to Captain Hettrick and Weiss was boiling furiously. Steam was rising up from it at a good clip. Weiss, who had been watching the coffee's maturation for some time, declared, "Captain, I believe that coffee has reached its prime."

Hettrick looked over at the cowboy and grinned. He could see, just barely under Weiss' wide brimmed hat, the fire's reflection in his moist eyes. He said, "My first sergeant will give me hell unless you can stand a spoon up in his coffee."

Weiss came back, his voice absent much of the tension that it had held last night at the graves, "Well Sir, I like a stout cup a coffee as much as the next feller, but by my observation this brew here is bordering on the consistency of molasses."

Hettrick laughed as he put a glove on his right hand and reached for the pot, "Alright, Mr. Weiss, we'll sample it." And then the captain lifted the pot off the hook beneath the apex of the tripod and turned toward Weiss, "Hand me your cup and I'll fill it."

Weiss looked down at a stack of tin cups sitting on top of a wooden box sized to fit a pannier. He picked up two and held them out while Hettrick poured. When both cups were full, he nodded, "Much obliged."

Hettrick set the pot on the ground next to the fire before taking his cup from Weiss' outstretched hand. Weiss was first to sample the boiling hot coffee. Even though his bushy black moustache buffered somewhat the heat of the coffee, there was no getting around the effects of the hot tin cup on his bottom lip. He cried out, "Damn, that's hot." He then looked over at the captain who was grinning and gently blowing on his coffee.

Hettrick said, "I guess you need to be in the army to recognize the limitations of tin cups."

Weiss shook his head, "I did my time in the army. Shudda known better."

Hettrick's grin dissolved, "You were in the war?"

Weiss nodded, "Same side as you."

"I take it one war was enough for you?"

Weiss snorted, "More than enough. The hell of it is, I can't seem to get away from it. It ain't like the rebellion out here but folks is gittin' killed regular like, whether it be the Indians or desperadoes wantin' your money."

The captain blew on his coffee again but did not try it. He said, "If we persevere, civility will come one day."

Weiss looked off to the east and the hint of light on the horizon. He said, without looking at Hettrick, "My fear, Captain, is we'll both be turned under before that happens."

Being a West Point graduate, Hettrick knew the history of war and mankind's propensity to never be satisfied with peace. And so, it occurred to him that he had misspoke. He now took a noisy sip of his coffee and grimaced, "I believe First Sergeant will approve of this brew."

Weiss did not follow the captain's purposeful digression. Instead, he went to what had been nagging at him since the day he discovered the Bellows family dead and Sarah missing. He said, "What are your plans to rescue Sarah?"

Hettrick was mindful of Weiss' attachment to the girl and the hopeful look in his eyes. Nonetheless, he did not feed those emotions with an unrealistic assessment of the situation. He said in a sober but compassionate tone, "What I have to offer Mr. Weiss is primarily force, men and guns. However, the Sioux are not easily intimidated. If it comes to a gunfight as the only way to recover Miss Bellows, she will likely be the first to die."

The flickering of comradery that was evident between them a moment ago was now gone from Weiss' face. He came back angrily, "So, you're not gonna do anything?"

Hettrick's response was quick and sharp, "I didn't say that but what I was leading up to is, as I see it anyway, is Miss Bellows is in a predicament."

Weiss' adrenaline overrode his common sense allowing his response to escape his mouth, "Well, any fool knows that."

Hettrick sighed and shook his head. He then purposely took a sip of coffee allowing Weiss' choice of words to hang in the air between them. He caught Weiss' eyes so he would know the gravity of what he was about to say, he began,

"The Sioux are off their reservation. They have committed serious crimes. I have no choice but to track them down. If this was a matter of them trespassing on the Blackfeet or Assiniboine reservation to hunt it might have been resolved by smoking their pipe and talking. But they've gone too far. Settlers hereabouts will want justice, and rightly so. Therein lies the problem, as your Miss Bellows will be in the midst of the violence that will likely accrue. So, Mr. Weiss, there is a plan. Not necessarily mine but rather it is what the times demand."

Weiss was somewhat taken aback. He was silent for a moment as he sieved the captain's words trying to find something good in them. At last, he said, "Maybe you could parley with them. Accept Miss Sarah in exchange for the Sioux going back to the reservation."

Hettrick struggled to suppress his incredulity, "Not a good precedent, Mr. Weiss. Rob and kill, but be sure to take a hostage to barter your way back to the reservation and safety."

Weiss appeared angry and frustrated. He lashed out, "Well, Captain, you go about this then like it was your wife you was trying to git back. I reckon you'd be mighty careful how you went about it."

Hettrick was about to respond when off in the distance a gunshot sounded. It was barely audible, suggesting it could be two or three miles away. Most all of the men had heard it. An immediate pall of silence fell over the camp. The men froze in place listening and looking in the direction of the shot. They strained to hear. Seconds ticked away punctuated by pounding hearts in ears and the diminutive chirp of a mountain bluebird. Then came another shot. No closer. From the same direction. And then another. More silence broken by a Western Meadowlark casting out its melodic song. From a nearby fire came the gravelly voice of one of the packers, "That ain't no gunfight. It's buffaler hunters. I'd bet money on it."

A fellow packer snorted, "That may be but, whose pullin' the triggers?"

Playing off the packer's conversation, Weiss said to the captain, "There was a bunch of Metis camped up on the Milk a while back. It's likely them."

Hettrick replied, "They've nearly decimated the buffalo in Canada, so they've come for ours."

Weiss noted the captain's assertion, he said, "Hell, Captain, the Metis been following the buffalo back and forth over the Medicine Line for years."

Beyond Weiss, the first sergeant called out, "Captain, whaddya wanna do?"

Hettrick shouted, "Likely buffalo hunters. After breakfast, we'll ride that way."

CHAPTER FIVE

In falling a tree, it is necessary to cut a notch shaped like a slice of pie on the side of the tree facing the direction you want the tree to fall. Once this is done, a five foot long whipsaw with a man on either end is used to cut through from the backside of the tree to the pie cut to drop the tree. It was James' turn to cut the pie. He swung the double-bitted ax with all the force that his 160 pounds could muster. Some of the wood chips surrendered by the big old hickory tree flew a good ten feet. One chip caused Billy, from where he sat on the ground smoking a roll your own Bull Durham cigarette, to dodge his head to the side lest it smack him in the eye. He called out in a lighthearted tone, "I dare say, Mr. Coumerilh, you have missed your calling in life. Why you should git yourself from this prairie country to the big woods. Become a bone-e-fied logger. Yes, sir, that's what my observations have led me to conclude. You're wastin' your talents on this kindlin'."

James paused and looked down at Billy. He was breathing heavily. Sweat was beaded up on his face. He said, "You call this tree kindlin? I'll guarantee you it's over a hundert feet tall and hard as granite."

Billy laughed, "Those riverboat people like that hardwood. Burns hot they say. Lot better than cottonwood."

"Well, it saws hard too so you might be well advised to save your energy for your side of the whip saw."

"Maybe I should take myself a short nap."

James' dark eyes flashed a sour look at Billy and then swung the ax into the notch. Chips fell away. He was bringing the ax back for his next swing when, from downriver, a shot rang out. It was followed by a shout, "Indians."

James dropped the ax and started for his rifle leaning on a downed log a few feet beyond Billy. The ax had barely hit the ground when another shot sounded, except this time he could not detach himself from its effect as he had done with the one downriver. The sensation in the meaty muscle on his right side, up high, under his arm, felt like he'd been poked really hard with the blunt end of a stick. The impact twisted his torso part-way around, but his adrenaline kept his legs moving towards his Winchester. James jumped over the log, which was about a foot and half high, and immediately dropped to the ground. Billy, who had been much closer to the log, had preceded James by a couple of seconds. He was laying on his back clutching his Spencer repeater across his torso. His cap had come off and was lying crumpled on the ground beneath his head. He looked over at James, his eyes wide with fear, "I reckon we're in for it now."

It had not been a random decision when James suggested earlier that morning that they lean their rifles against the big log they were now hiding behind. He'd noted the fact that most of the trees surrounding it had been cut and that another decent sized log was lying on the ground just beyond it. He said, his voice calmer than Billy's, "With these repeaters, it'll cost them to put us under."

Billy came back, still not looking any more confident than he did a moment ago, "I got 42 rounds total, so I hope they ain't too set on liftin' our scalps."

James did not say it, but he had slightly less ammunition than Billy. He said as the gunfire downriver crackled, "I'm guessing the Indians has got themselves spread too thin with the boys below us to break off enough braves to rush us. But you never know, Billy. If they do come at us, we got to rise up and pour it to 'em. If we don't, if we cower behind these logs, they'll run right up on us and shoot us like fish in a barrel."

Billy nodded as a bullet gouged a chunk of bark out of the log just above their heads. And then came another bullet thudding into the opposite side of the log. The fear in Billy's eyes was palpable. James saw himself there. It took him back in time. Almost ten years ago that a Yankee soldier came screaming over the remains of a log fence that James had taken refuge behind. He'd looked up at the man. His own musket, empty, lying in the dirt beside him. For a second he foolishly thought he'd be shown mercy. But then he watched as the soldier raised his rifle high and aimed the bayonet towards James' stomach. Down it came. The soldier screaming even louder to bolster his courage so he could see it through. Afterall, who does such a thing. And then as he saw himself writhing in pain the reality of the here and now came back. In their glee, their excitement to kill James and Billy, the Sioux came screaming and yelling. James said bitterly, "Not again," He rose up to his knees already having chambered a round in his Model 1866 Winchester. Straight out from him were three Indians running through the slash towards him and Billy. They were dodging and jumping over the downed wood. Their bodies naked, save for breechcloths and moccasins, were painted with red and white and yellow slashes and circles. It enhanced their ferocity even beyond that of the Union soldier. But it did not make them immune from the heavy .44 caliber bullets from James' rifle. Nonetheless, his adrenaline-charged fear caused him to jerk the trigger of his rifle before he had raised it to his shoulder to aim. The bullet went astray. He instantly cursed himself as he saw the emboldened reaction of the Indian closest to him pause and aim his rifle. James saw the smoke belch from the barrel of the Indian's rifle and, in that instant, he felt his high crowned hat being ripped from his head. Oblivious to having levered another round into the barrel of his rifle he concentrated on settling his sights on the Indian's chest. And then, in that milieu of terror, he saw the Indian's eyes grow wide with shock and his rifle fall to the ground before collapsing on a small log. The demise of their companion caused the other two warriors to drop to their knees behind downed trees that afforded them some cover. James fired at the one to his left not more than forty yards away. His haste, his excitement, caused the big 200 grain bullet to not go between the branches of the downed hickory tree and strike the brave in his chest as he had intended. Instead, it was deflected by the higher branch. In that instant, the brave to James' right fired. The bullet passed so close to his ear that he could hear it parting the air. The immediate realization that another two inches to the left would have embedded the bullet in his brain caused him to drop down behind the log. It was only now that he became aware that Billy had not moved. His reaction was spontaneous, "Billy, what the hell are you doing?"

Billy's eyes were filled with tears. He stammered, "I was a clerk, James. I ain't never killed anybody."

James' eyes shifted from the fear in Billy's face to the sounds of the two Sioux warriors who were shouting to one another. The possibility they were coordinating their assault diluted any compassion James had for Billy. He snapped, "Billy, they're coming for us. There's two of 'em. Ya gotta help me, Billy. One of 'em is hunkered down behind a mostly naked log straight out from you. Maybe thirty yards. When I say, raise up with me and give 'em hell."

Billy nodded, but not so it gave James confidence that he would do his part. He began to sob, "I don't know if I can, James. Look at me, I've pissed myself."

James looked hard at Billy. He couldn't help but see himself that day long ago lying there trembling and crying.

And knowing too that he deserted. He was no different than Billy. But they had no choice. He forced himself to say, "Ain't no shame in that, Billy. The shame will be if you don't come up from behind this log with me and shoot these boys."

Once again, Billy nodded. Tears now freely running down his cheeks. He said, the words barely audible, "I'll try."

James was laying flat on his back with his head twisted in Billy's direction. He said, "On three, Billy, we go. Alright?"

Again, Billy barely nodded, "Alright."

The thought flashed through James' mind that in a matter of seconds they could both be dead. No more sunrises or sunsets. No laughter. No blue skies. Just darkness. And then somehow, he heard them coming. His voice, urgent, afraid, escaped his lips, "Alright, Billy, one, two, three." He sensed Billy was moving but he did not look over. He was up on his knees, frantic to draw a bead on the Indian that had narrowly missed killing him a short time ago. He was clever, or maybe not, zigzagging left and then right. Predictable, James did not follow him with his sights but waited simply for the brave to dart back into them. The roar of his Winchester caused the Indian to collapse about 18 tall man steps away. However, at the same time, Billy pitched over backwards to where his legs were folded under him like some circus performer that was demonstrating his flexibility. And had it not been for the fact that the Indian was carrying an old single shot Sharps carbine, James might have suffered the same fate as Billy. But, as it was, the warrior found himself running straight at James, intent on clubbing him with his rifle. He was no doubt mindful, maybe even resentful, that his friend had failed to do his part in killing this white man. But, just like Billy, what choice did he have. And then James shot him dead when he could see, real clear, the hatred in his eyes. Not more than three tall man steps away.

For a time, he sat behind the log poised to shoot again. He tried not to look at Billy frozen in that contorted position, his eyes wide staring up at the blue sky seeing nothing but darkness. His white shirt stained with blood and sweat. His hands still gripping his unfired rifle. And then James became aware of it. A cacophony of silence had descended over the river bottom. He strained to hear over his pounding heart. It was competing with the ringing in his ears from the gunfire. And too, the naysayer in his mind. *You should have let Billy be. He gave no more fight than a prairie dog popping up out of his hole.* But then his rational side chimed in. *That second Indian was gonna shoot somebody. If not Billy, it would have been me. And then he would have ran right up on Billy and shot him dead as he is right now.* Mercifully, the torment in his mind's eye was interrupted by a faint shout from the trees still standing downriver, "Hello up there."

By James' reckoning it was well over a hundred yards to the tree line. He barely knew the other woodcutters as he and Billy had partnered from their hiring on three days ago. There was little doubt, however, in his mind that the person doing the shouting was one of them. He stood and cupped a hand to the side of his mouth and hollered, "Hello." His voice was swallowed up by the silence. Seconds ticked by to the point James began to wonder if he had been tricked by a smooth talking Indian. Such was his apprehension that he sat back down behind the log next to Billy. To his right, upriver maybe fifty yards, a gust of wind rattled the leaves of the cottonwood tree where they'd left their canteens and a Blue Bird flour sack that contained their noon meal. James looked over at the tree thinking, *behind that tree wudda been a good hide to shoot right down on us.* He then looked at Billy and the dead Indians out in front of him. It caused an involuntary shiver to course through his body. He whispered, "But for the grace of God I'm still taking in air." And then downriver he caught movement at the edge of the trees. It was the other woodcutters, or at least two of them. One was wearing a blue shirt. James remembered him from breakfast that morning at the woodyard. A talker. He'd been a wood hawk here for nearly a year. The other man, smaller, was taciturn. James knew nothing about him. He stood and waved. The man wearing the blue shirt waved back. His partner, who was wearing a dark colored shirt, appeared injured and did not acknowledge James. By and by, the two men made their way across the cutover area to where James was standing. From nearly fifty feet away, Blue Shirt called out, "Where's Billy?"

James shook his head, "Dead."

Seemingly unphased, Blue Shirt came back, "They got Caldwell too. Sons-a-bitches shot 'im in the back while he was notchin' a tree." He paused, studying the blood on James' side, he added, "Looks like they nicked ya purty good."

James nodded and looked at the small man whose left shoulder was bloody, "And your partner as well."

Blue Shirt blurted out before the wounded man could speak, "Oh, hell, he'll be fine."

James noted the irritation in the quiet man's face. At the same time, however, it occurred to him the casualness with which they talked of the dead, the same men they had eaten breakfast with. A glimmer of shame entered his mind, but it went away almost as fast as it had come. He said, "You reckon the Indians are done with this fight?"

Blue Shirt nodded, "I believe they've had their fill. I'm for certain we killed two of 'em and it looks like you boys hurt 'em. Payback, by hell."

James nodded, "We should take Billy and your friend, Caldwell, back to the woodyard. Bury 'em there I reckon."

Blue Shirt snorted, "Caldwell wasn't my friend. Just another pilgrim trying to make a dollar on his way to Montana." His fingers then fumbled to pull a plug of tobacco from his shirt pocket. Their trembling belied his display of indifference to the death that surrounded them.

James' heart was still hammering away faster than usual. Montana was where he was headed. Doubt that he would ever make it there flooded his mind.

CHAPTER SIX

Captain Hettrick had allowed the men to finish breakfast at a leisurely rate before giving the order to mount up. It had rankled Weiss some that he was treating the investigation of the gunshots they'd heard in this way. However, deep down, when he stripped away his desperate feelings to get Sarah back and his common sense could be heard, he knew that the Indians who had taken her and killed her family were likely, by now, a long way away. Several, if not many, days ride.

They'd ridden at a pace that the packers and their heavily loaded mules could maintain. In the distance, maybe a quarter mile, Weiss could see the mouth of a big coulee. He was about to point it out to Hettrick when the trooper who had been sent ahead to scout for signs of trouble appeared. He waved to the approaching column and dismounted to wait for them near a stand of chokecherry bushes that were four or five feet taller than he was. His horse, a big sorrel sixteen hands at the withers, was noisily sucking up a drink from the tiny brook that meandered through the bushes.

Within a few minutes C Company arrived at the coulee. The scout, a private newly arrived from Massachusetts had a wisp of a red moustache that did nothing to dispel the suspicion that he had lied about his age to enlist. He walked towards Hettrick calling out when he was close enough for conversation, "I found 'em, Sir. Frenchmen with Indian squaws. They're about a half mile up this draw. They killed ten or so buffalo. They're workin' on skinning 'em and cuttin' 'em up so that they can load 'em in these big two-wheeled carts."

Weiss looked over at the captain, "It's the Metis."

Before Hettrick could respond, the private, speaking out of turn, said in an uncertain tone, "Metis?"

Hettrick said, "They're half breeds, Private. Half French and half Indian. Maybe Cree or Assiniboine."

Weiss threw in as if he was afraid the captain would not go talk to them, "They could have seen the Sioux that we're lookin' for."

Hettrick squinted his eyes against the sun as he looked up the coulee at several black birds soaring overhead. He said, "Those vultures are going to eat well tonight." He paused briefly and then said to the private, "Did the fact you are a soldier make these people uncomfortable, Private?"

"I don't know, Sir. Maybe. They talk mostly in French or whatever Indian language they are."

Weiss said, "Sir, I've never had any trouble with the Metis."

Hettrick came back in a sharp tone, "That you know of Mr. Weiss. We know that the Sioux and other tribes are getting guns and ammunition and whiskey from traders that come across the Medicine Line. The savages that murdered the Bellows family may have been armed and motivated with liquid courage by these folks up the coulee from us."

The Metis that Weiss knew were good people. At the same time, though, he'd heard the rumors that Hettrick spoke of as fact. He said only, "So, what are your intentions, Captain?"

"We're going to pay these people a visit and see what their true purpose is in being on this side of the Medicine Line."

The captain gave orders for the packers and mules to come at their own pace while C Company cantered on up the coulee. The heavy grass sod was forgiving to the horse's hooves that were making a thunderous roar as they neared the first dead buffalo and several Metis working over it. They continued skinning a big bull buffalo right up until Hettrick and Weiss brought their horses to a halt when they were almost within spitting distance. The skinners, a middle-aged man and a plump woman with long black hair, stood upright and looked at their visitors. Their hands and forearms up to their elbows were bloody, as were the sheath knives that each held in their right hand. The boy, who was nearly as big as his mother, had been holding a big hind leg up so his father could get at it with his knife. He now dropped the leg and fell in slightly behind his parents. His father glanced nervously at Hettrick before making eye contact with Weiss, "Bonjour mon amie. Are you looking for more of your cows?"

The stocky, dark complected man before Weiss was familiar to him. He'd run into him last winter while looking for some missing cattle. Weiss said, "No, Mr. Coumerilh, our business is more serious today."

Hettrick cut in, "Sir, we're looking for a Sioux war party. They murdered a rancher and most of his family southeast of here. Have you by chance seen any Sioux recently."

Coumerilh's response was quick, like he'd just touched a hot stove, "No, not in a long time have I seen any Lakota." Hettrick, and Weiss too, might have let it go at that if not for the boy's reaction. At the first mention of the Sioux his eyes widened, and his expression became fearful.

Straight away, Weiss leveraged his past meeting with Coumerilh, "It's important, Antoine. The Sioux took a young woman. She means a lot to me."

The boy looked down and away from the eyes of the men on the horses. He knew they were on to him. But before either Weiss or Hettrick could question the boy a voice, speaking in French, called out from another dead buffalo about fifty yards away. Antoine turned quickly to the boy, "Go."

The evasion was clear to Hettrick. It caused him to play his trump card, "Mr. Coumerilh, I have reason to believe that the Sioux are getting repeating rifles, ammunition and whiskey from traders that have crossed over the Medicine Line. Do you have any knowledge of that activity?"

Antoine's dark eyes glared from beneath the brim of his gray, flat brimmed Stetson. "We are hunters who deal in meat and hides. That is all."

Hettrick went on like he hadn't heard the man, "Where are you camped, Mr. Coumerilh?"

Antoine, speaking louder with anger in his voice, raised his knife hand and jabbed the air towards Hettrick, "I told you, we're hunters. There's no need to go to our camp."

"That remains to be seen."

Weiss interrupted, his voice purposely softer and calmer, "Antoine, the Sioux we're looking for are bad for everyone in this country. It's not just the white man that will suffer from their plundering."

And then the woman, her demeanor now apprehensive, spoke up, "We saw the people you are looking for a day's ride to the north of this place."

Antoine scowled at his wife but saw too the futility in telling her to be quiet.

Hettrick asked, "How long ago was this?"

Antoine now offered, "Four days ago."

"Did they have a white girl with them?" pleaded Weiss.

Antoine nodded. "Oui."

"Was she ok?"

Antoine hesitated before saying, "I believe so."

Hettrick, with some sarcasm in his voice, said, "You sound unsure?"

Antoine came back, agitated now, "I saw her from a distance. I did not talk to her. She had some blood on her face, but she was alive. That is all I know."

Weiss asked, "Did they say where they were going?"

Antoine nodded to the north, "Across the Medicine Line."

Weiss frowned and shook his head, "My boss was raising horses to sell to the army. Good stock. Big thoroughbreds. We had seventeen head in a pasture near the house. We was going to take'em to Fort Benton." Visions of how the Sioux would likely treat the horses gripped Weiss' mind as he spoke. It caused him to pause briefly lest his anger bleed through to his words and then he asked, "These Lakota, was they pushin' a herd of good lookin' horses? Wuddda been all bays and sorrels."

Antoine was about to answer when a voice called out from behind him. The man approaching was maybe half Antoine's age. He had come from the dead buffalo where Antoine's son had gone to. The man's pace was brisk. His expression was angry if not fearful. He called out in the Cree tongue, *Uncle, do not give up my wife's people. It will bring much unhappiness to my lodge.*

Antoine turned to the man who was now within a few feet of him. Continuing in Cree so as to leave the white men in the dark, he said, *Louis, it is too late. I have told them what they wanted to know.*

Louis glared at his uncle, "These men are no friend to the Metis."

Antoine lowered his voice, "*and the Lakota are?*"

Louis shook his head in disgust before abruptly turning and walking away.

The tenor of the exchange between Antoine and his nephew was not lost on Hettrick. He said, "I take it he doesn't like you talking to us."

"No, he does not trust the American Army from times in the past when they have searched our camp for whiskey and guns or told us where we could or couldn't hunt."

Hettrick's demeanor took a sharp edge, "Do you deny there are some Metis who trade in whiskey and guns? Or others who hunt on reservations where they do not belong?"

Antoine replied ignoring the first part of the captain's accusation, "We go where the buffalo go."

Hettrick scoffed, "There are boundaries and rules that have to be abided by, Mr. Coumerilh. Even then, I fear the buffalos' days are numbered."

Weiss abruptly halted the repartee and its growing tension when he asked in a voice louder than theirs, "The horses, Antoine, did the Sioux have them?"

Antoine reluctantly turned away from the captain to Weiss. "Oui, they were driving many horses. I did not count them."

Weiss looked over at Hettrick like the theft of the horses was some revelation that changed things. That now the white elephant that everybody there knew would prevent them from getting justice would go away. That they could ride across the Medicine Line into Canada just like the Lakota had. But before he could verbalize his wishful thinking, Hettrick introduced reality, "I believe, Mr. Weiss, we are wasting our time. The Sioux have got too much of a head start on us. They are no doubt in Canada enjoying the fruits of their plunder."

Weiss made no attempt to disguise his anger, "So, you're not going to pursue them?"

Hettrick came back. "Since we're this close to the border we'll push on in the remote chance that the Sioux were overcome by stupidity and stopped on this side of the line."

Weiss knew the captain was right. Nonetheless, he asked of Antoine, "Would you happen to know where in Canada the Sioux might have gone to?"

Louis' father-in-law had been with the raiding party. He knew, as did Antoine, exactly where the Lakota would be camped. Antoine, however, guessed he'd done enough to damage family harmony as it was. He shook his head, "They did not share that with me."

CHAPTER SEVEN

Ezra Crawford had just pulled the whipsaw towards him with a push from the other side of the log by his hired man named Fred when he had heard the shooting commence. His reaction was spontaneous outrage, *Those sons-a-bitches are back.* There was just the two of them at the wood yard bucking up trees into three foot lengths. For a moment they had stood still listening to the tempo of the fight trying to put images to the sounds. Neither of the men were spring chickens. Gray hair protruded from beneath the flat caps they wore and from that grayness ran streams of sweat. Beneath the arms of their long-sleeved shirts more sweat collected. Previous days of labor were evident by the white salty stains on the dark cloth. Neither of the men wanted to be part of this gunfight but they knew they'd want somebody to help them if the tables were turned. So, they had grabbed their rifles and gone up the bottom of the coulee that was devoid of any decent cover save for a plethora of stumps cut real low to the ground on account of fire wood was money. All the while, their senses sharp as old age would allow. Looking, waiting for those savages to cut them down. But they did not. And now here they were faced with the task of burying Caldwell and Billy.

Blue Shirt was most vocal on the matter, "I say plant 'em right here. Ya ain't got no wagon or horse here to haul 'em with. But we do got a shovel."

James looked at the shovel lying nearby on the ground. Its wooden handle was cracked and weathered gray. Its metal head showed considerable rust. He came close to throwing in, *I don't know if that shovel is up to digging a grave.* But since his wound precluded him from digging, and likely cutting trees for a good while, he kept quiet.

Ezra said to Blue Shirt whose name was Arch, "I believe you have the right idy, Arch."

Arch spit a prodigious stream of tobacco juice, several feet to the side of where Billy and Caldwell lay on the ground. He said, "I know I do. Just bury 'em now instead of going back and gittin' the team and wagon and then haulin' 'em back to the wood yard."

Ezra nodded, "I agree. We got wood to haul."

James did not know Caldwell and knew of Billy mostly that his fear had paralyzed him and was maybe the reason he was lying here dead. He knew too that Billy would balk at lying in the ground next to some stranger in a coulee that no one would likely ever go to once the trees were cut. Even more, his kin would never find their way here to pay their respects. His conscience spun the words, "It ain't right, Mr. Crawford. These boys deserve to be buried back at the wood yard. It's at least a mark on the riverboat people's maps."

Ezra snorted "Two months' time and we'll have this coulee cut out. We'll be movin' on then."

"I still say kin of these fellas would have a better chance a findin' their graves down by the river than up here."

Ezra looked at James like he was being uppity, "I have no idy where these boy's kin is located. Do you?"

James met Ezra's hateful stare, "No, it just ain't right burying 'em here."

"Right or wrong it's what we're doin'." Ezra paused and nodded to James' blood-soaked shirt, "Besides, I reckon you ain't gonna be no help."

Absent the intense adrenaline, the pain in James' side was persistent. Blood had run down his ribs and seeped beneath the waist of his black cotton pants. He could feel the damp stickiness of it on his hip. In a way he felt guilty for not helping to dig Billy's grave. The feeling, however, did not hold up to Ezra and Arch's indifference. He came back, "No, I reckon I won't."

Ezra stopped short of showing genuine concern for James and the quiet man's wounds but said, nodding in their direction, "You two are worthless. You may as well go back to the yard." He paused and looked at Arch and Fred and then added, "I'll go with you."

"Like hell you will," snarled Arch. "You never know what those Indians are gonna do. The way I see this operation is one man diggin' and two men keepin' watch."

It may have been because Arch had been there from the beginning of Crawford's wood yard or maybe he made good sense that Ezra acquiesced to his insolence, he said, "Alright, Arch. Fred will start the diggin'."

Fred reluctantly picked up the shovel as James and the quiet man headed off downriver. In his left hand, James carried one of the dead Indian's rifles. It was identical to his own Model 1866 Winchester. Arch had taken possession of the other Indian guns or quiet man would have had one too. They'd not gone very far, but were likely out of earshot of the gravediggers, when the quiet man surprised James and spoke, "You reckon unscrupulous wood hawks sold that gun to the Indian you killed?"

James' conscience, his aversion to killing, caused him to be slightly taken aback in the way the quiet man had stated his question. His thoughts were competing with the innocence of the question and his guilt. He'd been raised to respect life. *Thou shall not murder*, echoed in his mind. They went several steps before his conscience reconciled the necessity of killing the Indians and freed his tongue, he said, "That's the rumor I hear."

Quiet Man came back, "It would be a foolish white man who would do such a thing."

James nodded, "Perhaps one day some of their customers will give them their comeuppance."

A grin briefly appeared within the week-old black stubble on the quiet man's face. After a couple more steps, it dissolved and he spoke again, "Name's Frank Murphy."

Even though he knew Frank had heard his name, James parroted back, "James Coumerilh."

"You a Frenchman?"

"I'm what you call Metis."

Frank flashed a blank look, "A what?"

Their pace, meandering through the stumps, had been steady until now. James paused to look at Frank whose breathing was slightly labored due possibly to the pain showing on his face, he said, "My father is half French and half Cree Indian. My mother is all Irish. I reckon a person could claim I'm a watered down Metis, but I don't see myself that way."

Frank winced, "I'm Irish."

James looked at the bullet wound in Frank's shoulder and sighed, "You need a doctor."

Frank forced a grin, "No worse than you."

James shook his head, "Mon amie, you are pale as river fog. Do you think you can make it to the wood yard?"

A surge of pain came over Frank's face as he struggled with the words, "Got to if I want a decent burial."

James snorted, "I was thinkin' more along the lines of hailing a steamboat to see if they got a sawbones on board."

"They ain't gonna stop unless they need wood."

"Well, I guess we'll hope for the best."

They went on. Several times Frank stumbled and fell. His wooziness would not allow his legs to work properly. He refused to let James help him up until finally he fell again. They were within sight of the woodyard. His stubborn pride was willing his legs to stand but he just couldn't do it. His breathing was quicker, almost panicky like. James reached down and took hold of Frank's good arm. Frank did not protest as he allowed himself to be pulled up. He rested his good arm across James' shoulders and leaned into him. They continued on. A hundred yards, maybe, to go. Big leafy green cottonwood trees towered over the camp. A log cookshack and bunkhouse. A privy, whose boards still retained their thick brown bark, was situated behind the bunkhouse. Across the coulee from these buildings was a corral with two bay horses in it. Next to the corral was a tool shed and a faded blue Studebaker wagon. But beyond all of this, next to the Missouri River, was a sea of wood stacks. A pier extended out into the deeper water. In the short time that he had been there, James had wondered if Ezra would cut the trees giving the camp shade and sell them too. He'd concluded that was likely.

Frank groaned, "Take me to the cookshack. I've got a cravin' for a drink."

James knew that Frank was not wanting water. The cookshack was Ezra's domain. He did the cooking. The men were not allowed in there except at mealtime. His rules forbid whiskey anywhere in the camp but the cookshack and he was the keeper of it. Not that he wouldn't share, but it was only when he said. With his free hand James opened the door and helped Frank across the room beyond the long rough plank table to Ezra's bed against the wall. He allowed Frank to collapse down onto the gray wool blanket giving no heed to his blood soaked shirt. The room was dim and smelled of the fried bacon they'd had that morning at breakfast. And too, the black river bottom dirt floor had a musty odor. Frank stared up at the splintery pine boards in the roof, his chest rising and falling as if it were an effort. He said, "I'll take that drink now."

From a shelf on the wall at the east end of the room, where all of the eating utensils were stored, James retrieved a plain clear glass. He then backtracked to a shelf on the opposite wall where Ezra kept the whiskey in between stacks of old newspapers, mostly out of St Louis, that he had gotten from the boat people. He set the glass on the table in the center of the room and then removed the cork from the gallon crock. He splashed about an inch of the auburn liquid into the glass and was about to set the jug down when Frank called out, "Don't be stingy now."

Having experienced the kick of Ezra's whiskey his first night there, James thought to question Frank's directive, "You sure about that, Frank? You're gonna pickle yourself."

Frank's voice was more serious than not, "Well, there ain't no undertaker here abouts so I reckon I'll have to do up my own self."

James gave a weak laugh and tilted the jug again, adding another half inch to the glass. "You better hope you die, Frank, cause I'm of the notion this is gonna give you one helluva hangover to add to your other misery."

Frank reached out and took the glass from James' hand. Straightaway he took a couple of gulps like he was drinking cold spring water. He closed his eyes and grimaced in response to the immense burning sensation the whiskey caused as it percolated down to his stomach. For a time, he lay there with his eyes still closed holding the glass like the good part of the whiskey was taking effect and he was savoring it. Sensing, no doubt, that James was watching him, Frank finally opened his eyes. His face showed less pain, he said, "The Indian who shot me musta had some piddly gun as the bullet didn't go all the way through."

James had seen a .36 Caliber Navy Colt among the guns that Arch had recovered from the dead Indians. He supposed that it might be the offending weapon, but more importantly, from the war, he knew bullets had to be removed as soon as possible. There was little doubt in his mind that Frank was in a bad situation, but he tried to not let on, "I betcha lots a these steamboats got doctors on 'em. We'll git one of those fellows to extract that bullet and put you on the mend. Why, I bet in a coupla weeks you'll be back to wood hawkin'."

Frank grinned, "I'll bet you believe in Santa Claus too."

James was pondering a response to Frank's sarcasm when a steamboat whistle sounded. It was faint. A good way downriver, but it was coming for wood. James looked Frank in the eyes, "Well, there ya go, Mr. Murphy, Santa Claus is coming."

Frank scoffed and drained the glass of whiskey, "We'll see." He then sunk his head back onto Ezra's feather pillow and closed his eyes.

James quietly left the cook shack, closing the door behind him and went down to the dock. He stood there watching the boat's progress. It was good sized. Black smoke flowed from its twin stacks. It sounded its whistle again, still a quarter mile away. He could see the people crowding its main deck. On it came, a stern wheeler. Its red paddles cascading the water into an endless white froth. He strained to read the name of the boat printed in bold black letters on a white background. He cupped his hands to extend the shadow afforded by his black slouch hat so he could see better. Finally, he could make it out: DESTINY.

CHAPTER EIGHT

The engineer had his back to the boiler and its open fire-box. He was looking off the port side of the boat at the fringe of trees clinging to the edge of the river and wondering how it was they could not take hold on the steep slope above them. But they did not, leaving that niche to waist high shrubs and grass. It was fortunate, but too late, that he heard a deck hand struggling to put a big chunk of wood into the firebox. He spun around and instantly shouted so as to be heard above the noisy workings of the steam engine, "You fool, I told you no more wood."

The big blonde haired Swede glared at the engineer who was a head shorter than him. His eyes read like an open book. He wanted to sink his meaty fists into the cocky little man's face. But he knew his place. Deckhands were easy to come by, engineers were not. He said, "I'm sorry, Mr. Piva. I forgot."

Piva stood with his hands on his hips staring into the firebox at the dark trough created by the three-foot length of hickory. At first the yellow flames licked at it gingerly, but now they were ravenous. He shook his head in disgust as he looked up at the deckhand and pointed his finger, "You're gonna clean this by yourself." Piva paused, his anger and frustration building as rapidly as the flames consuming the log, and then he snapped, "I should just put you off the boat at this wood yard."

"The Swede's desperation to get to Fort Benton overrode his pride and physical advantage, he pleaded, "Please, Mr. Piva, I'll do better."

Piva snorted. His black eyes locked onto the innocence of the young man's blue eyes, he said with newfound hatred, "No, it's too damned far to have to deal with you."

The Swede's demeanor suddenly appeared hopeful. From behind Piva, the mate asked, "What's the problem here, Mr. Piva?"

The engineer turned to face Isaiah Sherwood, the boat's mate, who was probably a decade younger than his forty years, and in his mind not deserving of any more respect than the Swede. He said sharply, "I told this kid that we were going to clean the silt out of the boiler at this wood yard and needed to let the fire die. But here he is chucking a big piece of hickory in the fire box just as we're pulling into Crawford's yard. I can't have it."

Sherwood could see the expectation in Piva's face that he support putting the kid off the boat. On the other hand, the kid's expression was begging to stay on board. And unlike Turk, who had refused to help him throw the corpse overboard, the Swede had given him no trouble. He was inclined to take the kid's side when the naysayer in his mind shouted, *The captain will side with Piva and you'll look to be a fool, a figurehead with no authority.* Nonetheless, Sherwood's ego did not give in to the reality in his mind, he said to Piva, "I've got a job for this boy."

Piva snorted and pointed angrily to the boiler, "We're comin' to a standstill, Mr. Sherwood, and he's feedin' the fire. You wanna blow up the boat?" He paused, thinking the mate was simply going to sentence the Swede to cleaning the boiler, he added, "I don't trust the kid to get the dirt out of the boiler."

Sherwood well understood the danger of generating too much steam pressure when the boat was not moving to utilize it. Often, they would take a scow loaded with wood in tow and offload the wood onto the steamboat as they went upriver. In this way, the engine continued to use the steam being produced. When they were done transferring the wood, the scow untied and floated downriver to their yard. But today, because of the muddy water they pumped from the river into their boiler, it was necessary to shut down and clean the dirt that had boiled out of the water. It required removing the entire head of the boiler so a man could crawl inside. And too, it required the fire to be reduced to warm coals. The boiler on the Destiny was thirty feet long and three feet in diameter. A man with claustrophobia wanted no part of crawling to the far end of that dark tunnel. But then, neither did most everyone else. Sherwood looked at the size of the kid, well over six feet and 200 pounds, he said, "The captain wants something done with the bodies below. Their kin won't have any part of tossin' 'em over the side so they're gonna be buried at Crawford's."

Piva grinned, "The kid's gonna help?"

Sherwood glanced at the kid and nodded, "If he wants to stay on the boat he is."

The big Swede protested, "This isn't right. Those people are bad sick."

It was an effort for Sherwood to maintain his indifference. His encounter with Turk and having to dispose of the other cholera victim himself was fresh in his mind. With the exception of one teenage boy, the kin of the dead below were too sick and weak to carry the bodies, let alone dig their graves. None of the other deck passengers, who had witnessed the misery of the dead and their kin folk, wanted anything to do with the burying. Sherwood said to the kid, still unaware and maybe not caring what his name was, "When we dock go below. The boy will be waiting for you to help him."

Anger consumed the kid's eyes. Like the proverbial mouse backed into a corner or maybe knowing that Turk had defied Sherwood and got away with it, he lashed out, "You're a bastard. A real bastard."

Sherwood, bigger than Piva but still smaller than the Swede, walked right up to him, close enough that he could smell the sour sweetness of his breath and see the anger in his eyes melt into puddles of fear. He paused and mustered his own anger that had been steeped in humiliation from Turk, he said slowly and deliberately. "By my reckoning we'll be docked in less than ten minutes. At that time, you either go below and do what I've asked or get off the boat."

Tears came to the kid's eyes. Sherwood's intimidation of him was complete. The kid said, his voice quivering, "You'll let me back on the boat if I do this?"

For a brief moment Sherwood felt bad that he'd broken the kid, but he saw how those people with cholera had died. He wanted no part of it. So, he nodded to the kid, "You do this and you can go all the way to Fort Benton."

CHAPTER NINE

James stood on the dock as the Destiny settled in next to it. The pilot allowed the vessel to gently bump the wooden planks while, at the same instant, the engineer cut the power to the churning red paddlewheel at the rear of the craft. People on the boat were pointing to James' bloody shirt and talking excitedly to one another. And then, in spite of the captain and the pilot both having made eye contact with James, the pilot blew the boat's whistle again, which made no sense to James. It was Sherwood who shouted down to him, "What happened?"

James looked up at the people leaning against the rail. They had a poor look to them because they were. Dull, drab, ordinary clothing. Days of living on the deck exposed to the elements had left them unkempt. Their eyes searched over James as if to suggest, *well, maybe here's somebody worse off than we are.* James called out to Sherwood, "Have you got a doctor on board?"

"Yes, but how did you come to be injured?

"Indians attacked us this morning."

James' response caused a ripple of gasps and even a muffled shriek from amongst the deck people. A middle-aged woman assailed her husband, "Hasn't this God-forsaken land caused us enough sorrow?" She then buried her face in his chest, a large man with a black beard, and wept.

Sherwood pointed to where Turk and another deck hand were securing the gangplank. "You're welcome to come aboard."

James shouted back, "We got another man lying up in our cookshack. He's got more need of a doctor than me. I'd be obliged if your doctor come to him?"

It occurred to Sherwood that the easy flow of words between him and the man on the dock could change once the cholera laden bodies came down the gangplank. It was important, he knew, that he and the doctor went down that gangplank well before the bodies did. He shouted, "Go tend to your wounded man. I'll fetch the doctor and be along directly."

From above and behind Sherwood, the captain yelled from the pilot's house, "What about wood? Are we free to load?"

James assumed that Crawford would want to sell the wood, so he looked up and shouted, "Go ahead and load your boat."

But then the captain came back quick, "Five dollars?"

James sensed an air of trickery, but in his three days as a wood hawk he knew only that he was getting fifty cents a cord and room and board. He wasn't certain what Crawford got for the wood. However, five dollars compared to fifty cents sounded like a healthy profit. So, he said, "I reckon that'll be good."

The captain nodded, "Alright, we'll load up."

James noted that Sherwood had disappeared while he was talking to the captain. He was debating if he should wait for him and the doctor when a surge of nausea came over him. It caused him to weave in place. He supposed it was due to the blood he'd lost and the heat and humidity. He said to himself, *I better head to the cookshack and wait for that fella and the doc like he said.* He turned and started across the dock, his boots scuffling over the rough boards. It was fortuitous that he did not turn around as, at that very moment, the Swede and boy emerged from below with the first of the bodies. It was wrapped in canvas so as to be indistinguishable, but the boy knew it was his father. The deck people gave them a wide berth. The dead man was large. Close to the size of the Swede. His pallbearers struggled under the weight. Their steps going down the gangplank were careful and deliberate. A weeping procession comprised of the dead man's wife, teenage daughter and red-headed boy, who was clinging to his mother's side, followed. They did not look well but what else were they to do? They would pick the spot where their father and another daughter, not yet brought up from the ship's hold, would rest forever. And they would be kept company by an old woman whose husband was delirious sick and unable to rise up from his blanket on the boat's deck, not even when they carried her past. All knew that in a day or two he would die and likely be thrown overboard. The God fearing amongst the deck people justified the separation of this husband and wife, *in the hereafter, the Lord makes certain loved ones find one another.*

The sound of the Destiny's whistle had carried up the coulee to Ezra and the others. Even though he hadn't yet taken a turn digging, Ezra announced that he was going to the yard. *There's wood to be sold.* Off he went, not knowing or likely caring that Billy Watkins would lie no deeper than three feet and Caldwell not even that. In less than thirty minutes, Ezra's 63 years' old legs carried him back to camp. He'd just cleared the maze of stumps from up the coulee and entered the mini oasis that they'd purposely left surrounding the wood yard. Right away he observed several deckhands taking wood from his stacks onto the Destiny. Neither James nor Frank was anywhere in sight. He grumbled aloud, "What the hell is this, load up on the honor system?" He went on, walking at a brisk pace to the dock. He ignored the laborers and looked for the man not working who he figured would be in charge. Soon he spied Sherwood, not on the dock but onshore, deep in the stacks of wood. Sherwood was pointing at the wood and giving instructions to a deckhand. Ezra started toward him. Momentarily he arrived to hear Sherwood tell the deckhand, "Take everything from here to the dock."

Ezra did not hide his irritation, he called out, "Well, Sir, just how much of my wood did you intend on helping yourself to?"

Sherwood's face showed surprise if not embarrassment. He said, his tone bordering on contrition, "I take it you're Mr. Crawford."

"I am."

Sherwood took a step towards Ezra in a conciliatory manner like he intended to shake hands and introduce himself, but he stopped abruptly when Ezra added, "Who told you to help yourself to my wood?"

Sherwood's demeanor took on a defensive look, "One of your men. Young guy. Said he'd been shot by the Indians."

"That would be about the greenest hand I got." Ezra paused and then added, "Just how much wood did my man say you could take?"

"We didn't talk about that?"

"How about price? Did you talk about that?"

"We did. Five dollars a cord just like usual."

Ezra shook his head, "There ain't no usual anymore."

Sherwood interrupted, "What do you mean anymore?"

Ezra spit a stream of tobacco juice onto a stack of wood to the left of where he was standing, he said, "Wood's gittin' scarce and Indians ain't. Not a good situation to do business. So, I'm thinkin' I'm gonna need ten dollars."

Even though it wasn't his money, Sherwood blurted out, "That's outrageous."

Fire came to Ezra's eyes, "Well, son, I'll tell you what's outrageous. Until I can find more men, the Indians pretty much put me outta the wood business this morning."

Sherwood was pondering how to respond to Ezra's dilemma when Ezra saw the Swede beneath one of the big oasis trees beyond the stacks of wood. A quizzical look came to his face. He took a couple of steps to the right so he could see around Sherwood. Right away, he saw the others and a pile of fresh dirt. He said, with some reverence, "You burying somebody?"

Sherwood's eyes gave him away, he nodded, "Yes sir, we have need to bury three people."

Ezra was no fool. He knew the diseases that plagued river boats. He came back in a sharp tone, "Cholera?"

Sherwood nodded again, "We had no choice."

"Like hell, you don't. I see bodies float by here on a regular basis."

Sherwood bowed up some, "Tell that to a grieving widow and her kids."

A modicum of shame briefly embraced Ezra's eyes before it dissolved, he came back shaking his head in disgust, "I got two men dead, two wounded and can't work, and now I got cholera in my camp. Not a good day."

Sherwood said, thinking it might ease Ezra's anger, "Our doctor is tending to your wounded."

"Well, they might just as well go on up the river with you and take their chances with the cholera. I ain't runnin' no hospital here."

"I reckon you can tell 'em yourself. The doc's with 'em now over at your cook shack."

Ezra came back quick as a whip being popped, "Your doctor, the same one I suspect that ministered to those dead people you're plantin' in my yard is in my cookshack?"

Sherwood said nothing. Instead, he watched as Ezra's anger ruminated into frustration. Ezra turned away and looked up the slope to the cookshack. Gray smoke was coming steady out of the rusty stovepipe on its roof. He placed both hands on a stack of wood next to him and looked down between his outstretched arms at the ground. He then sighed loud enough that Sherwood could hear it before spitting again. It was like he was trying to distance himself from everything that had happened to him that morning. At last, he said, "How many cords are ya needin'?"

"Fifty."

A calmer look, like he'd resolved something within himself, came over Ezra's face, he said, "That'll be $500 and passage for my wounded men to Fort Benton." He paused like he wasn't quite certain of what he was about to say but then he ejected the words before he changed his mind, "And when you come back downriver, stop here. Me and my other two hands will be going with you."

Sherwood was shocked by Ezra's declaration, "You're quitting?"

Ezra scoffed, "Not enough trees and too many Indians." He then started towards the cookshack to tell James and Frank to be on the boat when it left. That their fare to Fort Benton was paid.

CHAPTER TEN

The country was broken hills and coulees. Some with ponderosa pine and some not. They'd picked up the trail of the Lakota now two days ride north of where they had encountered Antoine Coumerilh and his family skinning buffalo. Their pace had not been leisurely but, at the same time, it hadn't been as aggressive as Otto Weiss would have liked. It grated on him. The naysayer in his mind taunted him with what the Indians were doing to his Sarah. *All them bucks will have had their way with her by the time Hettrick catches up to 'em.* For a time, this raiding party with likely over a hundred braves had scattered into smaller groups but now, well north of the Milk River, they had come back together. Their trail, with all of their stolen horses, was as plain as railroad tracks. It was conducive to riding fast. Catching them before they could cross the Medicine Line. But no one amongst Company C thought that was going to happen. The Indians had too much of a head start. Then they heard the shot out in front of them. Alarm showed in Otto Weiss' eyes. He shouted to Captain Hettrick, "I'll wager they bushwhacked your scout."

Hettrick did not respond to Weiss but instead brought the column to a halt not far from a stand of pines in the mouth of a small coulee that emptied into the much larger one the column was riding up. He barked orders, "First

Sergeant, direct the civilian packers and mules to stay under cover of that timber and leave six men to assist with their defense should the need arise."

The first sergeant saluted, "Yes, Sir." And rode off towards the rear of the column and the pack train.

There was a nagging tension between Weiss and the captain owing to their differences in how the pursuit of the Indians and the recovery of Sarah Bellows should go. It was as evident as smoke in your eyes. It was, therefore, a conscious effort on Weiss' part, in spite of his declaration about the scout being bushwhacked, to solicit the captain's thoughts out of respect for his authority, he said, "Whaddaya make of it, Captain?"

Hettrick sat on his McClellan saddle clutching the reins in his left hand while staring up the valley before them. Here and there, where the soil would allow, were small stands of yellow pine. But mostly it was a sea of grass and scattered sagebrush. In some places the grass stood belly high to a horse. Generally, however, the buffalo had left it as a patchy stubble peppered with wildflowers. Red, white and lavender. And a plethora of showy yellow ones that carpeted a sidehill on the west side of the valley. It was a setting that would have been pleasing to the eye had it not been tempered by the gunshot they'd just heard from somewhere in its depth. Hettrick relaxed his eyes from the thousand yard squint they'd held for the past few seconds and looked over at Weiss, he said, "I fear, Mr. Weiss that you are correct in the fate of my scout." Hettrick then turned his gaze back up the valley, not wide, maybe a half mile and peered into the heat waves dancing in the distance. He added, "Indians are peculiar."

Weiss dabbed a deluge of sweat with his glove hand that had pooled up in his right eyebrow before it could salt down his eye. He came back, "How's that?"

Hettrick's horse switched its tail at the hungry deer flies continually trying to feed on it. He glanced back and grimaced in sympathy, "Damned flies." And then added, "Had the Indians let our scout ride on by they could have had a much bigger prize when we came along."

Weiss snorted, "Hell, Captain, they still might."

Hettrick looked at Weiss as if to gauge his sincerity, "Surely, Mr. Weiss, you allow my abilities more credit than to ride into an ambush?"

Hettrick's challenge was left hanging in the air as the first sergeant came trotting up on his horse and called out, "Sir, the packers and six soldiers are deploying in the timber."

The captain caught the eye of the first sergeant and pointed up the valley, "I want two men on either side of our column out at the edges of this valley. They should precede us by about 200 yards, at a walk. And tell them, First Sergeant, if they see any Sioux to fire a warning shot and fall back to the column. As soon as those men are in place we will move out."

The first sergeant saluted, "Yes, Sir." He then turned his horse back to the column and began calling out the names of the men who would be the advance.

Weiss said somewhat irritated, "Do you think it's wise to fire a warning shot, Captain. Might not be the best way to start negotiations for Sarah."

Hettrick looked at Weiss with indifference, "I believe, Mr. Weiss, the first shot in this affair was fired just a short while ago. I believe too if my scout were still alive, he would have reported back to me what he knew about that gunshot." And with that Hettrick touched his spurs to the sides of his horse to purposely move away from Weiss. Grasshoppers boiled up from the dry grass and brush into the hot summer air. Weiss sat on his horse helpless to change how things were. He was caught up in an avalanche of blue. By and by the first sergeant returned and Hettrick ordered them forward.

They rode, at a walk, up the canyon. Their senses were strained to the point they began to see and hear things that weren't there. Every man thinking, knowing, seeing in his mind that bullet come from nowhere and smack him in the chest. Knock him backwards out of his saddle and if he had any life left in him it would run out right there in the brush and grass and Montana dirt. And then some Sioux warrior would descend upon him, jerk his head up and carve off his scalp. To a man they hoped, if that happened, they would already be dead.

On they went. No one talking as if the Sioux didn't know they were coming. The horses were hot, thirsty and weary of the incessant deer flies. Here and there they snorted and tossed their heads as they obediently placed their hooves in the tracks of their quarry. Men slapped at the backs of their necks silently cursing the repeated deer fly attacks. Oblivious to their misery, several ravens circled overhead chortling their guttural cry. And then, maybe fifteen minutes into this cautious probe, a short sage covered ridge spilled off the mesa to the right into the valley. The outriders, on that side, went up and over it and out of sight. Seconds later, the gunshot everybody hoped not to hear sounded. Back came the scouts riding at a good clip but not like their lives depended on it. Hettrick halted the column and waited for both sets of outriders to reach him. The troopers unsheathed their Spencer repeaters and rested the butts of their rifles on their thighs. Weiss followed suit pulling his Winchester from its forward pointing scabbard on the right side of his saddle and chambered a round. As he watched the rider's approach, he could not help that his pounding heart had replaced thoughts of Sarah with him dying in the next little while.

The soldiers who had fired the shot were first to arrive. They were young recruits still learning their trade. One of them, the one who had fired his revolver, was baby-faced with freckles and red hair. He was wide-eyed with fear while his partner, not much older as evidenced by his peach fuzz moustache, was not. They had not quite brought their horses to a halt in front of the captain and Weiss when Peach Fuzz shouted like he was tattling, "I told him not to shoot."

Hettrick ignored the fact that the soldier hadn't followed military decorum by saluting and addressing him as Sir, he said angrily, "So, did you see Indians or not?"

"No, I told Boyle not to shoot but seeing Harkness dead spooked him." shouted Peach Fuzz.

The first sergeant snarled, "No Sir, Private Meyers."

Meyers instantly corrected himself, "Sorry Sir. Guess I'm not quite used to Army ways."

Boyle defended himself, "Sir, it was plain to me that Indians killed Harkness. I reckoned they were lurking about, so I fired my pistol."

Meyers challenged Boyle's assessment, "Sir, he wasn't scalped. Weren't no arrows in him. Hell, his horse was standing not more 'an fifty yards away"

Weiss, perhaps out of turn, threw in, "Ain't no Indian gonna leave a scalp and a horse behind."

Hettrick looked at Meyers, "Private, what's the cover like on the other side of the ridge?"

Meyers, more conscious of being soldierly now, snapped back, "Sir, just knee-high sagebrush and grass. Ain't no trees or big rocks for a long-ways."

Hettrick appeared perplexed as he looked at the ridge and wondered what awaited him and his men on the other side of it. He sighed and shook his head, "Let's move out, First Sergeant."

On they went, their horses at a canter. Weaving amongst the sage. Sometimes crashing through it. Noisy grasshoppers flitting away. Within minutes they topped the ridge. Hettrick paused them there and surveyed the situation trying to visualize what had happened. It was as the scouts had said. Harkness' horse was grazing nearby while the yellow leg stipe of his uniform pinpointed his location in the gray sage. They sat on their horses in silence save for a raven circling overhead announcing his intentions if only they would leave their friend. Closer to the men, barely audible was the drone of bees working a patch of lavender daisy like flowers. From this lull of tranquility, Weiss said while studying a couple of juniper trees that looked to be over a quarter mile away, "Be my guess Captain, that somebody with a buffalo gun, shot your man from those trees that's to hell and gone out there on this mesa."

Hettrick scoffed, "I'd wager that's close to 700 yards." He paused, and then said, "Be a lucky shot."

Weiss spit tobacco juice on the sage to his right, away from the captain, "I'm hopin' that it was luck and not skill."

For those within earshot of Weiss, the significance of what he had just said was apparent in their faces sitting still on their horses as they were. Hettrick was not immune to this fear, but his position required him to conduct himself otherwise. In a mechanical tone, devoid of emotion, he ordered two men to collect Private Harkness and his horse and take them back to where the pack train was staged. And then they moved on toward the suspected redoubt of the lucky shooter hoping that he was long gone, if in fact he'd been there at all.

They cantered their horses up the bottom of the broad coulee without incident until they were on par with the juniper trees on the mesa above. Hettrick brought the column to a halt and looked up at the trees. The slope beneath them was steep. He sat on his horse studying it, as if considering his options, when he said to Weiss, "Are you familiar with this mesa, Mr. Weiss?"

Weiss came back, "I was to it one time last year. It's flat as a billiard table all the way to Canada, which ain't too far."

Hettrick paused only briefly before announcing, "We'll angle single file up this side hill, First Sergeant."

The words escaped the first sergeant's mouth, "All of us, Sir?"

"Yes, First Sergeant. I've got a feeling about this mesa."

Although the first sergeant's 28 years in the Army told him that it might be more sensible to send one or two men to check out the trees and the mesa beyond them, he did as a good soldier does and parroted, "Yes, Sir."

And so, they began with Weiss taking the lead going at an angle up the slope. Their horses slowly picking their way through the sage and rocks lunging, stumbling to their knees at times, until finally, one by one they reached the top. The men dismounted per the first sergeant's order. The horses' breathing was labored with some snorting their fatigue in the hot summer sun.

Weiss had seen it even before he got off his horse. An empty brass shell casing laying in a bed of juniper needles beneath the trees. He said nothing but jumped off his horse and went to it. The bottom of the case read .44-100. Weiss whistled softly.

Hettrick called out, "What have you found, Mr. Weiss?"

"Your man's bad luck, I reckon." Weiss held the cartridge out to the captain, "Buffalo gun."

Hettrick read the numbers on the casing and sighed, "I've heard of this caliber but never saw a rifle chambered for it."

"I don't recollect I have either," said Weiss.

From a slight depression that was almost within spitting distance of the shooter's hiding spot, the first sergeant shouted, "He tied his horse over here."

The captain and Weiss started toward the first sergeant. He pointed and said as they neared him, "Pile a green horse shit, Sir."

Weiss looked at the sagebrush near the manure. It was taller than the rest close by which mostly dissolved into short yellow grass that in the distance showed wagon tracks. His first impulse was that Metis had been here. *But why would they want to shoot a soldier?* He pointed north toward the Medicine Line, "Cart tracks, Captain."

Hettrick cupped his hand to the front of his forage cap to better shade his eyes and looked to where Weiss was pointing. His suspicious nature went to where Weiss was reluctant to go, "Metis trading in whiskey and guns I'll venture."

Weiss was hesitant but said what he felt, "I ain't never had any quarrel with the Metis, Captain. They've always treated me right."

Hettrick glared at Weiss, "A blind man can see what has happened here. They killed Private Harkness to delay us coming up on them and their ill gotten gain. I dare say, if we could catch them, we might find some of Mr. Bellows' horses that have been traded for new repeating rifles and ammunition and whiskey. Not a good combination, Mr. Weiss, in the hands of the Sioux."

On edge now, Weiss fired back, "Well, Captain, I reckon you need to decide who were 're chasin', whiskey traders or the Sioux?"

They allowed the horses to rest for a time as any urgency to pursue the shooter or the owners of the cart tracks was precluded by the fact that they could see all the way to the Medicine Line and Canada beyond it. It was a sea of yellow grass devoid of any places for their quarry to hide. By and by, Hettrick gave the order to proceed. They followed the cart tracks and what looked like a bunch of horses numbering maybe fifteen or twenty until off on their right they came to a pile of sod. It was conical shaped about five feet high and ten feet across at its base. Hettrick ordered a halt in spite of the fact, that just moments ago, they had spotted black dots far out in the yellow grass sea. He turned to Weiss, "Well, here we are, the 49th parallel. We have no authority beyond it."

Weiss knew what the captain had said was true, but unlike the captain, he was not obligated to refrain from making brash statements, he shouted, "For hell sakes, Captain, we have them in sight. A little hard riding and we'll be on 'em. Now is not the time to wither from your moral duty."

Anger flooded Hettrick's face but instead of laying into Weiss, as everyone expected, he turned to the black dots that were getting smaller and smaller. His eyes reflected frustration sufficient to go around. It was dead silent save for a gust of wind that straightened the Company C guidon gently snapping its pointed end. At last, he gave the order to go back, leaving Weiss to deal with his emotions in his own way.

CHAPTER ELEVEN

Their wounds, such as they were, did not lend themselves to either James or Frank working on board the Destiny. This was a circumstance that did not set well with the captain, a surly man named Asa Stauffer. He would not, in spite of the doctor's insistence, allow them to move from lying outside on the deck to inside on the floor of the cabin saloon away from the sickness which was rampant amongst the deck passengers. *Their being allowed on board at all*, Stauffer had bellowed, *was only due to the incompetence of Sherwood.*

They sat with their backs against the outside wall of a cabin and their legs stretched out on the deck in front of them. Frank said, his eyes barely open, "Do ya ever wish you could be like a ghost and just float right through this wall. Why I betcha there's a nice soft bed in there and pretty soon they'll call us to supper. I can see it now, James. Can't you."

James sighed as his stomach growled from hunger, "I can, but I'm trying not to."

Frank reluctantly opened his eyes to the reality surrounding them. To the left of him and James were wooden crates stacked chest high. To their right were people. Some standing. Some sitting and if they were sick, lying. He said, "Maybe that preacher's wife will share their supper with us again."

James came back with some irritation in his voice, "I believe I'd about as soon go hungry as watch the look in her kid's eyes while I'm eatin' what they should have. I can't abide it, Frank. I'd just as soon be at the mercy of the deck hands to toss us a scrap when they bring the leftovers out from the cabin passengers."

Frank snorted his disgust, "Back home, my dog got his meals the same way."

James forced a laugh against the misery that was surrounding them, "Well, I'll bet your dog was happy, wasn't he?"

Frank scowled at James' attempt to lift their spirits, "I reckon he was, but I damned sure ain't."

James' demeanor abruptly became serious. He nodded to their right at the new mate, a man named Ziegler. He was coming toward them. James whispered, "I wonder what he wants."

Frank mumbled, "Nuthin' good, I'll wager."

Ziegler was a big man with tar black hair and a droopy moustache to match. His dark eyes were sunk deep in their sockets making them even more difficult to read beneath the wide brim of his gray planter's hat. Since coming on the boat two days ago at Fort Sully, when the Destiny had stopped for wood, he'd not spoken to either James or Frank. Based on their observations of how he treated the deck crew and other deck passengers, they considered themselves lucky. But now here he was. His voice matched his size, "The captain tells me you two are special passengers. Says you're on the mend."

Neither James nor Frank made any effort to get up. Instead, they tilted their heads so as to make eye contact, James said, "We was wood hawkin' downriver when we got in a fracas with some Indians a week ago yesterday. Both of us took a bullet so since we couldn't work our boss cut us loose."

The mate laced the thumbs of both his hands behind the buckle of his pistol belt and scoffed, "Well, this ain't no damned pleasure cruise. I need at least one of ya to feed the furnace. I got a man down with this plague that the damned Irish has brought to us."

It was a reflex that overwhelmed Frank's common sense. He shot a hateful look at the mate, "You don't know who brought the sickness to this boat."

With some swiftness, the mate pulled his thumbs from behind his pistol belt and slid his right hand to where it was resting on the butt of his .36 Caliber Navy Colt that hung off his right hip. He seethed the words, "You calling me a liar?"

Frank's Irish temper caused him to instantly gather himself to get up in preparation for the fight that was coming. He made it to his knees before the mate planted the heel of his right boot in the center of Frank's chest driving him backwards and onto his side. The mate then screamed, "Call me a liar will ya, you Irish filth." He then kicked Frank again in the stomach. Frank gasped, barely able to breathe, unable to make a sound. The mate was bringing his boot back to kick Frank again when James tackled his legs bringing the big man to the deck. Not even the adrenaline of the moment could mask the intense pain he felt in his side where he had been shot. He was no match for the mate being a good forty pounds lighter. It flashed in his mind *he'll kill me if I persist.* But, like being caught up in an avalanche, what choice did he have but to ride it out? The mate was on his back and elbows, furiously kicking his legs trying to free them from James' grasp when suddenly he stopped. James looked up the big man's body to see that he'd drawn his pistol. It was pointed directly at James' face. Before he could release his grip on the mate, he said in an eerily calm but hateful voice, "I should kill you."

James' mind's eye went back to that day when he'd looked into the eyes of the Yankee soldier just before he bayonetted him. The feeling, the certainty that he was about to die, was the same. Still, he was not about to beg the mate for his life.

The need to do so was more than apparent, but groveling to a man like this was something he just couldn't do.

And then Frank regained his breath, "You kill him you'll have to kill me too as I'll put the law on you at the first chance I get."

Frank's declaration, and the fact that they were now surrounded by a good number of deck passengers, gave the mate pause. He kept the pistol trained on James as he pulled his legs back and got to his feet. He gestured with the pistol, its hammer back and his finger on the trigger, "Four o'clock. You be at the boiler ready to feed the furnace. If you're not I'll throw you overboard, so I guess it all comes down to how good a swimmer you are." And then he shook the barrel of the pistol at James as he laughed before walking away still laughing.

They watched the terrified deck people give the mate a wide berth until he was out of sight in the direction of the bow of the boat and the furnace. Frank said, "You know he'll come lookin' for you if you ain't there at four o'clock."

James touched his hand to the dampness on his side and grimaced. He said, "They say we'll be to Fort Benton in two weeks or less. I believe I can make that."

Frank looked at the dark red stain on James' blue shirt and then at the pain in his eyes, and snorted, "I believe pigs can fly too."

James came back, his voice edgy, "Well, I'll tell you something else I believe as much as I do the sun comin' up tomorrow and that is I'm certain Ziegler will throw me overboard if I don't feed the furnace."

Frank went silent for a time suggesting he agreed with James but then he said, "He'd never get away with it."

James' eyes widened, his demeanor derisive, "That's good to know, Frank. I thought my floatin' down the river for the catfish to feed on would be all for naught, but just knowin' the mate will git his comeuppance makes me feel a lot better."

Some shame for what he'd said came to Frank's face. He tried to make amends, "I kin barely raise my bad arm, James, or I'd help ya tote that wood."

James shifted his focus from the haggard cottonwood trees rooted on the river bank to the grassy bluffs above. The grass went uninterrupted to the horizon where it was squashed by billowy gray clouds with black and orange veins. His mind drifted to his uncle and grandfather who were somewhere deeper yet in this country. And then he became aware of Frank waiting for him to ease his conscience. He came back, "The fact of the matter is, Frank, we're both banged up and me being less so than you makes me the logical choice to feed the furnace."

"I'm sorry, James."

James remained fixed on the dark clouds. He did not look at Frank when he spoke, "Storm's comin'. Gonna cool things off tonight. Won't be so bad chunking wood in that furnace."

Frank played along, "Yes, Sir, I believe you're right. Those storm clouds could make it tolerable."

James laid back, resting his head on a blanket he'd wadded up for a pillow. He was looking straight up past the pilot's house. Roily black smoke spewed out of the boat's chimney's mostly obscuring the puffy white clouds overhead. He said, "What time does that pocket watch of yours say it is?"

A leather string ran from a belt loop on Frank's brown cotton pants to his right pocket. He pulled on the string to retrieve his cheap brass cased watch, "It's three-seventeen."

"Wake me at five till four, will ya?"

"Sure, James."

James closed his eyes. *38 minutes. That's all I've got.* He began to wonder if his wishful thinking about the storm clouds had any chance of coming true. He felt sick to his stomach and weak. Doubt crowded his mind. He would need the clouds' help. And he wondered too how the mate had become the cruel man he was.

The torture of trying to rest, let alone sleep while the 38 minutes ticked away was infuriating to James. He'd seen the deck hands poking pieces of wood four and five feet long into the boiler's firebox. He'd felt the heat flow out from it. Now here he was, not even succeeding at this in his fantasy.

At a couple minutes till four James was making his way along a lengthy stack of wood when he encountered a short, stocky black man coming toward him. James paused and looked at the man who was reluctant to meet his gaze. He nodded toward the furnace, "Is the mate back there?"

The man gave James a skeptical look, "You my replacement?"

The disbelief in the black man's face and words caused James' inner voice to cry out, *Am I that pathetic looking that a stranger who knows the work gauges my fitness for it lacking?* Aloud, he said, "I am, is the mate back there?"

The black man's eyes darted nervously from James' bloodstained shirt to the bow of the boat and then back. He said barely above a whisper, "You need be wary of Mista Ziegler. He's in a foul mood."

James scoffed, "Is he ever not?"

The deck hand purposely looked James in the eyes like he wanted to agree but then, after a few seconds of silence, he abruptly walked away.

James continued on past the chest high stack of wood to his left that formed a wall of sorts. To his right, not more than three feet, was a waist high white pipe railing. For a few seconds he took in the swiftness of the water as it rolled away from the hull of the boat. It looked cold and dark. In that instant, he envisioned how easy it would be for Ziegler to overpower him and throw him overboard. At five foot eight and 160 pounds and injured to boot, he would be no match.

He guessed the distance to shore at about a hundred yards. His inner voice tried to reassure him, *if I pace myself maybe I can make it.* But then the naysayer in his mind shouted at him, *hell if your cousin hadn't come to your rescue when you was 12, you would have drowned in the family swimming hole.*

"You're late."

James jerked his head in the direction of the voice. Ziegler was standing barely ten feet away. He initially thought to argue but said instead, "Guess my friend's watch is slow."

Ziegler frowned, "Well, if it happens again, you'll be leavin' the boat." He then laughed in an arrogant tone and added, "Follow me."

James fell in behind Ziegler staring at his massive shoulders while envisioning himself grappling with him to avoid being thrown overboard. Momentarily, the fantasy ended as they emerged beyond the wood wall and next to the open furnace beneath the boiler. The heat that radiated from the snapping and popping flames was intense. So too, was the noise from the engine. James' inner voice derisively called out, *you've descended into purgatory in the company of the devil himself.*

Lorenzo Piva, the engineer, a scruffy looking man with a black walrus moustache and about the same build as James was wiping his hands on a greasy rag. He glanced at James and then addressed Ziegler, his tone being sarcastic, "This is my new man?"

Ziegler nodded, "Best I can do with this damned sickness on the boat." He then walked off.

Piva eyed the blood on James' shirt and shook his head in disgust. He said, "You're here. There's work to be done and I expect you to do it. This boat going upriver depends on it."

James came back, "I'll give it my best."

Piva pointed toward the boiler, "We're having trouble making enough steam. Too much dirt has settled outta the water. The heat from the firebox can't get through it to the water. Savvy?"

James said, "Yes, Sir," even though he was still trying to visualize the problem.

The engineer's eyes were locked onto James' studying them to see if he truly did understand as he continued, "So, for the next three hours we've got to burn the hotter wood. That's the hickory and oak, not the cottonwood. You know the difference?"

James felt slightly insulted but said only, "Yes, Sir."

Piva nodded to the black deck hand who was coming up behind James with a piece of hickory about four feet long by about ten inches in diameter. The strain on his face suggested it was heavy. Piva said in a loud voice, so as to be heard above the noise of the engine, "Eloy here will show you the part of the wood stack to haul from before he goes off shift."

The black deck hand glanced at Piva as if to acknowledge what was expected of him and then heaved the big chunk of wood into the firebox. It landed hard on the hot orange coals causing an explosion of embers that were mostly contained within the furnace save for a few that took an odd flight and landed on the wood deck. Even though they were destined to die on their own, Eloy stepped on them. He then swept his eyes past James as he started to walk away and mumbled, "Follow me."

Because of the noise, James hadn't actually heard what Eloy had said but he guessed he was to follow him. He felt awkward, being an ex-Confederate soldier, following a black man. Nonetheless, they went single file out along the wall of wood beyond where they had first met. *I should tell him,* thought James, *my pa had no slaves. That he didn't hold with it.* Eloy abruptly stopped where the wall had been taken down to knee height. He said not looking at James, "They's good hickory from here thataway ten, twelve feet I reckon."

The toll the wood had taken on Eloy was obvious. His white undershirt was heavily soiled with dirt, crumbled bark and sour sweat. On the stomach and forearms, where he rested the logs, the shirt had tears and, in some places, bloodstains. The whites of his dark eyes were bloodshot from the constant flow of salty sweat that ran into them. James said, "I'm much obliged, Eloy."

Eloy came back not looking at James straight on but more of a sideways look that could be taken as indifference if a person was so inclined, "Keep a lively fire and Mista Piva will let you be."

"I'll try."

Eloy glanced at the wet blood on James' shirt. "They won't show you no mercy."

James caught the black man's eye and laughed sardonically, "Ziegler has made it real clear what will happen to me if I don't measure up."

Eloy lowered his voice, "The man's wicked. Ain't got a good bone in his body."

James nodded, "He's a bastard of the highest order."

Eloy quickly looked around before he allowed himself to briefly laugh. "I better let you get totin' wood."

James stuck out his hand, "My name's James."

Eloy looked at James' hand long enough that James didn't think he was going to shake it. Finally, he grasped it, not real firm, "You knows my name."

Eloy walked away as James took hold of a piece of wood and pulled it from the column. Right away he could feel the heft of it and the strain on his wound. It caused him to flex the muscle that the bullet had penetrated. In turn, the movement sucked more blood out. He held the four foot log carelessly against his waist until barely three steps toward the furnace a jagged stob, where a branch had been broken off, jabbed him near his belly button. He uttered a painful, "Oh, dammit" and instantly adjusted the wood while continuing his exaggerated heavy steps towards the furnace.

It was a little past seven o'clock when Piva stepped away from a gauge on the boiler that he'd been monitoring and motioned for James to come to him. He shouted, "No more wood. We're coming to the next yard. Gotta let the boiler cool off."

Emboldened by his hunger and fatigue, he said edging towards defiance, "Alright if I try an' find somethin' to eat?"

For a few seconds Piva's eyes settled on the enlarged bloodstain on James' shirt, suggesting to James that he was concerned. But that belief, that hope, evaporated when he laughed in a devious manner like he was playing a joke on James, "Go ahead. You're gonna need your strength."

James hesitated, but then said, "Much obliged," before walking away.

Piva shouted at him, deadly serious, "Be back here at eight o' clock."

James half-turned, mostly to show respect, and hollered, "Yes, Sir, eight o' clock." He then quickened his pace as best as what little energy he had left would allow, lest Piva change his mind and put him to work doing something else. His legs were weak. Inadequate, he feared, to distance himself quick enough from the furnace and Piva. But then he was beyond the last of the wood wall and coming to him and Frank's place on the deck. He stopped next to two big wooden crates piled on top of one another. They were three feet square made of fresh cut yellow pine lumber that up close smelled of the forest. Bold black letters that read, U.S. ARMY FORT BENTON were stenciled on their sides. On the deck beside the crates were their bedrolls and rifles, including the dead Indian's Winchester. It was their spot alright, but Frank was missing.

Mrs. Jessop, the preacher's wife, was standing a short way off at the rail. She had been staring into the murky water until she somehow sensed that James had returned. At first, after catching his eye, she did not move or even let on that she had anything important to tell him but now she was coming toward James. A stiff breeze and her inability to properly bathe over the past two weeks had left her blonde hair snarled. Several strands of it lashed the crow's feet at the corner of her right eye. Her blue eyes, tired as they were, registered some shock at the extent of the sweat and blood that permeated James' shirt. But she did not voice her concern as James thought she would, she said, "That vile man took Frank."

The words jumped from James' mouth, "Ziegler took him?"

Mrs. Jessop nodded while taking a white handkerchief from the pocket of her gray serge dress and dabbing at the wind generated tears coming from her eyes. She pointed, her voice barely audible over the wind and engine noise, "He's on the other side of the boat tending to a man who died."

James said, almost rhetorically, "Why Frank?"

The preacher's wife lowered the hankie from her face like she wanted James to know how it had been when Ziegler had come for Frank, she said, "Because Frank is Irish and the dead man is Irish and he has no one who isn't too sick to deal with his body."

James processed the injustice, or not, of having an injured man tend to a cholera victim. It was akin to a possible death sentence that normally was reserved for family and friends, really good friends. He said, purposely coating his words in sarcasm, "I'll wager, Ma 'am, that Mr. Ziegler did not solicit an Irish volunteer from amongst the cabin passengers."

Mrs. Jessop did not render an opinion on the matter of how deck people such as herself were treated in comparison to those who could afford a cabin and good food and some semblance of proper sanitation. She wondered, although never aloud, if God truly intended for her to occupy her current station in life. It was a conundrum of sorts that deep down she knew the answer to, but kept it buried there. In defense of her silence, she dabbed again at a trickle of tears from her left eye and said, "This miserable wind, Mr. Coumerilh, I can't abide it." She then turned her back to the wind and James and walked away.

James weaved his way through the deck people, some lolling against the outer wall of the cabins, some standing at the rail allowing themselves to be ruffled by the wind, and some lying on the deck against the wall too ill to move. At the stern of the boat, he paused briefly to watch the big red wheel thrash the water. It had slowed from its usual rate in anticipation of docking. A minority of the deck people were standing at the rail looking toward the wood yard, which was a few hundred yards away. Most of the people, however, showed little interest in it, focusing instead on Frank who was mopping the deck midway on the port side.

From a good way off, they made eye contact. Frank held it for few seconds before shaking his head and going back to mopping. A pall hung over this side of the boat. The weeping of a young red-haired woman sitting on the deck with her back against the wall occasionally rose above the sound of the wind and the workings of the boat. James halted at the edge of the deck's wetness. In spite of Frank's efforts, the air was malodorous. It caused James to briefly look around for the dead man. Seeing none, he stated the obvious, "What are you doing, Frank?"

Frank paused mopping long enough to say tersely, "Puke, James. I'm cleaning it up."

Noting the irritated look on Frank's face, James crossed into the wet area next to him. He said so only Frank could hear, "I heard Ziegler had you disposing of a man that died of cholera."

Frank glanced at the weeping woman and then looked into James' eyes so he could mostly read his lips and whispered,

"She's the widow. Ziegler made me bind up her husband's body in a blanket and throw him overboard."

James frowned and shook his head, "How you farin'?"

"Shoulder's seepin' some, but I reckon if I get some down time it'll clot up."

"You want me to finish this up?"

"I thought you had a job."

"Gotta go back to it at eight o'clock."

"Well, hells-bells, go lay down. I'll be along directly."

James dared not go around the bow of the boat where the boiler and Piva were located, and since he hadn't seen him on the way here, Ziegler too. He, therefore, backtracked and within minutes arrived at he and Frank's space on the deck. On the way he had vacillated on whether to go below into the belly of the ship where he'd heard the deck hands took their supper away from the rampant sickness and filth amongst the deck people. But the naysayer in his mind, who sometimes had some common sense, put the kibosh on that notion. *You been a deck hand all of three hours and you think those fellas are going to share the scraps they get from the cabin saloon.* He thought too of going to Mrs. Jessop for a biscuit, but his pride wouldn't allow it. So it was, he'd just laid down and closed his eyes trying not to think of the vomit smell on the other side of the boat and food at the same time. He was not succeeding at it when he heard Eloy's voice, "Mista James, you awake?"

James sat upright like he'd been poked with a hot iron. His voice bordered on fearful, "It can't be eight o'clock."

"No Suh," said Eloy as he held out his right hand, "Brought you some vittles."

James got to his knees and looked at the offering in the palm of Eloy's hand, a biscuit and chunk of cheddar cheese that had been pinched off a bigger piece. A partial finger-print that was defined by dark grime was evident on the surface of the cheese. James' hunger overrode his immediate curiosity as to why Eloy was doing this and the fingerprint in the cheese. He took almost the entire piece of cheese into his mouth and chewed three times before managing to say, "I'm much obliged, Eloy."

Eloy came back, "Mista Ziegler says you and me is gonna clean the boiler. Says we gonna be the inside men and Turk is gonna be the outside man."

James put the rest of the cheese in his mouth just as a door off to his right opened and a large white woman, older than James, emerged gingerly carrying a white porcelain chamber pot. She went straight to the rail and turned sideways so that her back was to the wind and tossed the vessel's contents into the river. That is, save for the urine mist that blew back on the deck people downwind of her. Women shrieked and a man, dressed better than most of the effected people, shouted angrily, "You ignorant bitch, do you not have any common sense?"

The large woman looked as if she might cry and ran towards the door while holding the pot with one hand at her side drizzling stubborn remnants across the deck. Within seconds she was behind the safety of the door.

James looked at the biscuit in his hand and then over to the rail where the woman had been standing and replayed in his mind the trajectory of the waste. He examined the biscuit for any suspicious spots while visualizing the path of the spray. Finally, he took a bite before saying to Eloy, "Food for deck people is hard to come by and you're giving me some that you cudda ate. Why is that?

Eloy was quiet, not meeting James' look till it became awkward and then he said, "I reckon it was just how I was raised."

James wondered if Eloy suspected he had fought for the Confederacy. *Surely, if he did, he wouldn't share his food with me.* He came back, "Well, you was raised right."

Eloy moved on, "Wear your poorest clothes tonight. Boiler cleaning is mighty dirty work."

"These I got on is so far gone, I reckon I'll just wear them."

"They's a colored woman that washes cabin people's clothes for money. She might do yours."

James put the last of the biscuit in his mouth and began to chew, its dryness making it difficult to talk, "I ain't got no money."

Eloy grinned, "She's sweet on me. Maybe I kin talk to her for you."

James' shame over his past was growing like bread rising on a warm day to the point he could not contain it, he said, "Eloy, you should know, I fought for the south. It wasn't cause I held with Jeff Davis, but a man has got to be able to show his face to his neighbors."

Eloy looked down at James who was now done eating and said, "I reckon I killed some of your neighbors."

"You was a Yankee?"

"I was. Last year of the war."

Oddly, James felt some relief but wasn't quite certain what to say, "I guess that kinda puts us on level ground."

The glint of comradery that had been flickering in Eloy's eyes suddenly went out, he said in a plain voice, "I reckon I'll see you come eight o'clock at the boiler." And then he walked away.

James watched as Eloy turned into an open doorway and stairs that went to the belly of the ship. His conscience was wrestling with the prospect that he had alienated Eloy when from behind him, Frank said, almost gleefully, "I brung ya a biscuit, James. Got a couple from the preacher's wife."

Frank's offer of a biscuit was like a dagger to James' conscience. *If I decline it, he'll think that is peculiar as hell with us starving like we are. He'll require an explanation.* But then his mind's eye went to Frank mopping up the puke and the stench surrounding him and the fact he'd thrown a dead man overboard. And he thought, *either way I'm not gonna get any peace of mind before it's time to go.* He opted for the truth, just flat out, "I already ate, Frank. You eat those biscuits."

At first, it was hurt. Then it tended more to anger that showed on Frank's face. James could tell that he was sorting through his words when he finally said, like a faithful dog, "Ok, James."

James leaned back against the wall closing his eyes to Frank eating his biscuits, he said, "You wanna holler at me when that watch a yours says it's ten till eight?"

Frank was struggling to swallow the dry biscuit such that he couldn't respond. Finally, he managed, "I could kill for a drink of cold mountain spring water."

James nodded to his canteen lying beneath their rifles that were partially enclosed in saddle scabbards, "I got a little spring water left from that last wood yard. You're welcome to it."

Frank moved the rifles and picked up the canteen. He took a long drink before saying, "As soon as we're tied up here, I'll go ashore and scout up some good water."

James leaned back and closed his eyes. He felt better now that he'd shared his water. He said, "Ten till, Frank."

Frank retrieved his watch and laughed, "Hells-bells, James. You sure you want to tease yourself like this?"

James did not open his eyes, "Like what?"

Frank laughed again, "You got 14 minutes."

James' was tired and hungry and his side ached. The naysayer in his mind showed his belligerence shouting, to hell with *Ziegler.* He said aloud, "Make it five till, Frank."

Fatigue can sometimes be a wonderous thing. It had taken James back home to a family dinner. His mother had made a venison roast and spuds with brown gravy and corn on the cob and rolls. But best of all, there was blueberry pie and ice cream. It was so good, so real that Frank actually had to shake him awake. Now here he was standing in front of the boiler. Piva and Ziegler had unbolted the head of it exposing a pitch black tunnel three feet in diameter and thirty feet long.

A smirk surfaced on Ziegler's face as he stood there looking at James and Eloy, "I hope you boys ain't adverse to tight places." He then allowed himself a full-blown laugh that caused Piva and Turk to join in.

From a bench nearby, Piva picked up two white canvas hats and handed one each to James and Eloy. The cap struck James as odd. He'd never seen one like it. At its front was a short leather bill with a metal bracket on the crown. Before he could ask questions Piva picked up a small lantern, shaped kind of like a teapot with a hook and a wick. He then took a match from his pocket and struck it on the table. The heavy smell of sulfur floated up from the tiny yellow flame as Piva touched it to the lantern's oil wick. Gradually the wick took hold producing a lazy yellow flame. James blurted out, "I believe that lamp makes more smoke than it does light."

Piva said in a stern voice, "Put your hat on."

James did as the engineer asked and put the hat on. Piva then hooked the lamp into the metal bracket. James could instantly feel the weight of the little lamp, but more importantly he was impacted by the smoke it produced. It caused his eyes to water. Beyond Piva he could see that Eloy had needed no direction in getting ready. He was standing at the entrance to the boiler with a short-handled spade like shovel and a tin bucket. Another bucket rested on the deck near him. Piva caught James' eye and nodded toward it, "Take that bucket and follow Eloy. He'll show you what to do."

From the corner of his eye, James could see the smirk on Ziegler's face. It was giving him some kind of mean-spirited pleasure seeing him and Eloy going into the tunnel. In that moment, it occurred to James that maybe Ziegler was fearful of tight places. *Why else would he make such a big deal out of it?*

Eloy went in first on his hands and knees. He tossed both buckets ahead of him ten feet or so and crawled with the spade in his right hand. James followed a few feet behind, already coughing on the floury dirt that rose up from their shuffling through it. When they came to where the buckets had landed, Eloy paused to allow the dirt in the air to settle so they could breathe better. Their lamps illuminated the swirling grains, thousands of them. James momentarily held his breath while he fanned the air in front of him. Eloy said, "It's gonna git worse once we go to shoveling and dragging these buckets back and forth."

James could not see Eloy's face owing to him being only partially turned around to where his lantern shined on the wall of the boiler. He said, "Sounds like you've done this plenty in the past."

"Gots to be done ever day. A man gits plenty a chances to take a turn in here."

From behind them came Ziegler's angry voice, "You two stop your jawin' and git to work."

James glanced back at the opening behind him that was now obscured by Ziegler's large mass. He whispered to Eloy, "That man surely does annoy me."

Eloy came back, "There'll come a day when he gits what's due him."

They crawled on, taking shallow breaths. The darkness gripping them tighter and tighter until it gave James the sensation of being smothered. The naysayer shouted to him, *as long as you're on this boat Ziegler will pick you to clean the boiler. Do it or go overboard.*

Eloy stopped. He said, almost casually, "End a the line."

James directed his headlamp to the side of Eloy. He could just make out through the smoke coming off Eloy's lamp, rivets in the iron wall. He said, "This is where we start?"

"Can't go no farther."

"So, how's this work?" said James, "We only got one spade."

"One fella loads the buckets. The other fella tote's 'em. By and by we'll trade."

James offered, "I reckon I'll start with the totin' part."

The beam of pale light emanating from Eloy's lamp bobbed up and down, "Alright."

They began with the dirt at the far end of the boiler which wasn't as deep as that closer to the firebox. Nonetheless, the scooping action made the consistency of the air sand like. Eloy filled the five-gallon buckets about two-thirds full due to the weight of a full bucket being hard to manage in the tunnel and the fact the bucket frequently tilted, which would have caused the dirt to spill.

To his credit, Turk had used a regular sized shovel to remove the dirt within his reach at the entrance to the boiler. It was a small but welcome surprise to James as he crawled on his side, crow-hopping the bucket of dirt a foot or two at a time. He paused the bucket at the very edge of the boiler's mouth so Turk could easily take it and dump it in a wheelbarrow.

Turk grasped the wire handle of the bucket and lifted it out, dumped it and set it back in front of James. He laughed, "How's the air in there?"

James scowled at him, "I'll trade ya jobs so you can find out."

Turk laughed again, "There's advantages to being a big guy."

James noted Piva and Ziegler's cold stares, grabbed the bucket's handle and crawled back into the darkness. Eloy's light was dim, smothered as it was by the cloud of silty dirt that floated around his head. It appeared to James to be much farther away than it was. The muffled sound of Eloy's coughing and cursing under his breath, however, defined the distance. Shortly, James crawled up next to Eloy with his empty bucket. Eloy said, his voice lively, chipper almost, "You's too quick, Mista James."

James noted that Eloy had the other bucket filled, he came back, "How's that?"

He laughed, "You shudda lingered out there and sucked up some good air."

James scoffed, "Not with Ziegler perched like he's got to keep track of the buckets."

"'Fore you know it, we be in Fort Benton and we can say goodbye to Mista Ziegler."

"Whaddaya aim to do there?"

"Find work. Maybe go strike it rich in the gold fields." Eloy laughed. "My sister, Nettie, lives there. She got a good job keepin' house for some army officer. Gonna look her up."

James was about to tell his plans when Ziegler's voice cut through the darkness, "What the hell are you two doing in there?"

Their lamps still showed the roily dust in the air. James offered, "You wanna swap say every other bucket?"

Eloy pulled the empty bucket to the side of the full one, "Naw Mista James, I be good for a few more buckets." He began to scoop dirt as James crow-hopped the full bucket back out the tunnel.

It was a tedious, dirty process but they had the boiler cleaned in less than two hours. Turk had not kept track of the number of wheelbarrow loads he had dumped over the side of the boat. At some point, that dirt would be sucked up again by a boat downstream. Regardless of how much dirt it was, he carried on like he'd had it as bad as James and Eloy. He said to Piva in the presence of James and Eloy, who had just come out of the boiler, "I'll tell ya, wheelin' this dirt ever day gits old."

It was clear by looking at James and Eloy, especially Eloy who had not surrendered the spade, that there was not a single orifice on their heads that wasn't caked with the fine white silty dirt that rose up from the floor of the boiler with the slightest provocation. Their eyes were bloodshot. All of their exposed skin was coated with the fine silt. Still, it came as a shock not only to Turk, but James, Ziegler and Piva, when Eloy mustered more sarcasm than he should have to say, "Well, I'll tell you Mista Turk, come tomorrow when we do this again, I'll swap places with you so that weary back a yours can mend itself."

Turk, who hadn't even really broken a sweat let alone filled his nose, eyes, ears and mouth with dirt came back in an angry tone, "Don't you be gittin' uppity with me cause I don't rightly give a shit what Abe Lincoln says about your people."

Eloy smiled, which instantly ratcheted up the tension, he said, "This ain't got nuthin to do with Mr. Lincoln. It ain't right me havin' ta go in the boiler ever day when there's other deck hands my size that could take a turn." Eloy paused like he knew better than to twist the tail of the tiger, but then he said, "And now here you are standin' upright in the good air complainin'." Eloy scoffed in a derisive manner as he cut off talking when he realized he'd gone too far. He turned away from Turk shaking his head. But the damage to Turk's fragile ego was done.

Turk started toward Eloy shouting, "You little sonovabitch, nobody talks to me like that and gits away with it. Least of all a colored man." Close now, Turk deflected a futile attempt by Eloy to hit him and grabbed him in a headlock. For a moment, they struggled with Eloy bent over under the hulking grasp of Turk. It was like an awkward dance with Eloy directing where they went while windmilling ineffective punches to the big man's torso. And then, as they careened off the boiler, Turk ended the dance when he suddenly threw Eloy to the deck. He hit hard. James thought that would be the end of the fight which, up to that point, had been mostly a shoving contest, but now Turk became enraged. Spittle escaped the corners of his mouth as he yelled, "Talk back to me, will ya? Well, I'll learn ya better." He then began kicking Eloy in his stomach and chest.

James took a step towards Turk shouting, "Stop it, that's enough."

Turk paused briefly and glared at James. "Stay outta this or you'll get a dose too." He then kicked Eloy again as he tried to cover his torso with his arms.

The impetus to tackle Turk came out of the blue. It overrode James' sense of self-preservation as he was fully aware of Ziegler and Piva standing there doing nothing, so long as the fight was going Turk's way. Even as he drove his shoulder into Turk's chest James had an awareness of what was likely to happen. It was like his mind's eye played the future, not by much, maybe a few seconds, but enough that if he had heeded it and not tackled Turk, what happened next might not have. It was a single gunshot. In the absence of the boat's engine noise, it was loud causing Turk and James to loosen their grips on one another.

A deck person, attracted by the ruckus, said in a voice almost indifferent to what had just happened, "You've kilt that man."

James rolled away from Turk and got to his feet. Eloy was lying face down. Blood ran from a bullet hole above his left ear down along the side of his face. His bloodshot eyes were wide open, staring ankle high out over the deck's dark wood and across the bow of the ship to the woodyard where men, alive and well, were carrying wood onto the boat.

Ziegler, who had not yet holstered his Navy Colt, said in a terse voice while looking at James, "I had no choice. He was about to help you thrash Turk. I won't tolerate my crew fightin' amongst themselves, especially if it ain't fair odds."

James came back angry and irrational considering Ziegler had a pistol pointed at him, "Kind of like the odds you gave Frank. Gunshot wound to the shoulder and you put the boot to him."

"Irish scum needed to learn his place."

James scoffed, "You're a fine one to be callin' anybody scum."

Ziegler's eyes widened mostly with surprise that James would insult him while looking into the barrel of his pistol. But then the surprised look gave way to a cruel, almost demented stare. Like an epiphany had materialized in Ziegler's mind. He abruptly took a step toward James and aimed the Navy Colt at his face. He seethed the words, "I'll not be insulted by any man. Least of all rebel trash such as yourself. Apologize, or you'll be lying next to your friend."

Fear, absolute physical fear, seized James' body such that he was uncertain if he could control his bodily functions. The prospect of never seeing the sun come up or taking another breath or just seeing what the future held terrified him. It was all about words. Seconds ago, they'd rolled off his tongue bold as you please but now, apologize to Ziegler?

Ziegler allowed a sick grin to come over his face as he took another step towards James. It was clear that he was enjoying the effect he was having on him. He stopped not more than five feet away and made an exaggerated effort of aiming for a spot between James' eyes. He said, with not an ounce of doubt, "Apologize, or I'll shoot ya, boy."

From beyond Ziegler, Piva said, "He means it, son. You better do it."

It seemed to James that there was so much to consider. That his mind had cast out a net and it came back with all of this stuff that would matter to a living person. It was strange, he thought, of all the things in the net what troubled him most is he would have to live with the fact he had groveled for his life to a man like Ziegler. He couldn't help but look at the bead at the end of the barrel and then follow on up past the cocked hammer and into the evil of Ziegler's eyes. It was now that he decided he wanted to live. His lips had barely parted when the hammer fell. Click. Shock, frustration, more anger in Ziegler's face. James felt himself charging towards Ziegler. Bowling him over backwards. Somewhere in this sudden onset of physical chaos he heard the dull clatter of the Navy Colt falling on the deck. And in the next instant that empty hand formed a fist that came crashing into the side of James' face. Adrenaline, however, is a wonderous thing. James took full advantage of the strength and temporary immunity from pain that it afforded him and drove his right fist into Ziegler's face. Ziegler, sensing his own vulnerability from his position of lying on his back with James on top of him, mustered his own adrenaline aided strength and shoved James off, unwittingly, in the direction of the pistol. James' side landed hard on the gun. Ziegler saw his mistake and instantly gathered himself to leap the four foot chasm between him and James. Percussion caps can be fickle but more times than not they fire. And this time it did. As luck would have it, the .36 Caliber bullet struck Ziegler in the heart. He piled up like a discarded towel. His head and shoulders coming to rest on James' legs. Frantic, somewhat in shock at what he'd done, James scooted away from Ziegler's body and got to his feet still holding the pistol. More deck people, Frank included, had been attracted by the gunshots. They now crowded the bow area looking at James standing next to two dead men with a pistol in his hand. Off to his right, Piva said, uncharacteristically, "You better git the hell off this boat, Son. The captain will be here directly and I don't believe that will bode well for you."

James fired back, "You can tell him what happened. I had more call to shoot Ziegler than him to shoot Eloy."

Piva shook his head, "No, what I saw is your negro friend stirred up trouble. It got outta hand. Ziegler tried to put a stop to it and then you stuck your nose in it and now Ziegler's dead."

James stared incredulously at Piva for a few seconds, wondering, *why would he tell it like that? I'll hang if there's any law hereabouts.* And then the naysayer shouted the more probable, *the captain will see to your hanging.*

Save for a few whispers, the crowd was silent lest they incur the wrath of this crazy man standing before them with a gun in his hand. James caught Frank's eye and started toward him. When he was close, he said, barely pausing in his stride, "I gotta leave the boat, Frank. Your choice if you stay or go. I reckon you know what you might be in for if you come along."

Frank looked over at the dead men. His eyes were desperate to piece together what had happened and to know if he should share James' trouble or stand still like they'd never met. The matter needed talking, but that wasn't an option. Later, when it was too late, there would be that time. One of the deck people found his voice. "There's law in Bismarck."

Sudden fear, beyond what he already felt, consumed James' face. He said abruptly, "Goodbye, Frank."

The crowd was so quick in making way for the crazy man with the pistol that a woman stumbled and fell causing a man, who was also part of the receding wave, to step on her hand. She cried out in pain which evoked an angry response from her husband. A chaotic distraction resulted which allowed James, who had stuck Ziegler's pistol in his waistband to gather his meager belongings and walk off the stern of the boat as if he had nothing to do with the commotion on its bow.

CHAPTER TWELVE

Paradise was about 25 miles north of the Medicine Line. It was so named because there was a little creek with good water and plenty of fish that ran next to it. For miles around, there was broken prairie and coulees with patches of timber. It drew people in. Some of the Metis, who had given up their nomadic ways, had taken to farming and ranching here. Claude Charbonneau was not among them. Many people, who were residents, suspected how he came by the buffalo hides and furs that he brought in to sell. It was of no consequence to them since all of Claude's business took place south of the Medicine Line in Montana Territory. For Andrew Hunt, it had been more profitable to turn a blind eye than question it.

Claude parked his big two-wheeled Red River cart in front of the Paradise Mercantile. There was no mistaking whose cart it was. His brace of white mules that ran a thousand pounds each were the envy of a lot of folks. Claude had barely jumped down from the cart's seat when Bonnie, the bigger of the two mules, relieved herself.

Andrew Hunt was sitting on a straight back wooden chair on the plank porch of his store. He frowned while deliberately staring at the pile of fresh green manure. He said, half kidding and half not, "You need to train those mules to do their business elsewhere. I just got things cleaned up around here."

A slight grin, albeit a sarcastic one, was hidden beneath Claude's full black beard, he said, "A little more work would do your fat ass good."

The storekeeper knew better than to take offense to Claude Charbonneau. Most people who knew him, or knew of him, did too. Hunt got up muttering under his breath, being careful that Claude didn't hear him. When the stiffness in his 61 year old back and legs finally allowed him to stand upright and take a couple of steps, he said, "What is it you're in need of today, Claude?"

"A hundred pounds of cracked corn and the same of sugar. A pound of yeast and a coupla cases of pint Mason jars." He paused before adding in a lower voice, "And Winchester cartridges. Five hundred, if you got 'em."

Hunt said, brazen, almost like he was goading Charbonneau's conscience, ".44 Rimfire ain't much good for buffalo."

Claude gave the old man a hard stare before testing his scruples, "I kin always take my business elsewhere. Might allow you to sleep better."

They'd never spoken openly about what Claude was doing, but only a fool would sell the things Hunt did and not know. In the past, before Andrew learned what Claude did with these items, Claude would go on about how his wife was going to put up lots of wild berry preserves and syrup and how slick and fat his mules would be on the corn. And then, on one of his visits, it was like he had tired of the ruse. He said nothing of putting up berry preserves or the mules. If it hadn't been for a drunken wolfer who had told Andrew Claude's secret, he might have probed the change in his behavior. But he did not. It became their unspoken agreement to not talk about how these goods were used. Andrew knew better than to ever let on to Claude or anyone else that he knew. But here he was taunting Claude about the cartridges that would be going to renegade Lakota who raided white settlers down in Montana. And the hypocrisy didn't stop there as Hunt had sold Claude the Winchesters. He said, "That would not be to my liking, Mr. Charbonneau."

Claude smirked, "I reckon not."

Hunt came back, trying to smooth over the uneasiness about the cartridges, "Be a shorter carry, Mr. Charbonneau, if you drive your cart around back."

Claude scowled as he stepped up onto the porch, "You got a hand cart, don't ya?"

Andrew looked at Claude's dark eyes long enough to nod. "Yes, Sir."

Charbonneau stepped so close to him that Andrew could smell the plug tobacco on his breath and see bits of it clinging to his brown stained teeth. Claude said, in a deep, irritated voice, "Show it to me. I'll truck my own damned goods from wherever you got 'em."

They stepped inside the store. Its walls were lined with pine board shelves that were rough to the touch. They ran from the floor to the ceiling. Opposite them on the far end of the room was a waist high counter that spanned the width of the room except for a gap to allow passage to the tables and shelves in the front of the store. It was right there, not ten feet inside the door, that 25 pound bags of sugar were stacked on a table. Claude saw them right off, "For hell sakes, Hunt, here's your sugar. I don't need no hand cart." With that, big as he was, he picked up two bags under each arm and started for the door. He was just about there when its frame was filled by a young man wearing a wide brimmed gray hat, who was not quite the size of Charbonneau.

The stranger quickly stepped out of the way, "Pardon me, Sir."

Claude nodded his head but said nothing as he tried to not look the man in the eyes lest he show his fear of the North-West Mounted Police badge on his shirt.

Hunt's guilty conscience caused his voice to quiver slightly. He said, trying to be cordial, "Morning officer, how can I assist you?"

The young man pulled a folded piece of paper from the breast pocket of his tan shirt and handed it to Andrew. "I got a list. There's five of us. We're going on patrol for ten days."

Hunt held the paper out at arm's length so he could read it. His hands were shaking just enough to be noticeable. Seeing that the officer had honed in on his fear, Hunt said, "It's hell gittin' old, son."

The officer came back, his upper lip barely visible behind his bushy red moustache, "You appear to be holding your own, Sir. My grandpa's trembles are far worse than yours."

Andrew felt some relief that the police officer thought his normally steady hands suffered today from old age and not fear. He looked up from the list, "How soon do you need this?"

From outside they heard Claude say, "Giddup, mules," as he gently rippled the reins over their backs. The big two-wheeled cart rattled and squeaked around the corner of the building and down along its side. The officer followed the cart noise with his eyes until Hunt felt it deserved explanation, "He's got other things to load out of the storeroom in back."

The officer looked a little puzzled but said only, "Oh."

Andrew said, "I can have your order put together in an hour. Will that suit ya?"

The young man glanced up at the wall to his right and a clock encased in dark oak. It had big black Roman numerals and a dull brass pendulum that echoed the seconds in the cavernous room. The clock read ten past eight. He grimaced, "Sarge wanted to leave by nine."

Andrew came back, "Well, alright then. Nine o'clock it is."

Having completed his assignment, the officer started toward the door calling over his shoulder, "Much obliged."

When the young man was out the door, Hunt went behind the counter and through the door to the storeroom. Claude was waiting for him, "When did the mounted police show up here?"

"A few days ago, but they're leaving in an hour."

"Where are they going?"

"Patrolling."

"Did he say where?"

"No."

Claude allowed a look of apprehension to consume his face before he abruptly glared at Andrew, "You know enough to be careful what you say to these boys, don't ya?"

Hunt came back with some edge to his voice, "I'll wager it's got nothing to do with our business. It's likely those Metis that ain't happy with the government."

Claude snorted, "They say Metis like me wander too much. That I wouldn't make good use of the land like white settlers. And now, the buffalo are getting harder and harder to find. That is why I wander. That is why I go south of the Medicine Line."

Hunt, a Scotchman, tempered his voice with empathy, "From what I hear, it's tough proving to 'em you got land owed to you."

"Their rules are like riddles," replied Claude. "I couldn't figure them out to the government's satisfaction. So, I do what I do."

Hunt shook his head and said, almost like he and Claude were friends, "It's a helluva note, it is."

Claude laughed in a bitter, angry, way before saying, "My wife is Assiniboine. We tried to go live with her people on the reservation, but they said no, that there wasn't enough game to go around."

Hunt had never had this kind of conversation with Claude before now. It eased his conscience a little for his part in Claude's dealings south of the Medicine Line.

CHAPTER THIRTEEN

The sun had been out of sight for over an hour on this long summer day when Claude finally spotted a wisp of blue smoke rising up from their camp on Goose Creek. It instantly gave him a good feeling. By and by, he could see into the coulee where the creek ran. There were three tee-pees and twice that number in white canvas tents strung out along the waterway that meandered through the grassland like a snake. Willows and quaking aspen clung to the water's influence. Cooking fires that had been robust earlier had been allowed to die in the summer heat save one that was tended by his wife, Pretty Bird. After she and their four kids had eaten and they'd gone off to play or fish, she had kept a vigil in the direction of Paradise feeding the fire small pieces of dead aspen. Just enough so that the yellow flames teased the bottoms of a pot of buffalo stew and another of coffee. The pots were suspended from an iron rod that was cradled between two other upright rods. Steam drifted up from the coffee pot's spout. Its aroma and that of the stew made Pretty Bird's fire inviting. Another woman, a girl really, just seventeen, saw Claude first. She smiled big and pointed, "There he is."

Pretty Bird stood and began walking to where the other carts were parked and where she knew Claude would stop.

Claude called out as he pulled back on the reins, "Whoa, mules."

Pretty Bird looked up at him not quite able, in the poor light, to make out his dark eyes hidden beneath the brim of his black Kossuth hat with its broad turned down brim. She was not so bold as to say what she thought, *I missed you. I missed being held at night.* She said aloud, "Are you hungry?"

Claude jumped down from the cart. He now met Pretty Bird's eyes in a knowing way and kissed her. He said, still holding her, "I am hungry. Haven't ate nuthin but pemican since I left Paradise yesterday."

Pretty Bird saw him first. It caused her body to become rigid as she pushed back from Claude. Her eyes had become watery and her face worried. He said, with some angst in his voice while still looking at her and not behind him, "What's the matter?"

She nodded beyond him, "I'll let Phillip tell you."

Pretty Bird walked away as Claude turned in the opposite direction. Phillip Trottier, a head shorter and thirty pounds lighter than Claude, was walking toward him. At about twenty paces, Claude read his demeanor as haughty. He spoke first, "What is it, Phillip?"

Trottier stopped a few steps short of Claude. He rested his right hand on the butt of the pistol on his hip. He said, his tone brusque, "Did your woman tell you what happened?"

Claude's heartbeat quickened, not because he was afraid of Trottier but because the man had a propensity for trouble. And he'd not liked the way he'd referred to Pretty Bird, he said, "My wife told me nothing."

Trottier now became hesitant. Faced with confessing what he'd done to Claude, the leader of their group, his courage began to drain away. He stammered, "I only did what I had to do."

"And what might that be, Phillip?"

"I killed an American soldier south of the line."

Claude momentarily closed his eyes in disgust and shook his head. Before he could open them to probe the circumstances of the killing, Phillip whimpered, "They was on to us, Claude. I had to slow 'em up."

"So, you shot one of them?"

"From far off. Killed their scout. Hell of a shot it was. Gave us time to escape as our carts were heavy with hides and we was driving stolen horses that we bartered from the Lakota. And we still had moonshine. Wouldn't a been good if the Army caught up with us."

Claude was quiet for a time, searching Phillip's face for signs he was lying. Finally, he said, "They likely picked up the trail of the carts and followed you to the line."

A smile escaped Phillip's face, "It is good, no?"

Claude sighed, "They're gonna blame the Metis. All of them."

Phillip, mostly absent any semblance of a conscience, came back, "All the better. They will not know which fish in the sea is guilty."

Claude glared at Phillip, "There's no point in provoking the American Army and at the same time our fellow Metis."

Phillip scoffed, "So, it is ok for the Lakota to kill the Americans with the guns and bullets we supply them, but not us?"

Claude's anger intensified. The hypocrisy of what they were doing, based on the faulty logic that they were justified because the government would not give them any land, haunted his thoughts. Now, Phillip, of all people, had stripped away the façade. He had no good answer for the misery they were causing. Desperation to ease his conscience caused him to say, "We all take different paths in life, but at the end of the day we all gotta eat."

The tension in Phillip's face drained away as he absorbed Claude's words. He said, giving ground to Claude's assertion that it was wrong to have killed the soldier, "Thank God for the Medicine Line."

Claude snorted and shook his head, "There are mounted police in Paradise now. They're patrolling somewhere out here. We need to be mindful of that." He paused and then added, "No bushwhacking' those boys. They'll bring the wrath a God down on us. Do ya hear me, Phillip?"

Phillip bowed up some. A smirk, that was not well disguised behind his bushy black moustache and goatee, spread across his face, he said, "And if they catch me tending the still, I'm just supposed to hold out my hands for their manacles and go merrily off to jail."

Claude snorted and tossed his head back slightly, "Shoot one of 'em and see what that gits you."

Phillip locked eyes with Claude like he had something hateful to say. It went on for a time. Seconds that seemed like minutes until, finally, he flashed a sour look and walked away.

Claude turned around to find that Pretty Bird had quietly unhitched the mules and taken them to the creek for water. He went to where she was standing at the water's edge, looking at the trout swimming back and forth methodically surveying the surface above them for supper. Every so often one of them would be rewarded causing a splash and concentric circles in the stream. It was soothing to watch. He put his arm around her causing her to willingly lean into his side. He said, even though she had done it many times before, "I didn't expect for you to tend the mules."

She said, "I know."

CHAPTER FOURTEEN

It was fortunate for James that the captain of the Destiny cared more about getting to Fort Benton on time than he did in tracking James down. He was angry that he had to take time to remove Ziegler and Eloy to a weedy area where the woodlot owner did not object to their being buried. No one from the boat had the stomach to go looking in the woods for James lest they end up next to Ziegler and Eloy. The captain, however, saw to it that he made James and Eloy out to be bad seeds. He'd planted those seeds with the woodlot owner. *That negro started a fight with one of my best deck hands. And when my mate tried to stop it, this Coumerilh fella killed him. Be careful of him if he should come back here. He's a killer.* So it was, that Ziegler and Eloy got buried no deeper than it took to finish loading the Destiny with wood and get steam up. For his part, Turk found a scrap piece of rough, splintery to the touch, pine board about three feet long. He did not know the mate's first name, so he scratched in two inch high letters, MR. ZEEGLER – KILT – JULY 30, 1874. Eloy got nothing.

James walked upriver all that day he had fled the Destiny. His progress was aided by visions of angry men and bloodhounds tracking him down and leaving him hanging from a tree. But they did not come. Nonetheless, he pushed himself, stopping once at a small creek, for too long he thought, to clean up. It felt good to have the white chalky dirt off his skin, and somewhat his clothes. On he went, so hungry he felt sick. He'd traveled, he reckoned, about ten or eleven miles when, near dusk, he heard a steamboat whistle. It was ahead of him, not far, around a bend in the river. He quickened his pace. His heart beating faster than need be in anticipation of what he would find. Still in the trees, he could see torches flickering in the evening breeze. He could hear voices and then he saw the boat easing up to the wharf already piled high with wood. It was his intention to get on another boat and continue to Fort Benton and from there find his relatives somewhere along the Milk River. But he had no money. All the time he had been walking he pondered the best way to get passage on a boat. Sneak on, trade his Indian rifle, or ask to work as a deck hand. In the end, the boat's mate, an older, grandfatherly type, put him to work loading wood. And over the next ten days he took his turn cleaning the boiler. Rumors of what had happened on the Destiny had been left at woodyards that preceded them. They were required stops at least once every 24 hours. The trepidation that he would be discovered at one of these yards was almost painful to James. Stop after stop, things went well until the day before they were to arrive in Fort Benton. It was their last pause for wood. A man bought deck passage. James had seen the man standing on the dock waiting to board. He was scruffy looking. His appearance, brown flat cap and full black beard, suggested to James that he might have come from one of the boat crews. It wasn't until that evening that he learned who the man really was. He was standing at the rail smoking a Bull Durham cigarette watching the bow of the boat knife through the water and its wake roll away when the man came up to him and said, "Well, I'll be go to hell, James Coumerilh. Back from the dead or should I say, the badly wounded."

It had been close to ten years since James had seen Zach Martin. Back home in Louisiana they'd been recruited from the same parish. Not exactly neighbors as civilians, they came to know one another while serving in the same company of infantry. James felt uneasy, fearful of where Martin would take the conversation, he said, "Didn't recognize you with all those whiskers, Zach."

Martin snorted, "Well, hell, last you saw me I couldn't grow much more than peach fuzz." He paused to laugh, his tone bordering on being derisive, and then he added, "I was just old enough, I reckon, to squeeze a trigger and maybe die."

James braced himself for what he figured Martin was working up to, he came back, "Army ain't too picky when it comes to pullin' people in."

For a moment Martin was quiet, studying James' face as if he were some kind of oddity. A smirk, that was only partially hidden by his beard, was fixed on his mouth. It complimented the mischief that danced in his eyes. He said, "We had great fun after you went home, James. Yes, sir, The Wilderness and Cold Harbor. They was great sport. You shudda been there, James."

James took a long draw on his cigarette and exhaled the smoke in a tight, forceful cloud out over the water. He looked at Martin and said with indifference, "The war's over, Zach."

Martin snorted, still not releasing James from the piercing look that he had held on him since walking up, he said, "You know, when you didn't come back after a coupla months I figured you died. But then one day I asked one a those paper pusher types, you know, one a those with a cushy job that keeps track a things, I asked him what happened to you. And you know what he told me? He said they couldn't find you. And so I says, well did you look in the cemetery? And so now this fella gets agitated. Thinks I'm just messin' with him. He says flat out, your friend deserted."

James scoffed and shook his head, he said, "Zach, until you've had your innards mixed up by a Yankee bayonet, you'll never know how I felt."

"There was others that was wounded and came back."

"Maybe they believed more in what they were fighting for."

"You don't believe in pride and honor?"

"I do, but there are those who'll use those feelings against you. Git you to charge into a wall of lead and you're wondering why you're doing it."

Martin became defiant, "you don't believe in the cause?"

Before now, James had been able to mostly keep the past at bay. There had been others, plenty of them, who'd not gone back after convalescent leave. He'd talked to a few of them. He took solace in what they'd said and done. He'd been able to rationalize how he wasn't a coward but now, with Martin who'd stuck it out, it was different. It was as if he was in the wrong. That it made perfect sense to be mowed down. To be part of that. Waves of men, falling like grass before a scythe. James took another drag from his cigarette and exhaled in a pensive manner, he said, "I killed men that I had nothing against. Just shot 'em and clubbed 'em and bayonetted 'm to death because I was told to. From time to time, some of these fellows visit me in my dreams. Most of them had a fair chance to kill me and but for the grace of God they did not succeed. So now, here we are, all these years later and you're wanting to add shame to my load. I think not, Zack." And with that James walked away.

Martin, like a schoolyard bully called out, taunted, "Coward." He paused to manufacture a loud laugh before adding, "I hope you sleep good tonight, James. Yes, sir, real good."

Martin's insults struck James as if they'd been blows from a whip. His pride shouted, *I should give him a thrashing*. But in the next instant, his common sense countered, *Do that and you'll give truth to the talk along the river about you being a crazy killer.* He sighed heavily in an effort to expel his anger and frustration and then willed his legs to keep walking. Seconds seemed like minutes before he went through the doorway and descended the stairs to the belly of the boat where he slept with the livestock. Martin did not follow. But it didn't matter. There would be the regulars. The ones who came to him on so many nights. The dead, the dying, the screams, but always the Yankee with the bayonet. It would not be a good night. Martin had seen to that.

CHAPTER FIFTEEN

The captain of the Prairie Rose was a Christian, a compassionate man who treated his deck crew fairly. At six this morning James had biscuits and gravy, bacon and coffee. It was a far cry from the cabin people's leftovers that the deckhands ate on the Destiny. It had been agreed that if he fed the furnace this morning, until they arrived at Fort Benton, he would have satisfied the payment for his deck passage and would not need to help unload the boat. At 10:15 the engineer had told him, *no more wood. We're almost to Benton. You're free to go.*

James now stood at the rail on the starboard side of the boat, the side the Fort Benton landing was on and watched, like some tourist their approach. The Prairie Rose had announced its pending arrival from a mile downstream. Hearing the long blasts from its whistle, people with a purpose, and a good many out of curiosity, had gathered at the water's edge to await its arrival. The noise and activity from them was like a swarm of bees, pointing, waving, all the while chattering and sometimes laughing. James heard the cessation of the big paddles at the rear of the boat but noted that its momentum was still taking it to its designated levee. Men on shore stood ready to receive ropes from the Prairie Rose while others were ready with planks to bridge the chasm of shallow water so that passengers and freight could disembark. It all looked innocent enough. Nonetheless, James searched the crowd looking for that man with a badge who could end his journey and maybe his life. He looked too for Turk or Piva. It would be their spin on what happened that would get him hanged. But he did not see them, so he gathered his rifles and bedroll and got in line. He started down the gangplank, mesmerized somewhat by the gentle caress of the water onto the levee's mud. The air had that river smell to it, damp and musty. Beyond and amongst the people was a clutter of crates, farm equipment, lumber, canvas and a boiler for a sawmill. James was glad to be off the boat and now, hopefully, able to put distance between him and all that had happened on the Destiny. He'd barely penetrated the crowd when he saw her, a young black woman, strikingly pretty, by herself, some distance from everyone. Since that day on the Destiny, in quiet times, he'd pondered if Eloy's sister would ever know his fate. He tried not to stare at this woman. She was well attired in a bright yellow dress with matching sun bonnet. He came to a halt next to several plows that were laying on their sides and pretended to be searching the crowd for someone. *Be mighty coincidental*, he thought, *if it were her*. It made him melancholy to think that not knowing exactly when, or what boat Eloy was coming on, she might come to the levee day after day to meet her brother. *There will come a time*, thought James, *she'll give up and think her brother has deceived her*. He sighed, *I owe Eloy this much*. and started walking toward the woman. When he had weaved through the milling people and emerged in the naked space between them, she spotted him. As he approached, it appeared that she was assessing his character, not out of fear but rather curiosity. She was first to speak, "How may I help you, Sir?"

James stopped a respectful distance from the woman. She was even more pretty up close than from afar. He had a knapsack with his bedroll tied on top strapped to his shoulders and a rifle in each hand hanging at his sides. He nodded his head as if to doff his hat to her and said, "Beg your pardon, Ma'am, but a friend a mine told me he was gonna meet his sister here. Was you by chance lookin' to meet your brother?"

The woman's face instantly evolved into a smile. She said, "Yes, my brother Eloy wrote me last winter that he hoped to come by boat in late July or early August he thought."

Seeing the joy in the woman's face and knowing that he was about to destroy it caused James to wish he'd kept on walking. That maybe she would be better off not knowing. That maybe she could continue believing that one day Eloy would come. And when that day did not come, somebody else could tell her. But then James telegraphed why he was there as he took a breath. The woman's smile was gone before the words tumbled from his mouth, "I'm sorry to have to tell you, Ma'am, but your brother won't be coming."

Tears were now puddled in her gray eyes needing, it appeared, only a slight provocation to spill over. She whispered, "Not ever?"

James shook his head, "No, he was killed in a fight on the steamboat Destiny a week or so ago."

Upon hearing what she feared, the woman's knees began to buckle. Seeing she was close to collapsing, James dropped his rifles on the ground and took hold of her with one arm around her waist and the other her right arm. He began to guide her to a nearby crate, saying, "It might be best if you was to sit down, Ma'am."

The woman, now openly distraught, allowed James to help her to a large crate, about three feet square, that was stenciled with black letters that read, FORT BENTON MER-CANTILE. She sat down with James standing before her. She sobbed, "I never knew fighting to be in Eloy's nature."

James came back, his tone somber, "I don't believe it was. Ma'am. Things got out of hand. His killing was not right."

The woman looked up. Copious tears streamed down her cheeks. "Did you see this happen?"

James nodded, "The man that done it was our boss. He was pure evil."

"Has this man been arrested?"

James shook his head, he said, his voice barely above a whisper. "I killed him. I tried to come to Eloy's aid but, like I said, this man was wicked. He was crazy with hate. It was him or me. But now, I'm fearful the law will come for me if they learn of my whereabouts."

Through her tears, the woman showed surprise, "You, why?"

"Because there's men on the Destiny that won't tell it how it was. Their friend would have killed me if he'd got a hold of me."

A surge of grief came over the woman, seemingly divorcing her momentarily from James' trouble. She said, "Where did they bury, Eloy?"

"I'm not certain, but I reckon it was about 250 miles downriver in Dakota Territory at a wood yard."

"You know this place?"

"Yes, Ma'am."

"Could you take me there?"

"It wouldn't bode well for me to go there now. Best I could do is maybe put an X on a map."

The woman took a handkerchief from her purse and wiped at her eyes and then her nose which was running onto her upper lip. She looked at James, her eyes red and blurry, "Maybe someday you could take me there, I would pay you."

James shook his head, "When the time's right I'll gladly take you, but I'll not accept any payment for doing so."

She came back, "My name is Nettie Bell. I work at the fort for Captain Hettrick. Please ask for me when you deem the time to be right."

James nodded, "I will, you can be sure. Eloy was good to me."

Nettie stood up from the crate, fully aware now that her grief was on display to a distant crowd of voyeurs, she said, "And your name, Sir?"

James removed his hat and introduced himself, "James Coumerilh, Ma'am."

A wave of grief hit Nettie. She buried her face in her hankie for a few seconds as James looked on. Finally, she snuffled before struggling to say, "You are French?"

"My father is part French and part Cree Indian. My mother is Irish."

Nettie bobbed her head, seemingly more in control now, "Metis."

"Yes, Ma'am. I've got kin hereabouts."

She said, her voice fairly clear, "My captain speaks often of the Metis. Perhaps he can help you find your relatives."

James' mind leapt ahead to the possibility that Nettie's captain would take him into custody if he got wind of what happened on the Destiny. He said, in a halting voice, "I'd be obliged, Ma'am, if you'd not mention my name to your captain just yet. If he becomes aware of my troubles, he may feel compelled to report me to the authorities or arrest me himself."

Nettie scoffed as if she was incredulous at James' fear, "With all the evil doings in this town, I should think it a sad day if the authorities were to come after a man like you. There are plenty of killers and thieves right here."

James was taken aback, "This is a rough town?"

"Purgatory on earth. Killings nearly every day. They got a street where these purveyors of liquor and gambling and women of ill repute are located. It is called the bloodiest block in the west. I would advise you to stay clear of it."

James forced a brief laugh, "I'm destitute, Ma'am, so I reckon since my pockets are empty folks on this wicked street will have little interest in me."

Nettie said, almost defiant, "To some it's sport, picking at old wounds."

"Old wounds?"

"There are lots of ex-confederate soldiers here. It is sport for them to get drunk and pick fights with soldiers from the fort." She paused and shook her head, "They just can't let go of the past."

James' mind flashed to it. *She's got to be wondering which side I was on.* He wrestled with it, just briefly, before confessing, "You should know, Ma' am, I fought for the south."

Nettie said, her demeanor calm, not like she was judging James' admission, "I suspect, from what little I know of you, that your motivation to fight for the Confederacy doesn't govern your behavior now or we wouldn't be talking."

James wanted to tell her that he would never in his life have been above talking to her, but he did not. *Best to not open that can a worms,* he thought. He said, "The war is a long time over, Ma' am."

Given the circumstances it was not within her to smile but there was something in her demeanor that suggested to James that her pain of a few minutes ago was at least tolerable now, she said, "You may call me, Nettie, Mr. Coumerilh."

James grinned, "James is my name."

"I know," replied Nettie as she opened her purse made of red yarn that was hand knitted by Mrs. Hettrick. From it, she took a five-dollar gold piece and held it out to him. "Here, so you won't go hungry."

James knew it would be the right thing to do to refuse the money, but he was flat broke, save for the Indian rifle and Ziegler's pistol. His hesitation caused Nettie to add, "You can pay me back after you find work."

James felt shame as he reached for the coin. "I will pay you back, Nettie."

"I know you will," she said as she placed the gold piece in the palm of his hand.

James took the money while looking at her red eyes, he said, "I'm much obliged."

Nettie came back, catching him off guard, "Do you reckon we can go to where my brother is buried before fall?"

It suddenly struck James that maybe the five dollars was down payment for taking her to Eloy's grave. He didn't want to think it, as he was not at all certain he could live up to his end of this agreement. "I don't know. I'll try."

Nettie came back, somewhat matter of fact in her tone, "The steamboats stop coming this far upriver in late October, sometimes mid-November if we're lucky."

A pang of guilt propelled James to say, "I promise, we'll go before the water gets too low."

A faint smile came to Nettie's olive colored face, she whispered as she started to cry again, "Thank you." And with that, she walked away.

For a moment, James stood and watched her, slender and buxom, walking briskly in the direction of the fort. He said to himself, *what am I getting myself into?*

CHAPTER SIXTEEN

Nettie was almost out of sight when a man driving a team of black draft horses pulling a flatbed wagon rattled up next to a loading dock and stopped. The driver, a skinny man, wearing a gray wide brimmed hat that was stained with sweat and dirt, jumped down from the wagon's seat. He walked to the end of the dock's retaining wall, which was constructed of creosote treated railroad ties, and turned up onto its dirt platform. Parked there was a new iron wheeled mowing machine with its five foot cutter bar in the raised position. From where James was standing, it reminded him of some giant bug. He watched the man climb onto the machine's cupped metal seat that was perched above the workings that drove the mower's sickle. For a time, he sat there studying how he envisioned the machine functioned. By and by, he began to look around and that's when he spotted James. There was no hesitation on his part. He stood up and motioned for James to come to him. Curiosity, mostly, caused James to comply. When he could see the man's eyes and that there was almost as much salt as there was pepper in his droopy moustache, the man called out, "I'd be obliged if you could lend me a hand loading this."

James shouted, his tone being extra cordial, "Be glad to." He then laid his knapsack on the ground at the edge of the dock and rested his rifles on top of it.

The wagon driver noted his actions and the fact he still had a pistol tucked in his waist. He chuckled, "You expectin' trouble, son?"

James managed a sheepish smile, "No Sir, I'm a peaceable person."

The man became quiet. His eyes roving over James like he was weighing the truth of his words before he finally stuck his hand out, "Name's Charlie Reed."

James looked the man in the eyes and shook his hand, "James Coumerilh."

Charlie looked back at the mower. "I'll hold the tongue if you'll push."

James nodded, "Alright," and placed his hands on the back of the machine's iron seat.

The end of the tongue, which was about ten feet long, rested on the top railroad tie at the edge of the dock. Charlie stepped down from the dock onto the wagon, a difference of less than a foot, and picked up the tongue. He said, louder than necessary, "Alright, son, push but don't send me off the other side of the wagon."

James leaned into the seat as he said, "I'll try not to."

Between the two of them, the mower abruptly surrendered to their efforts and lurched forward. The tongue and Charlie falling off the far side of the wagon and the mower making the drop from the top of the dock to the wagon bed with a loud bang. Charlie was on the ground, moaning. James instantly jumped down onto the wagon bed and then off the wagon to where Charlie lay on the ground. He was holding his side and glaring at a large rock that was sticking up out of the dirt. He winced in pain, "Son of a bitch, why is it these boat people leave such things laying where a man can land on 'em?"

James said, "Does it hurt to breath?"

Charlie barked the words, "It hurts all the time."

"But more when you take a breath?"

"What are you, a doctor?"

James recalled when his father had been thrown from a horse and broken two ribs. It had hurt him to breathe. He said, "They got a doctor here?"

Charlie grimaced, "They cost money."

"I'm sorry, Mr. Reed."

"Well, you damned well should be. I told you not to run me off the other side."

James thought to offer up what Charlie could or should have done, but he did not. He said, "Probably be best if you lay on the wagon and I'll drive you to the sawbones' office.

Charlie sighed in an exaggerated manner that caused him to suddenly catch his breath and contort his face in pain. He growled, "Alright, help me up."

James extended a hand to Charlie and began to pull while Charlie grimaced and uttered a long drawn-out guttural moan until he was on his feet, whereupon he declared, "I don't need this to be happenin'. I got hay to cut." He paused and checked his breathing and the movement of his rib cage as a means to retaliate against the pain. After a few seconds he exhaled, "Damn the bad luck." He then began walking gingerly around the horses and up onto the loading dock with James at his side. He stopped on top of the retaining wall and held out his left arm, the off side of his broken ribs, and said, "Keep me steady, son."

With both hands, James took hold of Charlie's forearm and bicep and guided his step down onto the wagon like he was a feeble old man well beyond his fifty years. Charlie sat on the bed of the wagon rather than climb around onto the seat. He said, "Head to town, son. I'll tell ya where to go."

It was at that moment James saw two men, a short distance away, pointing with some amusement at the mower sitting crosswise on the wagon bed. The bigger of the two laughed and called out, "You reckon to ride that mower side-saddle?" They both then laughed.

James looked down at that portion of the mower's tongue that extended over the side of the wagon bed. He was quick to see that a thinking man would have backed the wagon up to the dock so that the mower could have been loaded lengthwise instead of crosswise. Before James could respond, the smaller man says to his friend, loud enough so James and Charlie could hear, "You reckon they got instructions on how to use that thing?"

The big man replied, like it was his part in a play, "I dare say they're not smart enough to read 'em."

Charlie, who had been lying flat on his back, was now struggling to rise up, but owing to the pain was having considerable difficulty. James said in a low but stern voice, "Stay down, Charlie, no need to invite trouble." The pain, or maybe a flash of common sense, caused Charlie to wrinkle his face in agony and ease himself back down. James called out to the strangers who were now passing a pint bottle of whiskey back and forth, "How 'bout you boys give me a hand fittin' this mower on here right-ways? My partner here has got busted ribs. I'd be obliged if ya would."

Mild surprise registered on the stranger's faces. They were taken aback. Their taunts were not getting them the brawl for sport that they expected. It was the bigger one who was first to show some decency, he nodded, "Alright, Mister, we'll help ya." With that he and his friend began walking toward the wagon.

James felt some relief. With the three of them pulling and backing and twisting they finally got the mower situated lengthwise on the wagon bed. It was a far cry from how things had been resolved on the Destiny.

They had no choice but to drive up the bloodiest block in the west. Even though it wasn't yet noon, business was booming in the numerous saloons. It was a raucous environment. Music, loud profanity laced talk, and women's laughter floated out into the street. James had never seen anything quite like it. He swiveled his head from side to side, maintaining a wary eye for trouble. The brace of draft horses kept a steady pace. He was fortunate to not have to stop for any drunks in the street, not even in front of Madame Moustache's Cosmopolitan Saloon. Soon, they were by all of the depravity and onto a secondary street consisting of mostly log cabins whose walls were weathered gray. Some of the pine board roofs were covered with dirt and random weeds, while other, more affluent owners, had covered theirs with black tarpaper. James could see up ahead, where these structures petered out, a white clapboard house with a faded white wooden sign planted in the bare dirt and weeds out in front of it. James read the sign, *Doctor Archibald Perry,* while guiding the big horses to a halt in front of it. He twisted around on the seat that was perched on leaf springs high above the wagon bed and looked down at Charlie whose eyes were closed. He said in a low voice, "I reckon we're here, Mr. Reed."

Charlie opened his eyes but made no effort to move. Instead, he stared straight up at a kind of cream-colored cloud that resembled a batch of bread dough. Most of the pain lines in his face had dissolved, which suggested to James why Charlie had made no effort to speak or sit up. But then the Charlie that James was beginning to expect showed up. He said, still flat on his back and still not making eye contact, "You know son, I know for a fact there's a badger hole back up the street a ways. Maybe you should turn around and drive through it. Be a damned shame to come all the way from the levee to here and hit ever hole but that one."

From their right, towards the doctor's house, Arch Perry called out while not quite to the wagon, "Why you sorry old turd, if I was this young fella I'd a made you walk." Doctor Perry, who was slightly older than Charlie and known to him for some years, felt comfortable in taking such sarcastic liberty. He stopped at the edge of the wagon and looked down at Charlie, "What did you do to yourself?"

Pain had returned to Charlie's face. "I fell on a rock."

James added, "It was my fault, I reckon. We was loadin' this mowing machine"

Charlie cut in, his voice absent any sarcasm, "It just got away from us, Doc, and I couldn't git outta the way fast enough."

Perry, all business now, unbuttoned Charlie's tan shirt. His eyes immediately settled on Charlie's left side. A dark purple bruise the size of a saucer spanned several of his ribs. Perry sighed, not loud, but enough to worry Charlie who came back, "They busted?"

Perry ran a hand through his gray hair in a thoughtful way before saying, "I expect some of 'em are."

Charlie frowned, "Well, that's a helluva note. I got lots a hay to mow."

Perry shook his head, "You aren't going to be riding any mower or buck rake without enduring considerable pain for a good while."

It came to James that providence was looking him in the eye. He said, "Charlie, I'll cut your hay."

Charlie looked at James without speaking until it became awkward between them. Finally, he said, "I reckon I ain't got much choice."

James said, not knowing if he could or not, "I'll do ya a good job, Charlie."

Charlie mixed a look of doubt in with the pain that now covered his face on account of all the talking he was having to do. He said, "We'll see."

Doc Perry interrupted, "I need to bandage those ribs. Maybe get you something for the pain. Might be best if you spend the night in town."

Charlie glanced at Perry before sighing and looking at James, "Take the wagon and team to the livery. Tell Mac they're mine and I'll settle up before we leave town tomorrow."

James nodded, "Yes, Sir." It was a conscious effort for him to suppress a grin at his good fortune. He now had a job and a way out of Fort Benton.

After helping Charlie into Doctor Perry's office, James drove the wagon to the livery stable at the edge of town. It consisted of a big barn with connecting corrals on three sides of it. The business side was defined by large double doors that were now open. Above these doors, painted right on the weathered pine board wall was one word, LIVERY. The letters were close to two feet tall and the width of one of those big paintbrushes. They were showing their age as much of the white paint had curled and buckled and chipped off. Their appearance reminded James of a sunbaked dry water hole whose mud had cracked in myriad ways. He parked the wagon next to the corral that was north of the doors and jumped down. He was not quite to the opening when he heard talk inside.

A gravelly, old man's voice declared, "The deputy was just by here a little while ago. Said this fella shot a man on a boat coming upriver. Said to be on the lookout for him as he might be a tough customer."

The other talker, younger sounding, a little full of himself, came back, "Those damned boats bring all kinds a scalawags up here."

The old man cackled, "They sure as hell do."

"So, how's a fella to know this desperado," asked the bold man.

"Deputy said he was a young guy. Maybe your age. Had a French sounding name. Believe he said it was Coumerilh."

James, who had leaned against the barn's wall to eavesdrop was struck with the impulse to back away quietly and leave. He'd taken several backward steps when the naysayer in his mind stopped him, *where in hell do you think you're gonna go to with five dollars in your pocket? You go through that door and pass yourself off as somebody else, you'll have a job, something to eat and a place to sleep, if you can just git outta town without Charlie finding out you're wanted by the law.* James took a deep breath to settle his racing heart and stepped into the door opening. To either side of him were stalls, about half of them occupied. In the deep shadow at the rear of the barn were the talkers. He called out like he was carefree, "Afternoon, would one a you gentlemen be the proprietor?"

An old man with a snow-white moustache and a flat brimmed hat whose crown was sharply peaked came back, "What can I do ya for?"

James began walking toward the stationary livery owner and the other talker saying as he went, "I'm workin' for Charlie Reed. Got his team outside. Need ta board 'em for the night."

An odd look came to the old man's face, he scoffed, "I can't feature that skinflint puttin' out the money to overnight in town. Hell, it ain't but about three hours to his place."

James saw that the younger man was looking him over with more than what appeared to be casual interest. It caused the paranoia within him to rise up in his throat and take hold of his tongue such that it left an awkward silence. The stranger, who was now purposely locked on to James' eyes, filled the void, he said, "Did I hear you say, Sir, that you are in the employ of Mr. Reed?"

James nodded, "I am as of a little while ago. He busted some ribs loading his new mower. Appears I'll be cutting his hay."

Mild surprise showed on the talkers' faces with the younger one exclaiming, "The hell you say."

James came back, "Just this morning while we were loadin' the mower."

The younger talker shook his head, "You ever cut hay or run a buck rake before."

"No, Sir, but I reckon I kin git the hang of it in not too long."

The stranger's eyes darted to the Navy Colt in James' waistband and then back to his eyes as he stepped towards James. He held out his hand, "Name's Otto Weiss."

Panic seized James' insides. He was not an accomplished liar. The naysayer in his mind was screaming at him to be calm and for a new name. It came to him out of the past. A name, not an unusual one, that he heard at morning role call one time and again the next day on a burial detail. It rolled off his tongue in, he hoped, a convincing manner, "George Little."

And so, the ruse began, intact James hoped, until they met up with Charlie.

CHAPTER SEVENTEEN

It was over supper that James learned of Otto's past misfortune on the Bellows ranch and his quest to rescue their daughter from the Sioux. In turn, Otto learned half-truths. That, after the Confederacy surrendered, James had gone home to work on the family farm but had tired of it. And now he had come all the way up the Missouri River on the Prairie Rose looking to start his own ranch. And yes, he had heard about the murder on the steamboat Destiny.

They had taken their bedrolls to a grazed off grassy spot amongst the sagebrush out beyond the corrals. Throughout the night, James listened to Otto's raspy snoring that was incessant save for one time when he got up to relieve himself. James could hear it clearly, above the cricket symphony, the splashing of the urine on a patch of bare dirt. And then Otto tiptoeing in the half-moon light back toward his bedroll barely six feet away. But before he got there, he emitted a sudden but muffled, "ow, son of a bitch." There was then a controlled groan followed by a deep sigh and more tiptoeing. Soon, James could hear Otto wriggling under his blankets amid whispered profanity. By and by, it was as before with the crickets keeping time with Otto's snoring and James staring up into the darkness peppered with twinkling diamonds wondering if his good fortune would end when they tied in with Charlie.

So it went, until the bugler at Fort Benton blew reveille. It caused an almost immediate cessation of Otto's snoring. Nonetheless, he did not move, keeping his blanket shrouded back to James. After a time, he said, without turning over or sitting up, just staying as he was, "There was too damned many mornings that I had to jump outta bed just lickety-split on account of that tune." He paused and snorted a laugh, "but not anymore."

For a time, James said nothing, the wheels of his mind spinning with dread at what he knew was coming. Off in the distance, a rooster crowed an encore to the bugler. It caused James to consider, more seriously than he had all night, striking out in this dishwater light of dawn. He reasoned, *even on foot, I could cover some ground. Maybe enough so that when Otto tells Charlie who I am and they put the law on me, I'll be long gone.* It was then that the Naysayer chimed in, as he was so wont to do, *you fool, you got no food and no horse. You'll be in jail or dead by sundown.*

Otto rolled over in his blankets to face James. His hair was tangled from a week's worth of sweat and a hard sleep, he said, "I could kill for a cup a coffee, George. I'm of a mind we go to town and search one out along with some bacon and eggs. Maybe a stack a sourdough hotcakes too."

It seemed pointless to James to be thinking of food when he was in danger of losing his freedom by the day's end. His angst left him, at the moment, unable to speak.

Otto went on, seemingly oblivious to James' lack of participation, "I'll tell you what, George, it was a breeze of luck ole Charlie hiring me on. After the Sioux burned the Bellows' ranch down it purty much left me without a pot to piss in."

It was then that the impulse struck James. His fear was such that he was uncertain if he might throw up before he could rid himself of it. Right here, right now, he would put his fate in the hands of a stranger he had known for less than a day. He raised up on an elbow to better read Otto's face and then he just put it out there, "I lied about who I am, Otto."

Otto sat up in his blankets seemingly indifferent to James' confession, he came back, "The hell you say." He then casually reached into his shirt pocket for a plug of tobacco and bit off a chew. He worked it several times before allowing his tongue to push it over against his right cheek and draw off some of the juice which he launched beyond his bed into the sagebrush.

James nodded, uncertain how to take Otto's response, "Yeah, I lied. I'm sorry."

"Well, you know I kinda wondered about that last night. There was a time or two I called you George and you looked at me like I was talkin' Chinese or, like you forgot your name." Otto paused again to spit as is often the case with a new chew. After wiping his hand across his moustache, he asked the obvious, "So, what does your mama call you?"

"James Coumerilh."

Otto's face remained blank for a few seconds until finally an awareness came to it, he said, "You the fella that done the killin' on the boat?"

James nodded, "It was him or me. He would have killed me if he'd gotten ahold of me or the gun before me."

Otto shook his head as he looked off to the east and the still mostly dark outline of town. He sighed, "So, I'm assuming you telling me this you want me to keep it under my hat?"

James hissed the words, "The man was evil. He killed a friend a mine for no good reason."

Otto was now wide awake. Not knowing what to say, he spit again.

James pleaded, "Charlie knows my real name. He just doesn't know what I did, or at least when I left him at the doctor's office yesterday, he didn't. I know I'm asking a lot."

Otto snapped, "You damned right you are. Day one at this job and I gotta stand there with you and lie to the boss."

Other options began to play in James' mind, rapidly, like wind-blown tumbleweeds they were here and gone until one suddenly stuck. He met the resentment, anger even, in Otto's eyes full on, "Tell you what, I'll gather my stuff and head out right now. All I ask is you just say that when you woke up this morning, I was gone. And if they catch me, I'll not say a word about this conversation."

Otto pushed his top blanket down and gathered his legs under him so he could sit cross-legged, Indian style. Both of his gray socks had holes where his heels had worn them away. His black cotton pants weren't any better as they sported a hole over the right knee. It was obvious that he needed this job almost as bad as James. He continued to cogitate the matter, not looking at James. Instead, he picked up a small piece of dead sagebrush that he studied for a moment, like it mattered, before throwing it out into the retreating darkness. The silence between them was heavy. It seemed about to explode when the rooster, far off, crowed again, and a mountain bluebird, perched not fifty feet away in the top of a sage bush, cast out his diminutive call. Finally, Otto looked over at James, "I reckon I can just play dumb. Like I forgot hearing your name from the livery fella. But just so you know, if the law comes a callin' I'll swear up and down I had no knowledge of your past."

James sighed, not so it was noticeable, and said, "I'm much obliged, Otto."

Otto moved on, purpose like, "I'm gonna put on my boots and go find me some breakfast." He paused, knowing that James' situation would likely temper his response, he asked, "You comin'?"

James was hungry, so hungry that his stomach was growling, but he shook his head. "I better not. I'm too close to gittin' outta town."

Otto did not argue. He slipped on his boots and hat and got to his feet. He looked down at James who was still sitting in his blankets, "Well, Sir, I'll see you before the sun is all the way up." And with that he walked off toward town.

James watched him go. He wondered if he was being played for a fool and that Otto would go straight away and look up the marshal. But he made no effort to leave. He was tired and hungry. To run, with no horse and broke as he was, would only exacerbate those conditions. He laid back in his blankets, *I reckon I'll just roll the dice.*

CHAPTER EIGHTEEN

Chief Old Bear's camp was a half day's ride from the Metis on Goose Creek. He was the leader of the marauding Lakota that had attacked the Bellows ranch and killed them all except for their daughter, Sarah. Old Bear had been given his name even before he was old due to his being smart and cunning like an old grizzly bear that had survived the many attempts to kill him. He now had deep furrows in his face. His skin, a dark bronze color, did not contrast much with his black eyes.

Although they had little fear of retaliation for their crimes south of the Medicine Line, they still posted a lookout in a patch of timber on the ridge above their village. Moments ago, he had come to the edge of the trees and signaled that two riders were approaching. Because he did not give the danger sign, Old Bear allowed the people to continue as they were. Many were eating their noon meal. Children played along and in the knee-deep creek. Its water was cold and clear and good to drink, in spite of its name. The Lakota called it Skunk Creek because of a weedy plant that grew there that smelled bad when you crushed its leaves.

Not long after the lookout's signal, a half dozen dogs began barking and yelping at the south end of the village. Excited voices accompanied the canine cacophony.

From high on his horse, Claude Charbonneau spotted Old Bear standing near a cooking fire in front of his teepee. He was wearing his signature black Bowler hat that was adorned with a single eagle feather. The hat's previous owner had likely been a gambler or drummer, who was out of place here on the high plains of Montana. Before they were close enough to read one another's eyes, Claude raised his hand and shouted above the yapping dogs that were swirling around he and Phillip Trottier's horses, "Chief Old Bear, it is good to see you, my friend."

Old Bear raised his hand in greeting, "And you Claude Charbonneau. Get down from your horse. We will smoke the pipe of friends and then we will eat." Old Bear then spoke in his tongue to one of his wives who went quickly into their teepee to retrieve his pipe. No sooner had she entered the doorway than there was screaming and shouting and a white girl in a blue dress burst from the lodge's entrance running straight for Claude and Phillip yelling, "Help me, help me, please." She was nearly to them when a stocky Indian woman grabbed the girl around the waist and threw her to the ground. The girl, now crying uncontrollably but with her eyes fixed on Claude, managed to get to her feet. It was to no avail as a second woman came running up and punched the white girl in the face. The blow landed squarely on the girl's nose knocking her off her feet. Determined to reach Claude and Phillip in her belief that she would be rescued, the girl struggled to her knees. Blood was running out both of her nostrils and down over her lips and chin. It was obvious that her nose was broken. The Indian women began to shake their fists and curse at her causing the girl to remain on her knees until the stocky woman grabbed her by the hair and jerked her to her feet. The girl, still staring at Claude, moaned, barely above a whisper, "help me, please don't leave me here." And then the woman, the same one who had hit her in the face, planted her fist hard and fast in the girl's stomach. Her reaction was instantaneous. Her eyes grew big, and her mouth went wide, gasping for air. She fell silent as the two women each took an arm and began dragging her toward a teepee farther away and out of sight. The girl's limp body hung like a rag doll between the two husky women. Claude and Phillip, along with most everyone else, could not help but watch the spectacle. The girl and her captors were still visible when Old Bear looked away from them and to Claude and Phillip. His face was absent any emotion one way or another, he said, "She is slow to accept our ways."

Claude saw opportunity in the girl's grief. Unable to help himself, he said, thinking he was being sly in his intent, "Maybe she never will."

Old Bear became pensive, like he was seriously considering what Claude had said, but then the cracks in his face allowed a wry grin to come through, he said, "Some horses are like that."

Claude nodded, "Oui, I've owned a few that could not be broken."

"And what did you do with them?" countered Old Bear.

This is going to be too easy, thought Claude. *I will offer him the 500 rounds of ammunition and a gallon of whiskey.* Claude manufactured a brief laugh to further shape his proposition as a logical thing to do before saying, "I sold them to a horse trader and wished him well." He then laughed some more.

Old Bear did not laugh. He shook his head instead. He said, "If this one were a horse, I would do that. But no, I will break her. She is to be my wife."

Claude knew from previous dealings with Old Bear that the two women who had dragged the girl away were his wives. They were plain looking. A little portly from having given Old Bear five kids between them. And the puncher, the one who had caused the most pain to the girl, was missing two front teeth from a time when she was thrown from a horse and landed face first. It was clear to Claude why Old Bear would want this buxom young girl to share his bed. He suspected his entreaty would be pointless, even as the words escaped him, "I'll trade you for the girl. Five hundred bullets for the many shoots guns that I have brought you and a gallon of whiskey."

Old Bear's response was quick, "No trade. She is to be my wife."

Claude hesitated, trying to read Old Bear's eyes. *He could be stonewalling me knowing that I'll bump my offer.* In the next instant, the cautious part of him shouted out, *you don't even know if her kin have got money.* And then his conscience showed up late to the deliberations, *you can't just leave the girl.* He said aloud, "I will have to come again with the rest, but I will give you a thousand bullets for the Winchesters and five gallons of whiskey for the girl."

Old Bear scoffed, "You desire her in your bed as much as I."

Claude came back, "No, my culture does not allow for more than one wife. With me, this is business. I am a trader. In the end, I may lose, or maybe not."

Old Bear shook his head, "No matter. I no trade."

Beyond Old Bear, Claude saw the less aggressive wife enter Old Bear's lodge and come out with his pipe. He knew better than to persist in getting the girl.

It was several hours before they left leading four sorrel horses that wore Amos Bellows' Rocking B brand. In return, Claude had given Old Bear five hundred rounds of .44 rimfire ammunition and a gallon of whiskey.

CHAPTER NINETEEN

From where he sat in the privy behind the mercantile, Andrew Hunt could see through a knothole in the door that Claude Charbonneau and another man were coming. They were driving six horses that appeared mostly cooperative. He grumbled as he pulled up his pants, "Dammit, a man can't even do his business in peace." He sighed and pushed the privy door open. The bright sunlight caused him to squint hard as he started walking towards a pole fence that defined a small pasture behind the store. At one time, the land inside the fence had supported waist high grass. Now it was grubbed out, save for clumps of weeds here and there that were so unpalatable the horses wouldn't eat them. The pasture was a rectangle that took in about five acres. It ran down to and across a little creek that a man, with a running start, could jump across.

It was a week ago yesterday that Claude had been in Paradise. Today, he and Phillip rode up to the swing gate entrance to the pasture, as usual, like it belonged to them. They took it for granted that Hunt would buy their horses, he always had. Claude got down from his horse and swung the gate open while Phillip and a black and white dog named Wolf held the horses in check. Momentarily, they followed Claude as he led his horse through the opening. He continued on into the pasture, about fifty yards. The horses followed, eager to go around him and get to the creek for a drink. Claude watched until they reached the water before turning around and starting for the gate. He'd had a sense, a feeling when his back had been to Hunt. It had been awkwardly quiet. He now looked at Hunt, leaning into the fence while resting his forearms on the chest high top pole. He was generally not a talker but today he seemed particularly taciturn. From shouting distance, Claude called out, "Good looking horses, don't you think?"

Claude took five more steps in silence before Hunt said, cold and indifferent, like he feared somebody else more than he did Claude, "I can't buy your horses."

Claude stopped abruptly and drilled an angry stare into Hunt's eyes, he said, "What?

Hunt did not wither as Claude had expected. Instead, he said, "Unless you got a bill of sale I can't buy your horses."

Claude fired back angrily, "Where's this coming from?"

Hunt dug in, "Mounted Police. They been by here twice since that day you was here. They asked if I had bills of sale to prove where the horses I got in my pasture came from."

An anxious feeling gripped Claude, he said naively hopeful, "I always thought you worked up some phony papers to cover that."

Hunt snorted, "No, I take in the horses on good faith. That you traded for them with the rightful owner so that made you the new rightful owner."

Claude laughed sarcastically, "You're a miserable liar, Hunt. You know damned good and well where the Sioux get these horses."

Hunt shook his head and seethed the words, "And so does the Mounted Police. That young one that was in here the day you was, he came back later with his boss. Said they know I been selling you material to make moonshine and buying your stolen horses and buffalo hides that you get by trading whiskey to the Indians. He said, "it's gotta stop.""

Claude scoffed, "What proof has he got of this?"

Hunt looked incredulous, "If it comes down to them having to show you, Claude, you'll likely be in manacles."

Claude glared at Hunt before looking away and shaking his head in silence. It was clear to him that Hunt was afraid of the police and that business between them, as he'd known it, was over. He put his hands on his hips while staring across the pasture to where the horses were. The US brand was clearly visible on the left flank of a big gray gelding. And then there were the two with the Rocking B brand but the other three were slick. They were not as good looking as the branded horses. It was probably why Old Bear gave them up for bullets and whiskey. Claude's inner voice defended his actions, *I knew I shouldn't have taken those branded ones. They'll cause trouble if their owners ever come north of the Medicine Line.* Finally, he turned back to Hunt. It was galling to see the look of confidence, arrogance almost, in his face. His watery green eyes, always bloodshot, exuded victory over Claude even though it would cost him money in the long run. At last, Claude said, his tone bitter, "The ones without a brand, will you at least take those?"

Hunt sighed and rubbed his hand thoughtfully across a four day stubble of gray whiskers. He appeared to be studying the horses in question for some time until finally he said, "I'll give you ten dollars a head."

Claude's response was explosive, "You sorry bastard. Why don't you just put a gun to my head and steal 'em?"

Although his voice trembled some, Hunt did not cower from Claude's outburst. He came back, "That boss policeman told me that the bigshots in Ottawa are fed up with how things are out here. They're afraid that if folks like you keep trading whiskey and guns to the Lakota and they keep killing and robbing white people in Montana, that the American Army will cross the Medicine Line to put a stop to it and never go home."

Phillip, who was still sitting on his horse, had been taking in the exchange between Claude and Hunt. He now blurted out, "You don't put any stock in what those old fools think, do you? If they was fair-minded they'd give the Metis land to call their own and there'd be no whiskey trading."

Hunt came back quick, not knowing Phillp's temperament, "The scrip commission was this way not long ago. You should have made your case."

Phillip scoffed, "We did almost two years ago and we're still waiting to hear from them."

It may have been that the police had emboldened Hunt beyond what was prudent given his circumstances. He said, almost flippantly, "There's been some folks that gave up their scrip payment for whiskey. Since you're in the whiskey business maybe that's a means for you to acquire some scrip to buy land with."

Being half Cree Indian, Phillip had known some of his mother's relatives that had been swindled out of their scrip payment and lost their chance to own 160 acres of land. It was insulting to Phillip that Hunt thought he would cheat his own people. He nudged the sides of his horse and rode next to the pasture fence where Hunt was standing. His expression was hateful as he looked down at Hunt and said, "If you weren't such a foolish, loose tongued old man I'd get down from my horse and give you a good thrashing."

Fear flooded Hunt's eyes. He immediately took several steps back from the fence and looked at Claude to restore civility. Claude said in a sharp voice, "Let it go, Phillip."

Phillip scowled at Claude and then Hunt, before saying, "It don't bother you that this old shit thinks we'd cheat our own people?"

Hunt, an Englishman, looked at Claude as if to gauge his desire to keep Phillip at bay and then proceeded to fan the flames of discourse that he had created, he said, "Your outrage is almost amusing, Mr. Trottier. Are you not half white? Look at the misery your actions are causing to those people south of the line."

Phillip instantly started to get off his horse when he was frozen by Claude's shout, "Stay on your horse, Phillip. Don't set foot on the ground."

Hunt looked relieved, appreciative even, that Claude had stopped Phillip from assaulting him. He said, his voice unsteady, "I'll give you twelve dollars a head for the unbranded ones. The others, take with you."

Claude grimaced, "The others are sound animals. Much better than the ones you're buying. You can have them for the same price."

"And have the mounted police haul me off to their jail? No, take them with you."

"Surely, you –"

Phillip shouted, "Stop it, Claude. You're begging like a dog."

Claude went silent and glared at Phillip. Before he could speak, Hunt said, "Take what I've offered and leave. It will not bode well for me if the police were to come by here and those American horses, and you, were here."

Claude looked at Hunt and shook his head. His inner voice shouted, *you're a scoundrel Hunt. I'll never trade with you again.* But he kept quiet as he knew Hunt had the upper hand.

CHAPTER TWENTY

Dusk enveloped Antoine Coumerilh's camp. His hunting party had pitched their white canvas tents and teepees along Cottonwood Creek, which was well south of the Medicine Line and two days horseback west of Fort Benton. Their big two-wheel carts were in a line just beyond their lodges. Up away from the creek, where it was drier, the prairie grass was all yellow. But close, within rock throwing distance, the soil supported a fair amount of green grass and even some late summer wildflowers that were mostly lavender and white. For now, until they grazed it off, their horses were picketed here. As the creek's namesake implied, there were cottonwood trees overshadowing the water. It was a fine place to camp, even if the buffalo hunting hadn't been very good. Antoine's wife, Angelique, sat cross-legged next to a flickering buffalo chip fire. A long skirt, made of burnt orange cotton cloth that Antoine had traded a buffalo hide for in Fort Benton hid her slender, muscular legs. In her lap she held a wooden bowl full of dried chokecherries that she was pulverizing with a palm sized rock. Later, she would mix the powder like fruit with dried buffalo meat, ground to a similar consistency, and fat. The end result would be pemican, which they could sell at the various trading posts. Angelique often hummed while pounding the chokecherries, but not tonight. Sitting across the fire from her was

Antoine, her nephew Louis, and his Lakota wife, Doe Eyes. Their conversation was terse.

Louis said, in a haughty tone, "So, Uncle, you have decided to become a farmer?"

Antoine ignored how Louis was being and replied, "The buffalo are nearly gone. Without them, we cannot live as we once did."

A wry grin came over Louis' face, "You've gotten lazy and timid in your old age, Uncle. There is game. We just have to go where it's at." He paused and then smiled in a devilish way, "The white men have plenty of slow elk. They taste good." He then laughed.

Antoine squinted slightly while making a perfunctory effort to fan the acrid smoke away from his eyes. An irritated look came over his face, "You know the soldiers will remove us if they catch us hunting on the Blackfeet's reservation, or any other where we're not welcome. It is to make trouble for ourselves to hunt where we are not allowed." And then he added, "Stealing the white man's cattle will get us all killed."

Louis scoffed, "So, you're just going to give in to the soldiers like an old woman?"

"There are rules, Louis."

The fire's flames reflected in Louis' eyes accentuating his contempt for what his uncle was saying, he said "It doesn't mean we have to follow them."

Antoine leaned forward and spit tobacco juice into the fire. It was consumed quickly save for a few drops that landed on a white rock that was part of the fire ring. The spit danced frenetically for a few seconds before evaporating. They had all watched the distraction knowing that Antoine was about to settle the matter of following rules. He looked at Louis in a manner that suggested there would be no forgiveness, no tolerance, if he chose to break the law and said, "If you choose to go down this path of lawlessness you cannot be part of us."

Louis snorted as he tossed his head back in defiance before saying in a loud, angry voice, "Your sister's son. Your own blood. You're casting me and my family out?"

Before now, Antoine had purposely not pointed out that what Louis advocated doing was the path his wife's people were following. He said, "Perhaps it would be best if you and your family went to live with Doe Eyes' family."

Louis looked over through the drifting smoke at his uncle. He held the look for a good while in the silence of the fire popping and in the distance snippets of conversation and laughter, sharp and clear. And then, when at last he'd weighed the consequences of his decision, he abruptly stood up and looked down at his uncle. His words were bathed in arrogance, "I will be warm this winter and have plenty to eat in Old Bear's village." He paused before saying contemptuously, "You will have your rules to keep you warm and fill your belly." He then snorted and pushed Doe Eyes in the direction of their tent and walked away.

Angelique saw the sadness in her husband's eyes and said, "Maybe he will change his mind after a while and come back."

Antoine shook his head, "No, there will be no coming back. If he goes down this path of breaking the rules, the soldiers will look at him as bad and all those around him. To let him come back after he breaks the law would be like inviting smallpox amongst us. It would eventually kill us all."

The sun was not yet up when Louis, Doe Eyes, and their daughter, Ariele, set out for Old Bear's village.

CHAPTER TWENTY-ONE

The Grubstake Café was on the next street over from where the saloons and brothels of Fort Benton had concentrated themselves. It was quiet relief from the raucous debauchery of the saloon district where drinking, gambling and daily killings were the norm. The solitude of the little cafe drew in decent people, regulars like Doctor Archibald Perry. And on this night, there was a newcomer.

Frank Murphy had stayed on the Destiny, enduring Turk's taunts and the menial work that was assigned to him, all the way to Fort Benton. Odd jobs unloading freight, cleaning stables and the like had kept him from going hungry. But tonight was a celebration of sorts. In two days, he would start a new, permanent job as a shotgun messenger on the stage that ran between Fort Benton and Helena.

The dining area was big enough for six tables. There were four round ones with four chairs each and two smaller, rectangular ones against the wall on the left side of the room. The little tables each had two chairs. It was not coincidence that Frank, a man of few words and friends, sat down at one of the little tables. Some of the same rationale probably applied to Doctor Perry as he often dined alone. He sat at the little table next to Frank's. They were both sipping coffee and reading month old papers from St. Louis with even older news while they waited for their supper. And although they were facing one another in a space of about ten feet, they each extended to one another the courtesy of not invading their privacy. Given the fact that two of the other tables besides the doctor's, were occupied by couples, Frank was particularly grateful for the abandoned newspaper. There had been other nights when he had to feign an insatiable thirst for coffee by taking repeated drinks or an intense curiosity about the design of the red and white oil cloth that covered the table. But not tonight. He was still on his first cup of coffee when the door to the street opened. A stocky man dressed in a dark suit with a gray wide brimmed hat, came inside. A Colt revolver rested on his right hip. It was obvious that it was one of those new kind that took metallic cartridges as there were many loops on his belt that contained them. Frank kept his paper low enough that he could pretend to be reading while watching what the stranger was going to do. It wasn't long before he saw the man's eyes light up with recognition as he started towards the doctor's table, who was unaware that he was coming. Shortly, the stranger arrived, "Evening, Doc. Mind if I sit down?"

Doctor Perry looked up and folded his paper saying, "Not at all, Marshal. Pull up a chair."

Frank's senses ratcheted up a bit. It'd only been a couple of days ago that he'd heard Turk, who had quit the Destiny, going on to a half-drunk audience how he saw this Coumer-ilh fella kill the Destiny's mate in cold blood. *Just shot 'im like a dog. Execution it was.*

The marshal glanced at Frank before dragging his chair back across the rough plank floor. The chair made a loud scuffing noise that was contrary to the ambience of the room. Frank paid it no mind but an older, pretty woman sitting at a table in the middle of the room frowned at the marshal like he was some uncultured oaf.

Doctor Perry allowed his guest to settle himself into the chair before beginning, like he thought the marshal's reason for being there was social, "Has it been hot enough for you?"

The marshal bobbed his head in a downward slash, "Purgatory couldn't be any hotter."

Perry gave a polite chuckle, "I've seen it like this before. Going into September this hot and then the weather gods ambush you with a foot of snow or some such."

Before the marshal could add his part to what both of them knew was the foundation for the marshal being able to state his reason for inviting himself to Perry's supper, the waitress arrived with a steak and all the fixings. "Anything else, Doc?"

Perry did a cursory inventory of the table, "Maybe more coffee."

The woman nodded and looked at the marshal, "Are you eatin', Jim?"

Jim Hays smelled the warm aroma of the steak and fried spuds. It caused him to hesitate until his mind's eye leapt forward to when he and Perry would get down to business. It could be he wouldn't be welcome after that, he replied, "Just coffee, Irene."

Perry made no attempt to encourage the marshal to eat. He sat silent until the waitress was out of earshot and then he gave him a look that said there would be no more weather talk. He said as he cut into his steak, "So, what's on your mind, Jim?"

The marshal, still trying to be cordial, came back, "I been hearin' that you treated old Charlie Reed for some busted ribs."

Perry knew what was coming. Nonetheless, he forked a bite of steak into his mouth and chewed several times, like he had no worries, before responding, "I did. Said he broke 'em loading a new mower down at the levee."

Hays nodded, "That's what I heard."

Irritation percolated through Perry's mouthful of steak, "Well, why are you asking me then?"

Irene was now back with the coffee. A smile that she'd purposely ginned up just before she got to the table vanished as she read the tension between the two men. She set the coffee down without speaking and walked away.

Hays leaned in slightly towards Perry, "Alright, Doc, I also heard this Coumerilh fella, the one that did the killin' on the Destiny, was helpin' Charlie. I heard he brought him to your office."

Perry nodded as he took a bite of spuds, "Yeah, a young man brought Charlie to me on the bed of his wagon."

Hays' eyes became intense, "And Charlie didn't introduce you to this young fella."

Perry was at a crossroads, a conundrum of sorts. Charlie had introduced James but, at the time, neither knew that he was wanted by the law. It wasn't until a couple of days later that he learned James Coumerilh was wanted for murder. His initial thought, upon hearing this, was he needed to report it. But then he thought, *if I do, it'll leave Charlie high and dry. He needs to get his hay cut and hauled to the stage stop on Porcupine Creek or come winter he'll be destitute.* He said, "I don't recall if he did or not, Marshal. Obviously, if he did the name didn't stick with me."

Hays did little to hide his disbelief. He came back, "So, how did this fella strike you? Is he a rough customer?"

Perry shook his head, "I don't think he would give you gunplay if you were to come upon him."

Hays snorted, "Well, the word at the livery is this mystery fella and another guy drove Charlie out to his ranch. I reckon tomorrow I'll ride out there and see how good a judge of character you are. But, hell, it might not even be this Coumerilh fella." He laughed in a derisive way before pushing back from the table and walking out, leaving his coffee untouched.

Frank had heard every word of the conversation between Doctor Perry and the marshal. He was pondering what allegiance, if any, he should have to James when the waitress arrived with his steak. He made momentary eye contact with the woman as he said, barely audible, "Thank you, Ma'am." He then began to eat, all the while thinking of his moral obligation to James. The events after he was shot by the Indians and his time on board the Destiny were seldom far from his mind. And even now, as he cut another piece of steak, his recollection put James in the middle of it all. His conscience shouted out to him, *who knows how things would have turned out if he hadn't got that sawbones off the Destiny to patch you up?* Frank was still on this teeter-toter of guilt and indecision when Irene brought Perry his dessert, apple cobbler. He knew it wouldn't be long now and his dilemma would worsen if the doctor left before he could talk to him. So, he paused in his eating and looked in Perry's direction saying, "Best part of the meal."

Perry returned Frank's gaze and grinned while taking another bite of cobbler, "It's the fresh apples. A fella coupla miles south of town has an orchard."

Frank nodded, "Yes Sir, nothing like fresh apples to make a good cobbler."

It was Perry who allowed it, an awkward silence to come between them. Their words hung in the air like pointless fluff. He could read it in Frank's demeanor that the conversation made him uneasy. And then Frank committed himself, just as the naysayer in his mind was admonishing him, *down the road that doctor will tell on you.* He said it anyway, "I'm new here. I was wondering if you could give me directions to Charlie Reed's place. I've heard he might be looking for a hand."

The coincidence of Frank's request came across as peculiar to Perry. He briefly considered playing along and telling him what he wanted to know, like he was clueless without an ounce of suspicion as to why this stranger, who had obviously eavesdropped on him and the marshal's conversation, would now be asking how to get to Charlie Reed's ranch. But he said on purpose to see what response he would get, "Charlie isn't hiring. He took on a couple of men not long ago to put up his hay."

Frank came back quick, hoping to overshadow his embarrassment at having his lie challenged, "That ain't what I heard in town."

Perry looked straight at Frank so he could read his lips if need be and said, "Be truthful with me and I'll tell you what you want to know."

Frank glanced over at the people sitting at the tables in the center of the room. They appeared unconcerned with he and Perry's conversation, so he nodded to the doctor, "Alright."

Perry came back, "Is this Coumerilh fella your friend?"

"Yeah."

"Did he do what they say?"

"Folks are lying about what happened."

"You sure about that?"

Frank nodded, "I am."

Perry paused while he studied Frank's face for signs he was lying. Finally, he described in some detail how to get to Charlie's ranch. He concluded with, "I'm trusting you to not tell a soul how you came by this information."

Frank replied, "I keep my word."

Perry locked onto Frank's eyes in a look that bordered on threatening before looking away to take the last forkful of his cobbler. In short order he followed it with several quick sips of coffee and dabbing his gray moustache with his napkin before pushing back from the table and walking away as if he and Frank had never talked.

CHAPTER TWENTY-TWO

Had it not been for the fact that Frank, on occasion, had cleaned stalls and otherwise tended the horses at the livery, the owner might not have been agreeable to renting him a horse so late in the day. At first, he'd admonished Frank, *you go trapsing off across the prairie on one of my horses and bust a leg in a badger hole an' I'll take it outta yer hide. And don't think just because I'm an old man I can't git the job done.* But even with this footing of trust, or not, between them, it took another lie to override the logic of riding at night. In response to the demand, and high prices of the brothels in town, a hog ranch had sprung up two miles west. Frank countered his sometimes boss, like he was embarrassed, *if ya gotta know I'm headed to Polly's. Be back in the morning.* The livery owner had howled with laughter while struggling to say, *remind me to not have you watch my sheep.*

It was full on dark, save for a quarter moon, by the time Frank reined in his buckskin horse on a ridge overlooking a broad coulee. He'd been following a two-track wagon road that was not well defined in places but good enough to keep him from getting lost. In the coulee below him, next to the creek, was Charlie Reed's ranch headquarters. It was as Perry had described it. A rock walled cabin with a dirt roof built that way because rocks were plentiful and so were Indians who might want to burn your house down. A good-sized barn with a loft, whose doors were open showing it to be near full of hay, stood away from the cabin along the creek. Corrals tied into the back of the barn. Next to them was a log building that appeared to be a shop as Charlie's new mower was parked in front of it. A sickle cutting bar was leaning against the wall of the building next to a grinding stone that was likely used to sharpen it. To the south of the cabin was a root cellar and on the north side, a privy.

Frank whispered aloud, "This has got to be it." He then nudged the sides of his weary horse and started down the gentle slope toward the cabin. A thread of blue smoke drifted up from its rusty stovepipe. Dim yellow light showed through small four pane windows, one to either side of the door. Frank had just about reached the toe of the slope when two dogs charged out from where they'd been laying on the hard-packed bare dirt in front of the cabin. Their excited barking caused faces to appear in the windows. Moments later the door cracked allowing a sliver of light to escape. James dangled this bait to any would be ambushers for a time before he suddenly flung the door back and dashed outside in his stocking feet. He did not stop until he had reached the heavy shadow at the corner of the cabin. His heart was pounding hard as he peered out in the darkness of the yapping dogs. He called out as if he was a sentry in the Army, "Who goes there?"

"Frank Murphy."

Some of James' fear instantly drained off. Still, he kept his Winchester at the ready. He hollered back, "Frank, what are you doing out here?"

"Well, can I come on in so we can talk.?"

"Are you alone?"

"James, I came to warn you."

It was almost instantaneous, the muffled voices inside the cabin. James grimaced and sighed. He stepped out from the wall and shouted, "Badger, Toby that's enough." Immediately, the dogs, good dogs they were, stopped barking and started back to the cabin. James shouted again into the darkness, "Come on in, Frank."

James eased the hammer down on his rifle and cradled it across his chest and into the crook of his left arm. Frank's horse had just become visible in the faint moonlight when Charlie and Otto came alongside James. True to his word, Otto had offered no explanation inside the cabin causing Charlie to ask, "What has he come to warn you about, James?"

James was glad the ruse was over. He'd not liked deceiving Charlie. He said, straight out, "The law's after me."

"For what?"

James hesitated and shook his head before saying, "I'm the guy who killed the mate on the Destiny."

Charlie was clearly taken aback. He became quiet and looked away as he ran his fingers, trembling some, through his gray hair. For a good while no one spoke, not even Frank, who had ridden up and immediately recognized what might be going on. He was still on his horse when Charlie finally turned back to James and said, in a calm voice, "I can't believe that you'd kill a man in cold blood."

"I didn't, Charlie. He'd already killed a friend of mine and was intent on killing me."

"There must be people saying otherwise or the law wouldn't be after you. Why is that?" said Charlie.

James snorted and shook his head, "If you knew some of the people running things on the Destiny you'd have your answer."

Charlie gave a deep sigh and looked away from James to Frank who, absent an invitation to get down, sat on his horse, "And you, Sir, you've come to warn James about what?"

"A deputy marshal is coming here in the morning looking for him."

"How is it you know this?"

"I overheard him and Doc Perry talking about it."

A surprised look came to Charlie's face. He said to Otto, "Did you know of James' trouble?"

Otto gave an embarrassed sigh and nodded, "I did. I'm sorry."

Charlie looked down towards the barn and the meadows along the creek beyond it where they had cut grass hay. He shook his head and said, "You boys helped me when I couldn't do for myself. So, I guess we're in it now."

James thought to offer, *I'll take my leave of your place Charlie, and just ride out now.* But in that same instant the naysayer reminded him, *you don't own a horse.* He said, "If I strike out now, Charlie, I reckon I can make those thick woods up on Willow Creek."

Without hesitation, Charlie came back, "You can take, Buster."

James shook his head, "No, Sir. Horse tracks would be easier to follow than mine. I'm light. And besides, if the law catches up to me with your horse, they'll be right quick coming to your door."

Charlie paused, thinking more logically of what was at stake before agreeing, "Alright, maybe it is best you hide out for a while."

James said, even though he thought it unlikely, and he reckoned Charlie did too, "I'll hunker down in those woods for a time and then come back an' give you an' Otto a hand hauling hay."

Charlie nodded and said in a voice that was not convincing, "Yes, Sir, I'll wager four or five days you layin' low and then you come on back and we'll be right as rain with the world."

James looked at Frank. "I'm obliged you came."

Frank nodded, "You know we both had our differences with Ziegler."

James said, his words more defeated than angry, "So, who is hell bent on sicin' the law on me?"

"Near as I could tell, it was the captain."

"He wasn't even there."

"I suspect Turk and Piva filled his head with their version."

"But there were others that saw what happened."

Frank snorted, "Deck people, James. You know they don't count."

James shook his head, "Well, I reckon I better git my belongings packed and maybe a little grub if that's alright?"

Charlie said, "Oh, hell ya, we'll fix you up good." And then he looked at Frank. "You're welcome to spend the night. There's oats in the barn and good graze along the creek."

Frank touched his right hand to his hat, "Much obliged."

"Follow me," said Otto as he started walking toward the barn, "I'll git you situated."

James and Charlie were mostly quiet as they went about their respective tasks of gathering things. It was too quick. Just a few minutes and what had become an almost father-son relationship would be over. They both knew it but neither wanted to say it for sure. It was time to go. Charlie held out a Blue Bird flour sack that he had filled with biscuits, a jar of jam, coffee and a big tin cup. "Ain't much, but maybe you can shoot some sage chickens to go along with it."

James took the sack, "I appreciate it, Charlie." He then held out the Winchester that he had taken from the Indian that he had killed in the fight above the wood yard. "I owe you this."

Charlie shook his head, "No, I can't take your gun." He then turned away to a small dresser by his bed and took some money from it. "Here, your wages and for the Indian rifle if you want to sell it."

James looked at the gold pieces in Charlie's hand. They amounted to fifty dollars. He stood still looking at the coins and then the total sincerity in Charlie's eyes.

Charlie said again, "Take it."

Finally, James gave in to the reality of his circumstances and took the money with one hand while handing the rifle over with the other. "I'm much obliged, Charlie."

Charlie came back, "Watch your backtrail."

James picked up his things and went outside with Charlie following. At the corner of the cabin, he paused and nodded towards the barn, "Tell those boys goodbye for me, will you?"

Charlie said, "You probably got that kinda time, don't ya reckon?"

James was quiet for a few seconds like he agreed, but then he said, "I better be going." And then he started off, up along the creek, his way being lit by a sliver of moon and the stars.

CHAPTER TWENTY-THREE

In the daylight, it was a three-hour ride from Charlie Reed's place to Fort Benton. Frank was two hours into his return trip when he saw a man on horseback silhouetted by the sun, which was still partially mired in the coulees and buttes to the east. The rider was a good quarter mile away coming straight at Frank on the same two track road that he'd ridden the night before. It had occurred to him that maybe he should take a different route back to Fort Benton. That there was a chance he could run into the marshal on his way to Charlie's. But his fear of getting lost in the morass of sameness that surrounded him had caused him to stay with what he knew. He grimaced and cursed himself for listening to his cautious side. His rented horse continued on at a walk toward the stranger who appeared to be cantering his big bay horse. When the stranger was less than ten seconds away, Frank could see that it was the deputy from last night. Same stocky build, dark suit and black moustache. And, as he brought his bay to a jerky halt, it was clear he recognized Frank. The deputy called out, "How was your supper?"

Frank purposely played dumb, "Supper?"

A wry grin came to the deputy's face, "Last night at the Grubstake. I was sitting at the table next to yours."

"Oh, I'm sorry, I reckon I'm not too observant."

The stranger nodded, "I'm Deputy Marshal Jim Hays."

It flashed in Frank's mind to lie about his identity, but he quickly abandoned the idea, and came back, "Frank Murphy."

Hays paused for a moment, seemingly processing the logistics of a man being at the Grubstake in Fort Benton at suppertime last night and this morning already heading back to town. He said, "You don't favor sleeping much do you, Mr. Murphy?"

Frank could see it in the deputy's eyes. It was a look that suggested suspicion. But even more, it was evident that he was deriving a smug satisfaction in making him uncomfortable. Frank gathered a glob of tobacco juice in his mouth and turned his head to the side and spit, as if to indicate he was not rattled. He locked onto the deputy's grin and said, "I'm startin' as the shotgun messenger on the stage to Helena tomorrow. Gotta git back to town and tend to a few things."

Hays appeared a little surprised at this information, "you know what happened to the last one, don't ya?"

Frank nodded, "Indians already tried to rub me out when I was woodhawkin' down on the Missouri. I'm hopin' my luck will hold."

Hays snorted, "I'm afraid it's gonna take considerable luck to hang on to your hair in that job."

Frank wondered if Hays thought he wasn't fit for riding shotgun. His speculation about Frank's longevity fueled the self-doubt that had swirled in his mind since he'd accepted the job. He resented the deputy rekindling this doubt. It came natural to say, with some edge to his voice, "A man's gotta eat."

Hays moved on, not caring that he'd stoked the fires of doubt in Frank, to the peculiarity he saw in him being where he was, "so what was the purpose of your ride out here last night?"

It came to Frank's mind to snap at the deputy, *what business is that of yours*? But he said, "I owed money to a man. I wanted to pay him before my new job kept me away."

Hays' arrogance stopped short of calling Frank a liar, "That man wouldn't reside at Charlie Reed's ranch, would he?"

Frank instantly felt his face become flush as his heart stumbled. He forced a laugh and said in a tone that came close to insinuating the marshal was some pilgrim that didn't know the lay of the land, "Hell, Marshal, a man ain't got many choices as to where to go out here."

Hays was quick to snort a sarcastic reply, "Just a lucky guess on my part, was it?"

Frank felt totally naked in his deception. He was certain that his eyes were giving him away. Nonetheless, he continued the ruse, but was unable to look the deputy in the face as he said, "I reckon so."

Hays' demeanor turned cold. He glared at Frank, "You know, Mr. Murphy, I put folks in two categories, those that tell me the truth and those that don't. Those that tell me the truth," he paused and smiled before adding, "why hell, I might buy 'em a sarsaparilla sometime.' He paused again, briefly, as if to let his words marinate Frank's conscience. He went on, "But those folks that lie to me," he sighed deeply and shook his head, "well, Sir, I can't abide it. Those folks, I'll follow to the gates of hell to get my satisfaction. So, I'm gonna give you one more chance to make amends." Hays paused again like a cat playing with a mouse.

There was considerable angst on Frank's face such that he blurted out before Hays could speak again, "I'm not a liar, Marshal."

Hays smiled and shrugged, he said, "Well then, Sir, did you see a man by the name of James Coumerilh at the Reed Ranch?"

Frank's mind exploded with indecision. He and Charlie had agreed that if the law showed up, Charlie would say that James had moved on a few days ago for parts unknown. For Frank to say anything else, right here and now, to the deputy, would get Charlie in trouble and maybe lead to James' capture. On the other hand, it could cause Hays to follow Frank to the gates of hell. Frank looked at Hays and sighed like he had succumbed to the deputy's threat and said, "I came upriver on the Destiny with Coumerilh. That shooting on the boat was self-defense. I came to warn James you was gonna pay him a visit but turns out he lit out several days ago."

Hays was slightly taken aback, but at the same time smug with himself at the confession he had obtained. For a few seconds, it was quiet as he and Frank stared at one another from the backs of their horses. It was as if they were assessing one another's character. Hays' horse broke the silence when it snorted wearily. Hays said, catching Frank off guard, "You swear on the good book that what you just told me is true?"

Frank was a God-fearing man, but it was like he'd jumped off a roof with this lie. He had to ride it to the ground and explain to God later. He said, "I do, Marshal. Mr. Coumerilh took leave of the Reed place some time ago."

At first Hays' face went blank, almost like he was confused. And then he smiled wryly and shook his head, "I suspect I'll be talking to you at the gates to hell." He then nudged the sides of his horse and trotted off toward Charlie Reed's place.

CHAPTER TWENTY-FOUR

There were a half dozen rust colored chickens scratching the ground and pecking at bugs in Charlie Reed's yard when the marshal rode into it. No one, not even Badger or Toby, was around. He sat on his horse listening to the contented clucking of the chickens and pondered his options. He'd had plenty of time, since talking to Frank, to evaluate the likelihood that James Coumerilh would, on a whim, abandon a cozy situation such as this. It angered him that he'd been made to be a fool. From his perch he could see that there were meadow hay fields hugging the river both above and below the ranch headquarters. *A man would stick to cover*, he reckoned. *But which way would this Coumerilh fella go*. After a time, Hays reined his horse to the west, upriver, because his gut told him that if he were running from the law, that's the way he would go. And so, it was just dumb luck that he was on James' trail. About thirty minutes into his pursuit, he found boot prints in a stretch of near bare, soft ground along the river that James had walked across in the dark last night. Hays stepped down from his horse and knelt beside the tracks. They were firm and well defined. No leaves or twigs had blown into them. Not a hint of crumbling. He snorted, "Lit out several days ago, my ass." Suddenly, it occurred to him that this killer might, at this very moment, have him in his sights. The thought of it caused a shiver to engulf his body for a few seconds before letting go. Hays remained in a crouch and looked around. There were big cottonwood trees, not real thick, in the river bottom. Beneath their dark green canopy were scattered wild rose bushes and willows. What grasses there were had been grubbed out by buffalo and cattle. Vegetation on the slopes of the coulee leading up to the prairie above was sparse. The yellow grass growing there was grazed down too. Cover here *ain't favorable for an ambush,* he thought. It was almost involuntary that Hays stood up. He felt a little embarrassed that he'd allowed fear to get hold of his judgement.

About another hour's ride up the river James had made a cold camp. The willows, and cottonwoods too, were thick here. He was eating a biscuit that he had ladled wild plum jam on when a raven, perched high up in a nearby tree, abruptly flew off cawing incessantly. If there was anything that James had learned while wood hawking it was to pay heed to the ravens and squirrels. He watched the bird's flight. It went upriver a short way and then began to circle and call. *Gotta be something there*, thought James. *Buffalo, or maybe antelope, come in for water.* And then it occurred to him, *or Indians.* His heartbeat quickened as he stuffed the last of the biscuit in his mouth and picked up his rifle and belongings. He was torn as to what to do. Stay where he was, go back down river a ways and wait until whoever or whatever was ahead of him left, or go see what was there. He was still mulling his options when beneath the circling raven he heard a voice shout, "Whoa, mules."

The sound of the voice caused instant relief in James as it was unlikely that a lawman or Indians would be driving a wagon. Other voices, some women and kids now chimed in, but not loud enough for him to make out what they were saying other than much of it wasn't in English. James shouldered his bedroll with the flour sack of food tied on top and set out for the voices. The willows were thick. He pushed their branches away mostly with his left hand as his right was filled with his Winchester. Soon the voices became louder, discernable, such that James paused to listen, he whispered, "They're Metis. Maybe they know Uncle Antoine." A good feeling that he was safe now, came over James. He quickened his pace, not caring that he was making noise and flushing birds, as he believed these people were close to family. He did not notice that the voices had gone silent until he stepped from the willows into a small grassy clearing and was confronted by three men with rifles. They stared at him for a few seconds until the biggest of the three said, "I'd accuse you of sneaking up on us, but you're clearly no good at that. So, what are you doing out here on foot?"

James could see that the men were expecting some sort of lie to explain away him being this far from civilization without a horse or camping gear. But while they expected it, it was clear they weren't going to tolerate it. In spite of his predicament, James said, "I'm looking for my family. They're Metis."

The demeanor of the man to the right of the bigger man was surly, hateful by James' estimation. He said to James, "Monsieur, there are no Metis as stupid as you appear to be. I feel sorry for your family." The surly man, as well as the man next to him, but not the big man, laughed.

The big man frowned, "What is your name?"

"James Coumerilh. My uncle is Antoine Coumerilh. Do you know him?"

The reaction, not only in the faces of the three men with rifles still pointed at James, but the onlookers of women, kids and other men behind them that were within hearing, was immediate. James read it as somewhere between fear and respect. "I take it you do know my uncle?"

The big man nodded, "Oui, he is known to me."

"Do you know where I could find him?"

The big man shrugged with apparent indifference, "Wherever the buffalo are."

James tried to suppress the anger that was building within him from being advertised on his face. His inner voice was no help in that regard, *this fella likely knows where my uncle is but for some reason he's not saying. He's a scalawag of some sort, I reckon.* Aloud, he said, "Do you recall where you might have seen him last?"

Before the big man could answer, the surly man cut in, "Maybe you should tell us why you're stumbling around out here on foot with no outfit? Let's get beyond you lying to us before we tell you what you want to know."

The big man scowled at the talker before turning back to address James, "I last saw Antoine Coumerilh north of the Milk River. He was headed for the Medicine Line."

James came back quick, his voice being excited, "When was this?"

The big man shook his head and offered a wry smile, "I have told you some truth. Now it is your turn. What are you running from?"

James felt sick inside. He could see it in their eyes. *They'll turn me away or worse yet put the law on me.* Too long had gone by before he finally stammered, "I told you I'm looking for my uncle."

The big man snorted, "leave our camp." He started to turn away when an attractive Indian woman came from behind him and said to James, "My husband will treat you fairly if you are honest."

The big man looked at his wife, "Pretty Bird, this man is trouble. We should be done with him."

She came back, "Claude, he will not survive out here with no horse and what little he has."

James' mind ebbed and flowed with indecision. It was on impulse that he finally blurted out, "I killed a man, in self-defense mind you, but the law is after me."

The surly man instantly pounced on James' confession, "I told you he was trouble."

Claude glared at Phillip Trottier, "You should talk." Trottier's haughty look melted away so quickly it drew attention to his fear of Claude.

Pretty Bird looked up at her husband, "This man has told the truth. It's your turn to tell him what you know about his uncle."

James kept quiet but looked expectantly at Claude as he turned his attention back to James, he said, "I last saw your uncle in the spring. It was west of here on the Blackfeet Reservation. There were plenty of buffalo. He was having a good hunt, but he was not welcome there. The Indian agent sent the army to chase him off the reservation." He paused, "And us too."

Trottier scoffed under his breath, "The Blackfeet are selfish."

Claude took no exception to Trottier's comment but added, "Times are changing. It is difficult for Metis to live as they always have. Across the Medicine Line we have to beg for land to call our own and even then, our claims fall on deaf ears."

Trottier said sarcastically, "Ottawa wants us to stay in one place and be pig farmers."

"Someday," said Claude, "we may have to accept that life."

James looked beyond Claude and the others to several big two-wheeled carts parked in the yellow grass above the river bottom. He could see that one of them was piled high with buffalo hides. He nodded toward the cart, "It looks like you have found plenty of buffalo."

Silence abruptly enveloped them. It was like James had said something wrong. He was trying to read in Claude's face what that might have been when Trottier declared, "Unless we happen onto our own buffalo, we're traders."

Upon hearing the term, 'traders', James' mind went back to the unscrupulous wood hawkers that traded whiskey and guns to the Indians. He had no doubt that the Sioux, who had attacked him and Frank, were probably armed by such traders. His mind's voice begged to ask Claude, *what goods do you trade*? But his common sense told him, *that could spark trouble and an invite to move on.* He said, "So, you have no idea where my uncle might be?"

Claude was ashamed to admit that his reputation for trading whiskey and guns often dictated who wanted to share a camp with his group or their plans of where they were going. He was being honest when he shook his head, "Non, Monsieur, he did not tell me where they intended to hunt."

Trottier scoffed, "They think they are too good for us."

It was reflex that James looked at Trottier and absorbed his words. He then said to Claude like their reputation didn't matter to him, "I'd be obliged if I could travel with you folks for a time. Maybe run across my uncle or someone who knows his whereabouts."

Before Claude could answer, Trottier shouted, "And the law. How far behind you are they?"

"I don't know," said James, "Hours I'm guessing. I got word last night they was coming for me today."

A look of incredulity came over Trottier's face, "And you want us to take you in? I say no. Tell him no, Claude."

Claude endured the stares and whispers of his people for a time until finally he said to James, "If the law catches up to us, we will claim to not know of your past, only that you are looking for your Metis uncle."

Trottier came back, "And what if they search our carts?"

Claude shrugged, "You think with the way things are, the American law wouldn't do that anyway?"

"It may be," began James hopefully, "the law didn't pick up my trail. It could be this marshal gave up and went back to town. You might not have any call to worry."

The desperation in James' voice was clear. Trottier seized upon it, "Send him on his way, Claude. It will not go well if the law searches our carts. You know that."

Claude looked at James and sighed before spitting a dark stream of tobacco juice on the ground in front of where he and Pretty Bird were standing. His face suggested that he was annoyed with James' presence and the trouble he brought with him. But, at the same time, there was a hint of compassion. Its origin was more Pretty Bird than him. Regardless, he said, "I'll loan you a horse. You can travel with us until I tire of you, or we cross the Medicine Line." He paused and spit again, as if to emphasize the seriousness of what came next, "If you tell anyone of our business dealings, I'll kill you."

James was taken aback by the directness of Claude's threat. It suggested to him that his suspicions about the nature of Claude's trading were not wrong. His inner voice shouted at him, *you'll be getting in bed with the devil.* But he did not listen. It took a concerted effort to steady his voice, "Sir, I'll not cross you up with a loose tongue."

Trottier snorted defiantly before turning and walking away. Claude noted his departure and then shouted purposely in his direction an order meant for everyone, "We'll water the animals here and then move on." He paused and then added, not stating the obvious reason for doing so, "We need to be quick about it."

It was almost two hours after Claude Charbonneau's group left the creek bottom that Deputy Marshal Jim Hays came upon the tracks where they'd watered their stock. They read like a book, or maybe a sketch that somebody had drawn and left behind to taunt him. He had followed James' boot prints right into this clearing where the ground was churned up by a plethora of people and animal tracks. He could see that the tracks poured down from the crest above the creek where the yellow grass began. They went across the meadow and into the creek. Hays surmised that the tracks had been left by Metis even before he walked up the slope to satisfy his belief that James had taken up with them. The wheels of their heavy carts had mashed the grass down such that it was not likely it would right itself this year. It would take another growing season to erase their impact. But even then, where the ground was forgiving, there would be those parallel lines headed north toward the Medicine Line. Hays held his hands so as to extend the brim of his hat and the shade it afforded his eyes so he could see better. He followed the marks of the wheels out through the yellow grass until just short of the horizon. He sighed and whispered, "He's gotta be with 'em."

He shook his head and said to no one, but his bay horse, "It's a sad day when I can't catch a man on foot." And then he did not say it aloud, not even to the bay horse, *thirty minutes hard ridin' and I'd catch these people.* And then, before he could think it, his mind's eye played out his fear. The Metis and this killer from the Destiny were throwing down on him and just like that he could see himself lying dead in the yellow grass. To his credit, the deputy stared at the lines in the grass for a good while before he got on the bay and turned it toward Fort Benton.

CHAPTER TWENTY-FIVE

With the exception of Phillip Trottier, the Metis in Claude Charbonneau's party treated James well. He'd garnered the treatment by gathering buffalo chips, or wood when it was available, for Pretty Bird's cooking fires. And he helped with the stock, hitching and unhitching teams. But his biggest contribution was helping herd the horses that they had acquired in trade from the Lakota. No one spoke about where the Indians had gotten the horses until the fourth day. James had taken breakfast with Claude and Pretty Bird before they'd broken camp. Not long after that he noticed two Sioux riders materialize from a coulee off to the east of the caravan. The Indians, who were mounted on good-looking sorrel horses, rode straight to the lead cart where Claude was riding alongside it on horseback. James was too far away to hear what was being said but he could see that there was considerable pointing at the horse herd and north toward the Medicine Line. He continued to watch from afar this animated conversation for several minutes until one of the Lakota abruptly made a dismissive gesture with his hand before he and his friend rode off, at a quick pace, in the direction from which they'd come. The Indians had not gone a hundred yards when James' herding partner, a young man who had a wisp of black chin whiskers and barely a shadow of the same above his top lip, nudged his horse to within talking distance of him. He caught James' eye, "The Lakota will not be happy if Claude told them what I think he did."

It seemed obvious to James that the kid wanted to tell him what this was, or he wouldn't have baited his hook and cast it out as he had. James obliged the boy, "What was it you reckon Claude told 'em. It appeared to me they left mad."

The boy, whose name was Joe, just Joe, came back, "The big shots in Ottawa don't want the American Army crossing the Medicine Line to take back what is stolen from their people down here. I believe Claude told the Lakota this and that he will only trade for unbranded horses."

James had wondered about this trade in stolen horses when Otto Weiss recounted to him the destruction of the Bellows family. It gave him considerable pause to think there were enough people, without a conscience, that would buy these stolen animals to sustain this illicit trade. It occurred to James, *the owners of those unbranded horses are likely just as dead as the branded owners.* But, not being a fool, he said, "I'll grant ya, it's a tough spot to be in."

Joe came back like he genuinely believed that James was sympathetic to their plight, "We generally pick up two or three times this many horses. But Claude, running scared on this avoiding branded animals, is gonna put us in the poor house."

It was a surprise impulse that James spent some of the credibility he'd earned over the past four days, he said, "You know, Joe, if you keep on like you are you could be swapping the poor house for one with bars."

Joe frowned at James, "Well, if you can conjure up some buffalo, I suspect Claude would be happy to tow the mark."

It was like James couldn't turn off the spigot of irrational words, "Do you do whatever Claude says?"

Joe looked at James and shook his head, "You are not truly Metis." And with that he reined his horse around and trotted off to the other side of their small bunch of horses.

Regret was gripping James as he watched Joe ride away. His conscience, now a faint voice in his mind, tried to reassure him, *what they're doing isn't right. You can't be a part of it.*

CHAPTER TWENTY-SIX

James had not seen it happen, Joe talking to Claude. It could have been when he was out gathering buffalo dung for the evening fire but, by the next morning at breakfast, the change in Claude was clear. He did not come right out and call James on his assessment of how they made a living trading whiskey and guns. Instead, it was in his body language, the tone of his voice. And, to James' dismay, this malady of indifference had infected Pretty Bird too. As nice as she had been, she now seemed incapable of smiling. So, they sat there, Claude and Pretty Bird on one side of the fire and James on the other. Their children were playing near the creek with several other kids. Happy talk and laughter, oblivious to the adult drama, was audible above the occasional crackling of the fire. The day was moving on without them. It seemed to James that everybody in the camp knew the reason why but him. The sun, a perfect orb of brightness, floated just above a flat top butte to the east. *They don't trust me*, thought James as he brought his tin cup of lukewarm coffee to his mouth and strained a sip through his moustache. An hour ago, he had welcomed the taste of it. Now he drank it, they drank it, to give purpose to their waiting. His taste buds were in rebellion. But what was he to do? Claude dictated what went on in this camp. So, he stared into the lazy white smoke that drifted up from the fire. From time to time, the acrid fog lolled about his head. It caused him to squint his eyes and hold his breath while pawing the air in front of his face. Sitting, saying next to nothing as they were, gave rise to the angst within his mind to escape. It had now overtaken his body, including his bladder. James welcomed the excuse to be away from the fire and the tension that lingered there. He set his coffee cup on a small rock and stood up, "Gotta make a nature call."

Claude looked at him as he took a drink of his coffee but said nothing. James absorbed the slight and walked away toward where the big two-wheeled carts, seven of them, were parked all in a row. He hadn't gone far when he could hear, but not make out, Claude and Pretty Bird talking in low voices. Anger, mixed with the hurt of rejection, took hold of his inner voice, *I've got to take my leave of these people. They are the ones Otto warned me about.* On the far side of the carts, out of view of the tents and teepees and smoldering breakfast fires along Dead Dog Creek, he unbuttoned the fly of his pants and began to relieve himself. The sensation was calming. His mind's eye went home. For a time, he savored the vision until it was interrupted by those who knew of his past. That he'd not returned to the army after convalescent leave. That he had no reason other than he did not want to die senselessly. And now, here he was running from the law because he didn't want to be hanged for no good reason. He opened his eyes. There was no escape from what he had done. He was doing up the last button of his pants when he saw them. Coming down Dead Dog Creek. At this distance, a good half mile he reckoned, it was hard to get a count as their horses were strung out along the creek. He'd barely cleared the tongue of the cart he'd been behind when he ran into Joe who grinned and said, "Time to do business."

James felt like an outsider. They'd done no trading in the short time that he'd been with them. He said, "What do we do?"

Joe's look became serious, "Whatever Claude says."

James looked at the approaching Lakota and then back to Joe. He said rhetorically, lest he stand mute, "They've come to trade?"

Joe, ten years younger than James, smirked, "Well, it ain't no social call."

James glared at the insolence that danced in the boy's eyes before shaking his head and walking away. He took maybe a dozen steps before pausing to allow the Lakota raiding party to stream by him. They were formidable in their appearance. Some near naked with only a loin cloth and moccasins, while others wore white man's pants or vest. And, here and there, a bowler derby or a misshapen black felt hat. A single feather, sometimes two, adorned their head gear or a braid of hair. But to James the visual effects of their garb were secondary to the streaks of yellow, red and white paint on their exposed skin. Even their horses wore bizarre markings. All of it was intended to strike fear in the hearts of their adversaries. But, as intimidating as it was, it did not cause James to involuntarily shiver as did the sight of the bloody scalps that hung from the waists of some or the saddles of others. He tried not to stare, but one was red, almost orange colored, and another mostly gray. His mind's eye added faces to these. He could see them. The redhead, young and pretty. Fighting to live. And the old lady, feisty but going down with a single blow from a war club. Suddenly, James was plucked from this kaleidoscope of horror. A man, close to his age and dressed like the Metis, came riding by on a pinto horse in the midst of the Lakota warriors. He seemed at ease, if not exuberant, with his being part of the group. With his eyes, James followed the young man. Slender, with shoulder length black hair and a smooth face. James' inner voice spoke up, *He's mean, he just looks it.* And then, apart from the main body of fighters by a hundred yards or so, came the horse herders. There were five mounted riders and close to twenty stolen horses and mules.

It was clear they were headed toward where Claude and the leader of the raiding party were greeting one another. There had been some high-pitched whooping and hollering from the Lakota as they entered the Metis camp, but now they sat on their horses saying nothing. The silence was such that James could hear a meadowlark's cry on the far side of the creek and a gust of wind pulse through the yellow grass. On purpose, he studied what he could see of the stolen animals. At least half were branded.

Claude called out, his voice disingenuous even from where James stood, "It is good to see you, Old Bear. You have brought many horses to trade."

Old Bear made no attempt to get down from his horse or suggest they smoke the pipe of peace before doing business. He knew what Claude had already told his two braves that had come calling a few days ago and yet here he was with branded horses. He pointed to the animals and then looked at Claude, "We trade for all."

Claude took a couple of steps towards Old Bear as if to demonstrate he was not afraid of him, when in fact he was. James could see it in his eyes. *He's likely done the math on our chances if a fight breaks out. Gotta be fifty or sixty of them and less 'an a dozen shooters amongst us.* Claude said, "You are my friend, Old Bear, so I am telling you truth that it is different now across the Medicine Line. The white father in Ottawa is afraid the American soldiers will cross the line and take back what you have stolen from their people. He is afraid that if they do, they will stay and take the land too."

Old Bear scoffed, "I do not fear the pony soldiers. I have killed many of them." He then held up the Winchester repeater in his right hand and stabbed the air in front of him. "With the guns you bring us they die like flies."

Claude shook his head, "It's not just the pony soldiers we have to deal with. The mounted police have come to Paradise. They intend to stop our trade." Claude paused and shook his head again, "No, Old Bear, there are too many to fight."

The deep wrinkles on Old Bear's face contorted into a look of disgust. He snorted, "You have become like an old woman without teeth who is weak and afraid."

Claude came back, "Insult me if you want, Old Bear, but it won't change how things are."

James could see it. A palpable fear in Pretty Bird's face, and beyond her, Phillip Trottier's, that was as obvious as rain clouds. Like most everyone else within earshot of Claude and Old Bear, they sensed what was about to happen if Claude said the wrong thing. In a slow, casual way James felt his pistol. Charlie had given him a castoff holster for his Navy Colt. It was strapped to his right hip, but it gave him little comfort that he would survive if a gunfight broke out.

Old Bear turned to the warrior sitting on a roan horse next to him and began speaking in Lakota. His voice was an even tone, but James saw the look of surprised concern that came to the man's face within seconds of Old Bear beginning to talk. His mind's eye immediately played out how it saw the opening moments of the gunfight. Claude would die. Maybe Pretty Bird too. And he would as well if he didn't make it to the cart where his Winchester was. Even then, he saw himself living only a little while longer before the Lakota overwhelmed him. They would scalp him and leave him in the yellow grass along Dead Dog Creek for the ravens and coyotes. And then, just as James was about to accept this vision as his fate, Old Bear said to Claude, "It will be your choice, my friend, if you trade as we always have, life will be good. But if you take the path you speak of now, I will not allow it. We will have no choice but to take what we want and give you nothing in return. Maybe not even your lives."

It was a toss-up as to which emotion, anger or fear, dominated Claude's face. He had no chance to sift through them to see which one would win out, before Pretty Bird was next to him, she whispered, "Trade with them like always."

Old Bear, now cocky, tossed some pitchy wood on an already hot fire, "Listen to your woman." He laughed, "She wants to lie with you tonight. You are no good to her beneath the blankets if you are dead." Other nearby Lakota, who understood enough of what Old Bear had just said, laughed along with him. He then added more insult, "But do not worry, I will keep your woman warm." And then there was general laughter amongst the Lakota while the Metis maintained worried looks.

There was no longer any fear in Claude's face, rather it was a look of helpless rage. Trottier was now at his side. "Make the trade, Claude. We have no choice."

Claude hesitated, while Trottier stared intently at the side of his face as if that would compel him to trade. Finally, he sighed angrily, not caring that it was obvious to Old Bear, "Alright, we will trade like always."

Old Bear nodded and continued the tenuous façade between them as he said to Claude, "It is good, my friend, that we do business as we have in the past."

It was not spoken, but James sensed it, a collective easing of the tension as they went about making the trade. Nineteen horses. Eleven of them with brands, and the others with no proof of purchase. The futility of taking any of them to Andrew Hunt's store ate at Claude all during the trade. But his anger peaked when he handed over five 'Yellow Boys' or Model 1866 Winchesters with fifty rounds each and two gallons of whiskey. It was good the Lakota did not linger after that.

CHAPTER TWENTY-SEVEN

After the trade debacle with Old Bear, Claude was out guns, ammunition and whiskey for horses that would be difficult to sell in Canada. And south of the Medicine Line, trying to sell them to a white man might get him hanged. He was at a loss of what to do, short of acquiescing to Ottawa's desire they become pig farmers on land they were reluctant to give them. Nonetheless, Claude directed his people west toward the Blackfeet Reservation. It wasn't until right after breakfast of the second day that he called them together to satisfy their grumblings of, *what are we doing?*

They were camped in a grove of cottonwood trees next to the Teton River. It had been a comfortable place. There was good grass and water. And hooks from the mercantile in Paradise baited with grasshoppers had produced cutthroat trout for both supper and breakfast. For the first time in some days, James felt at ease. It was tempting to think that he was one of them.

Counting women and kids, there were 31 of them. They were all there. Even the horse herders had been told to come. Claude stepped up onto the stump of a tree that had been felled with a whipsaw. Its surface was as smooth and flat as a kitchen table. He looked out at them. Their faces were innocent, expectant that he had something good to tell them. That Old Bear's wrong would be righted. Claude was no smooth talker. He shook his head before saying straight out, "These horses that Old Bear forced on us we cannot sell to Andrew Hunt."

James stood near the edge of the crowd in the very back. A middle-aged man standing next to him snorted before whispering, "For this, I did not finish my breakfast."

Claude went on, "I have decided that we will travel to the land of the Blackfeet and trade with them for buffalo robes. Those we can sell or trade in Paradise."

The same man who had groused about not being able to finish his breakfast spoke up, "What are you going to do if the Army or the Indian agent catches us there with stolen horses?"

Another man shouted, "We have no permit to trade there. If the Army or the law catches us, they'll take everything we have. I say we go home."

From the crowd there were four or five shouts of, "Yeah, we should go home."

Claude was taken aback by the people's reaction. It was plain to see that they did not respect his judgement anymore. However, in defiance, he shouted back at them from his elevated perch, "Go home? What is home? It is here today and over there tomorrow. Without the buffalo there is no life as we know it. You are naïve children if you think we can cross back over the Medicine Line and everything will be ok."

Trottier spoke up, his tone arrogant, "We have outwitted the American soldiers before. We can do it again."

To James' surprise, Joe, who was standing only a few feet away, shouted, "You can't bushwhack them all, Trottier."

Trottier scowled at Joe, "It's unfortunate you don't have a backbone for such things. Life for you must be miserable."

Trottier's words had barely cleared his lips when Joe started through the crowd to get at him. In that instant Claude jumped down from the stump. He shouted as he went towards Trottier, "enough, you two."

But he was too late. Joe had pulled a sheath knife. Several women screamed to no avail. The report from Trottier's pistol caused the knife and Joe to fall to the ground. The people surrounding Trottier and Joe fell back like ripples of water from a big rock being tossed in a still pond. Talk amongst them was excited and emotional. Some kids were crying and Joe's mother too. She pushed through the crowd with her husband, a burly man who could easily exact revenge against Trottier if it weren't for the fact he still held his pistol. Joe's mother, who was half Assiniboine, collapsed on her prostrate son's body and began to wail. Her husband, knowing that his son was dead, stayed on his feet looking wild-eyed through the black smoke that hung in the air in front of Trottier's gun. He screamed, "You evil son of a bitch, you did not need to kill him."

Before Trottier could respond, Claude stepped between the men. He looked at Trottier and said angrily, "Give me your gun, Phillip."

Trottier smirked and nodded towards Joe's father, "And have Raphael jump on me? No, I am not a fool."

Raphael shouted, "You are a coward. That's what you are. Afraid to fight a man fair."

Trottier came back, "Your son would have stabbed me if I hadn't shot him."

Claude now stepped directly in front of Trottier's pistol, so as to block the view the two men had of one another. He said in a level but angry voice, "This is your last chance, Trottier, give me your pistol or pack your things and leave camp."

Trottier remained quiet, nervously pensive, until finally he gestured with the barrel of his revolver beyond Claude to where Raphael was standing, "What about him?"

Claude held out his hand to receive the pistol, "We'll talk this out. Neither side here is free of guilt."

For a long moment it was totally silent save for the leaves of the cottonwoods rattling gently in response to a gust of wind. At last, Trottier succumbed to the hateful looks of his peers and eased the hammer down on his .44 Caliber Colt revolver. He then held the grip out to Claude who took it and turned to Raphael, "Let's go talk."

Raphael snorted, "Talking ain't gonna fix this."

Claude was about to respond to Raphael when the stillness was pierced by a shriek as Joe's mother leaped up from the ground wielding Joe's knife. She was close to Trottier. Maybe three steps, but even in her buckskin dress she covered that distance so quick that Trottier had barely time to raise his hands. There was little doubt as to her intent. She plunged the ten-inch blade into his chest all the way to its brass hilt. It sliced off the lower part of Trottier's heart causing him to gasp in surprise that he was dead. He fell away, not real fast, from Joe's mother. As luck would have it, he ended up falling face down until his forehead and the big knife protruding from his chest contacted the ground. At this point, he groaned and went to his side and then his back, barely a foot away from Joe, who was lying face up only because his mother had turned him over. The both of them now, their eyes wide open with regret, lay there staring up at several puffy white clouds in a sea of blue. It could have been such a fine day.

There was no more talk of where they were going and the consequences of trespassing on the Blackfeet Reservation, at least not now there wasn't. James had his doubts that Joe would have done the same for him, but he helped dig his grave.

CHAPTER TWENTY-EIGHT

Captain Hettrick brought the column to a halt. They were in a broad coulee that ran a trickle of water called Rock Creek. Up ahead about a half mile he could see his point man's gray horse entering the charred remains of a ranch headquarters. It was the second burned out ranch that Company C had come upon in the six days they'd been gone from Fort Benton and the good life civilization afforded them there. Even though the first sergeant knew the routine, Hettrick said to him, "We'll wait here until Private O'Reilly has checked it over."

"Yes Sir, a man can't be too careful."

The company was riding two abreast. In the third pair behind the captain and the first sergeant a horse nickered its fatigue. Its rider spit tobacco juice to his left before whispering to the man on his right, "I believe the captain has got a healthy respect for that sharpshooter since Harkness got his self bushwhacked."

The other private had seen the damage that the buffalo gun had done to Harkness. He came back, "I'll sit here all day if it keeps me from getting shot with the cannon that killed Harkness."

The first sergeant, who was shading his eyes with his hand so he could see O'Reilly better, said all of a sudden, "He's waving us on, Sir."

Hettrick squinted his eyes in the direction of the point man for a few seconds before telling the first sergeant, "Alright, let's move out but everyone needs to be alert. If that fella with the 44-100 that killed Harkness is lurking about, death could come from a long way off."

The soldiers within earshot of the captain immediately looked to the bluffs above the coulee. They were naked save for yellow grass, rock outcrops here and there and a smattering of sagebrush. And then the first sergeant waved the column onward, shouting "Move out. Stay alert."

They rode at a good clip coming to the blackened buildings and the horror that awaited them there in short order. Ravens and vultures hopped about within the walls of the house and barn. They refused to leave until the soldiers had dismounted and started towards them.

The first sergeant and Hettrick dropped the reins of their horses and started walking slowly towards what was left of the house. They'd taken only a few steps in that direction when a young private, not more than three months in the Army, reached the house before they did and abruptly turned away. He began to retch until he spewed his breakfast onto the hardpacked dirt. It was quiet save for one man who had been in the Army almost five years and was still a private that shouted, "Calkins, how could you waste good army chow like that?" And then he laughed alone until Hettrick yelled at him, "That's enough, Private. Show some respect for the dead." He paused and then scowled at the man, "Get a shovel and start digging a grave beyond the house."

The man showed no shame. He was barely able to wipe the grin off his face as he came back in a lazy voice, "Yes Sir."

Hettrick walked on past the young private who had been made ill by what he saw. The acidic stench of the vomit rose up from the ground causing him to nearly gag.

They'd gotten good at digging graves, three at the first ranch and now five here. Only two of the victims had been killed with arrows. More evident was a plethora of spent .44 Caliber Rimfire shell casings ejected on the ground. They were not clustered at a single fighting spot such as inside the cabin near a window or a barn door. The soldiers had found only two such locations and then only one of those was marked by .44 Rimfire casings. The .44 Rimfire cases were seemingly ubiquitous. It was an observation that caused Hettrick to comment, "The Lakota are armed better than we are."

The first sergeant, whose name was Billy Greer, looked down at the mutilated naked bodies of the two women. They had both been scalped but enough of their hair remained to identify the younger woman as a redhead. The other woman's hair was gray, which coincided with her sagging, wrinkly skin. Greer sighed and shook his head, he said, "It is a mystery to me how some folks could trade guns and whiskey to the Lakota knowing, most likely, that this is what would happen."

Hettrick did not have to ponder his response. He came back quick, "It's easy money. Once a man gets a taste of it, there's no weaning himself off it."

Greer replied, "Some things money shouldn't be able to buy."

In that instant, Hettrick found himself staring at the younger woman's nakedness. An uptick in the wind caused the woman's pubic hair to shimmer ever so slightly. Straight away his conscience flooded him with shame, *have you no decency*? The possibility that Greer had observed his voyeurism caused him to shout so quick that he almost stumbled on the words, "You men, find some blankets. Cover those women." He paused and shook his head in a deliberate manner, kind of like he was on stage, before adding, "For hell sakes, allow these poor souls some measure of dignity."

One of the soldiers standing near the corpses shouted, "Yes Sir," before running off towards where the pack mules were located. First Sergeant Greer, on the other hand, showed a faint grin beneath his black walrus moustache. And for a moment, he savored the moral superiority that came with it.

CHAPTER TWENTY-NINE

To say there was disharmony after the killings in the cottonwoods would be accurate. James sensed it. Hushed conversations that abruptly went silent or changed to some trite subject at his approach had become common. And at night, every night since the killings, he'd heard the crying. Nonetheless, they continued on toward the Blackfeet Reservation. On the fifth day, since the sadness and doubt of Claude's leadership had begun, they crossed onto the Blackfeet's land. James knew this only because one of the other herders, a sixteen-year-old boy named Pierre, had told him.

There was still plenty of light left in the day when Claude came riding back to the horse herd. Usually, he relayed his orders to one of the others, but today he came to James. He brought his horse to a jerky halt next to James' and allowed it to rock his head up and down a couple of times to adjust the bit in its mouth before he spoke, "James, we're gonna camp here. There's plenty of bug killed pine nearby." Claude paused briefly and added like he needed to justify this simple decision, "There's good water and grass here too. Fish in the crik. It'll hold us for a while."

James was surprised, even suspicious of the change in Claude's behavior toward him. The naysayer in his mind cautioned him, *he's looking for an ally in case his people turn against him. If that happens, taking his side might not be the smart thing to do.* James showed no emotion, one way or another, and said, "We'll bed the horses along the creek."

Claude looked at him, as if he expected James to say something more, until the silence became awkward. He then said, "Keep a sharp eye out. The Blackfeet are like ghosts in the night when it comes to stealing horses."

Thus far, they'd seen no Blackfeet. So, it was only natural that, for a second or two, James thought the dark mass way out on the horizon was them coming to see who was trespassing on their land. But something didn't look right. *Maybe it's a herd of buffalo*, he thought. Then he saw it, a flicker of color in the black dot. His heart immediately picked up its tempo. He looked at Claude and nodded to the country behind him, "They're coming."

Surprise mostly came to Claude's face, "Who is?"

"The Army."

Fear now seized Claude's eyes as he twisted around in his saddle to look. At first, he didn't see them.

James pointed to a tall pine tree on the edge of the creek. "Look to the left of that big tree way out there. You can just make out their guidon."

Claude reined his horse around so he could study the approaching soldiers. For a good while he looked at them. Not saying anything, just shaking his head before he announced, without looking at James, "They've got us."

James' inner voice had started in, the moment he realized that he was looking at soldiers, *you better skedaddle while you can.* But he said to Claude, "I reckon they do."

Claude came back, "You're not gonna make a run for it?"

James' mind flashed back to how it was that he came to be with Claude, he said, "I got no food, no camp outfit. And here I am on the Blackfeet Reservation looking more like a white man, thanks to my mother, than Metis. Those are circumstances that I fear won't bode well for me if I were to encounter them."

The dark mass was discernable now as cavalry. Claude looked away from it to James, "And what do you think your chances are with the Army?"

"As far as I know they don't know what I look like, only that I'm Metis."

Claude glanced back at the soldiers and then to the people setting up camp along the creek. He said, "Everyone here knows who you are and what you're running from."

James sighed and shook his head as he watched the Army getting closer and closer. He could see the people in camp were now shouting at Claude and pointing to the soldiers. Finally, he looked at Claude, fairly intense, so he would know right from the git-go if he was wasting his time, and said, "From here on, my name is Jack Doyle. I was on my way to the gold fields in Idaho when Indians snuck into my camp three nights ago and stole my pack mule and horse. Left me afoot until you came along and took me in."

Claude snorted and tossed his head. "I don't know with all of my people knowing who you really are if we could float that lie for very long. And when those soldier boys figure out we was all trying to deceive them, it could go bad for all of us."

James shrugged somewhat dejectedly, "Well, Claude, this is the only card I got in my hand."

There had been something brewing in Claude's mind and now it had jelled in his eyes such that James could see it and was hopeful of Claude's response, he said, "I'll lie for you if you will for me."

"And what might that be?"

Claude scoffed, "Ain't no gittin' around the horses being stolen. But the buffalo hides aren't. I intend to tell the Army we traded coffee, beans, sugar, blankets and the like for both the horses and the hides. They'll likely pull you aside and ask you. As an outsider, they might believe you. But me, they know me. A lot of people do."

The soldiers were now about a quarter mile north of where the carts were parked along the creek. It appeared they had stopped to size up the Metis camp. James couldn't help but look at them. His initial reaction was that Claude's request was reasonable. But then the naysayer in his mind challenged that, *you'll be admitting to being part of a serious offense. You could still go to jail.* The soldiers started moving again towards the camp. It caused James to temper his response along the lines of the naysayer's advice, he said, "Would it wash with you, Claude, if I was to tell them I didn't see any trades while I been here."

A hateful look came over Claude's face, he came back, "You go right ahead with that, and I'll introduce them to James Coumerilh, on his way to the Idaho gold fields. And I'll act real surprised when they tell me you're wanted for murder."

The soldiers were at the creek now. Some of them were splashing their horses through the knee-deep water to the Metis camp. It was clear to James that he had no choice but to go along with Claude and run the risk of adding trading guns and whiskey to the Indians for stolen horses to his problems. He could see Pretty Bird looking up at a soldier on a horse and pointing toward him and Claude. The soldier, an officer he reckoned, touched his gloved right hand to the brim of his cap before reining his horse around and starting toward James and Claude. Another soldier rode beside him.

Claude glanced in the direction of the soldiers and laughed derisively before turning back to James. His expression became serious, "Do we have a deal?"

James reluctantly nodded, "I reckon we do."

The hooves of the soldiers' horses pounded the sod-like grass. The sound of their approach drifted up the slope. Claude smiled and said, "Alright then, Jack Doyle, we'll see where these lies will take us."

The pounding hooves gave way to the labored breathing of the horses as they came to a halt. Hettrick said, in a wry voice, "Bonne apres-midi, Monsieur Charbonneua."

Claude hesitated, pondering the sincerity of Hettrick greeting him in French like he respected the Metis culture, before he came back close to indifferent, "Good afternoon, Captain. How may I help you today?"

Hettrick became curt, "We've traveled this road not two years ago, Claude. And so, I'll ask you just like last time, do you have a permit to trade on the Blackfeet Reservation?"

"You know I don't."

First Sergeant Greer, who had been looking at some of the horse herd just beyond James and Claude, pointed to a white horse, "Sir, that horse is branded."

Hettrick shifted his attention to the horse. Before he could respond, Greer added, "Sir, that brand, /Y. I recollect a branding iron in the barn at that last ranch where we tended to the dead. It looked just like that."

A sudden surge of adrenaline propelled James' heart to an even faster pace. His inner voice chastised him, like he had a choice, *of all the people to tie up with.*

Hettrick looked at Claude and nodded towards the white horse. "How'd you come by that horse?"

"Traded for it."

"With who?"

"A Lakota by the name of Old Bear."

Hettrick shook his head in disgust, "It didn't occur to you that it was likely stolen? That he killed white people to get it?"

Claude's eyes showed anger that crept into his voice, "What does it matter if he trades the horse to me on this side of the Medicine Line or to someone else on the other side. Either way, it is just how things are."

Hettrick spit the words back at Claude, "It's going to stop if I have my way."

Claude shrugged with a cold look on his face, he said, "Take the horse, give it back to the owner."

Hettrick snapped, "He's dead, Claude. Him and all of his family, butchered."

There was now shouting and voices arguing in the camp by the creek. James, as well as Claude, could see that the soldiers were going through the carts tossing everything out onto the ground. Claude's anger grew exponentially from what it had been just seconds ago. He bobbed his head in the direction of the camp, "What the hell are you doing? You have no right to do that? Just because we don't have your stupid permit. You can't do this."

Hettrick's anger was now the equal of Claude's, "You, Mr. Charbonneau, are the one who is in the wrong. You are lucky I don't seize everything you have." He paused and drew in a breath to calm himself before adding, "who knows, maybe I will."

James was unaware that the Metis had more whiskey and guns in their carts. He'd thought that Old Bear had taken it all plus some legitimate items in exchange for the horses. But now he could see a soldier inside a cart handing down several brown crock jugs to another soldier on the ground. And then, as if it could only get worse, the soldier in the cart came up with two 'yellow boy' Winchesters that he handed to the man outside the cart. The rifles and liquor attracted more soldiers to the one holding the rifles. The shouting became louder and more heated.

First Sergeant Greer, who had been observing the goings on in the Metis camp, said, "Sir, it appears they've found whiskey and repeating rifles."

Hettrick turned in his saddle to study the situation for a moment before looking back to Claude. He snorted and shook his head, "You disgust me, Charbonneau."

Claude fired back, "You judge me and my people when you know nothing of what it takes to live as we do. So, stop with your insults and do what you're going to do."

Hettrick scowled at Claude and pointed toward the Metis camp, "You're dealing death and misery to people just trying to make a living."

"And the Metis are not allowed to make a living?" replied Claude.

An incredulous look came over Hettrick's face, "Not trading whiskey and guns to the Sioux, they're not."

Claude came back, "Those guns and the whiskey is for our use. It is not for trade."

Hettrick laughed while Greer broke into a smile. Hettrick said, "I am no fool, Charbonneau. I'm taking the stolen horses along with those guns and any other new Winchester repeaters we find amongst your belongings and your whiskey." He hesitated before adding, "And all of your buffalo hides."

Charbonneau exploded, "You sonovabitch, you can't do that."

"Everything you are doing here is illegal. So, you are going to pay the price."

Claude caught James' eye, as if it was time for him to honor their bargain, and pointed to him, "This man is Jack Doyle. He can tell you what we traded to the Sioux."

James could see the shiny brass receivers of the yellow boy Winchesters as several soldiers passed them back and forth. He could see too jugs of whiskey on the ground beside the men. But in his mind's eye he saw a gallows, he said to the Captain, "I have been with these people only a few days. In that time, I saw them trade with the Indians on one occasion. It was mostly coffee, tobacco, beans, sugar and the like."

Hettrick was taken aback by what James had said. He looked at him for a few seconds as if to be able to see the lie, which he was certain of, in some material form. Finally, he said, "You are not Metis?"

The shame of denying his heritage was insufficient to override James' fear of the gallows, he said, "No, I am Irish."

It was at this point that the tense shouting near the cart where the whiskey and guns were found, shifted several carts away. A soldier could be seen standing in the back of the cart holding a rifle when he abruptly shouted excitedly, "Sarge, it's the buffalo gun. It's a .44-100. It's the gun that killed Harkness." Soldiers from up and down the line of carts immediately collapsed on the buffalo gun's location.

Hettrick became enraged, "Who owns that rifle?"

Claude said in a smug voice, "A dead man."

"What's his name?"

"Phillip Trottier."

"How did he die?"

"He insulted the wrong man."

Hettrick abruptly looked at James, "Is this true Mr. Doyle?"

James felt himself slipping even deeper into Claude's trouble. The angst within him had caused an undo amount of saliva to blend with the chew along his right cheek. He debated spitting lest he look arrogant to the captain, but then he swallowed a little of the juice out of reflex. It burned going down to his stomach. In the next instant, out of necessity, he turned his head to the side and spit. He then ran his gloved hand across his moustache to clear it of tobacco juice that had hung up. He looked the captain in the eyes, like they were equals as opposed to him being a criminal and the captain not, and said, "Mr. Charbonneau is telling you God's truth concerning these matters."

Hettrick scoffed, "Sir, I fear that you are cut from the same bolt of cloth as Mr. Charbonneau."

James took a shallow breath through his nose, so as to steady his voice, before replying, "That is your opinion, Sir. I am only telling you what I have observed."

It was at this point that a corporal, somewhat out of wind, came jogging up the hill with the buffalo gun. He stopped beside Hettrick's horse and looked up saluting as he did, "Sir, Sergeant Hall asked me to bring you this rifle. He thinks it's the gun that killed Private Harkness."

Hettrick reached down and took the rifle from the corporal. He held it with both hands reading the markings on the barrel. "Remington-Creedmore. .44-100." He worked the lever of the single shot rolling block action and then eased the hammer down with his thumb. But then he deliberately paused before snorting and shaking his head while lifting the folding ladder sight at the rear of the receiver. He mumbled, "This is the gun, alright." He then put the rifle to his shoulder and aimed at a distant rock. He looked at Claude, "This has got to be the rifle that killed my man."

"Or one just like it," countered Claude.

Hettrick responded, his voice stern and arbitrary, "No, Charbonneau, I would bet my life that this is the gun that killed Private Harkness."

"You can't prove that."

"I don't have to."

Angry shock came to Claude's face, He shouted, "Well then-"

Hettrick shouted louder with more anger to cut off Claude's objection, "You fool, you've got stolen horses, whiskey and guns and you're on the reservation trading without a permit. Adding murder to that list would cause me to take you, or whoever pulled the trigger, to the United States Marshal in Helena and a date with the hangman. But you are right, Mr. Charbonneau, I can't prove murder." Hettrick paused and stared down at the buffalo gun for a moment pondering, it appeared, what to do. Finally, he looked at Claude and sighed, "Here is my decision. I am seizing these stolen horses, this rifle, the yellow boy Winchesters and whiskey, and all of your buffalo hides and the carts and teams pulling those carts."

Claude erupted with anger, "You bastard. You can't do that. It is how we make our living. We'll -"

Hettrick raised his hand for Claude to be quiet and then added, "Some of my men will drive the horses and carts to Fort Benton while I and the rest of my men will escort you and your people to the Medicine Line."

Claude pointed his finger at Hettrick, "You are an evil scoundrel. I will get even someday."

"Are you, a non-citizen, threatening an American Army officer?"

"Take it as you wish."

Hettrick calmed himself a little before saying, "This time when you cross the Medicine Line you, nor any of your people, will be allowed to come back. If you do, I will see to it that you are jailed for conspiracy to commit murder and repeat offenders of trespassing to engage in illegal trade."

The words tumbled from James' mouth before he'd really considered the wisdom of it, "I'm an American citizen. This doesn't apply to me, does it?"

Hettrick smirked at James and shook his head, "No, I believe you to be a liar but beyond that, I believe that you have fallen in with bad company. You are free to go."

James could not believe his good fortune. He was quick to solidify it with, "Thank you, Sir."

James' salvation still hung before the group when Claude piped up, "Captain, maybe we can bargain, at least for my hides."

Hettrick sighed impatiently as if he was having to deal with a recalcitrant child, "what might you have that would be valuable enough for me to give back the hides you obtained illegally?"

"First, you tell me is it possible to parley for my hides?"

Hettrick frowned at Claude, "Tell me what you want to trade, and I'll tell you if it's worth the hides."

For a moment, everyone went quiet. They listened to the distant voices at camp and up close the incessant flies buzzing around them and the horses. It was a concession to Claude while he sat on his horse gauging, it seemed, if the captain would trade if he offered first. At last, he said, "I can tell you where the Lakota have a white girl that they took south of the line."

It was obvious that Claude's proposition had tempted Hettrick. He looked at him in silence, much like he might study terrain for a possible ambush. He was still pondering the wisdom of dealing with a man as evil as Claude when Claude gave some credibility to his offer, "Her name is Sarah Bellows. Got long blonde hair, she does. A pretty thing."

At the mention of Sarah Bellows' name, James' look of passive relief that his true identity had gone undetected by Hettrick abruptly changed to surprise. He knew the Bellows name well from the many times Otto had pined over their demise and the abduction of his sweetheart.

Hettrick sighed, "I suspect word of the Bellows massacre is common knowledge amongst the Metis. "He paused as if he was leery of Claude and then he sighed again, "If this girl is alive and she is across the Medicine Line, there's little I can do about it."

I should say something, thought James. *It's the least I can do for Otto.*

And then Claude, seeing all of his ill-gotten buffalo hides being taken away, spun a lie as smooth as water slickened rocks, he said, "Alright, Captain, I will tell you anyway just to show you that I am a good person. The girl is in Old Bear's village. It is about three days ride west of Paradise. For the right amount, he will trade for her."

Hettrick came back, "And what is that amount?"

"Five hundred dollars worth of goods is what he told me."

"Is she being treated well?"

Without the slightest hint of remorse Claude responded, "From what I saw she was. But just because she has a favored place in Old Bear's lodge today doesn't mean she will tomorrow."

Hettrick looked to the west and the rugged mountains a day's ride away. His silence, save for a raven cawing overhead, gave Claude some hope that Hettrick was considering his proposition. That maybe he would be allowed to at least keep the buffalo hides and the carts and teams that transported them. But then Hettrick looked at him. He could tell, James too, that it wasn't going to be good. He said, "That Bellows girl may as well be on the moon. The Army's got no money for such trades nor the authority to go into Canada."

Unaware that Claude was lying, James jumped in, "If a bargain could be had, why couldn't Old Bear bring her south of the line and make the exchange. Wouldn't that work?"

Hettrick nodded, "I suppose it would, but someone would still need to come up with the five hundred dollars."

An uneasy look came over Claude, but before it manifested itself into something requiring justification, lest he be smoked out as a liar, James blurted out, "Surely the Army, or maybe relatives of this girl, could put up the money."

And then the First Sergeant threw in, "Sir, some years back when I was stationed down in Kansas folks there took up a collection to pay the ransom the Indians were demanding for a white woman. It worked, at least that time it did."

James said, "Well, there you go, Sir. It can be done."

Hettrick said, "It's an idea with some merit but I foresee there being lots of obstacles to it coming to fruition. Besides, I think you're all forgetting how fickle and devious Indians can be."

James came back, "You could parley for Miss Bellows, couldn't you, Claude?"

It was an effort for Claude to hide his lie. And even more, that Old Bear was adamant he wouldn't trade at any price for the girl. But he was desperate to get his hides back, he said, "I believe I can do that. I get along pretty well with Old Bear."

It was only now that James locked on to Claude's eyes. His inner voice said, *that sonovabitch is lying.*

And then Hettrick abruptly ended the speculation, "No, there's no money for such a trade. I believe once Mr. Charbonneau crosses the Medicine Line this fantasy concerning Miss Bellows will evaporate. So, no, my decision stands. You're lucky I don't take everything you have for being accomplices to murder."

Claude glared hatefully at Hettrick, "You're not God, Captain. Someday, that fact will become known to you." He then reined his horse to the side of Hettrick's and rode on, without permission, towards camp.

Claude's departure left James face to face with the captain and the first sergeant. Hettrick said to him, "My advice to you, Mr. Doyle, is to part company with these people. They are of a poor moral caliber. Besides, they will be headed north and you, west. Am I not right?"

"You are, Sir. Going to Idaho Territory to make my fortune."

Hettrick nodded, "Good day, Mr. Doyle," before nudging the sides of his horse and heading up the slope, with the first sergeant following, in the direction of the stolen horses.

After collecting what little belongings he had and a sack of pemican, biscuits and coffee that Pretty Bird gave him, James played out the ruse of his going to Idaho. He struck out to the south, making it known to Hettrick his intent was to get off the Blackfeet Reservation and pick up the Mullan Road, as the captain had suggested. In truth, however, he was going to follow Pretty Bird's advice and ride until he came to the Teton River. *Follow it downstream*, she had said, *it will take you to Fort Benton.* That was not his destination but rather three hours ride west of it to Charlie's ranch.

He rode that first night till it was almost dark before stopping to make a cold camp, still not confident that one of Claude's followers might tell the Army who he really was. Or maybe just as bad, the Blackfeet or Lakota would come upon him.

CHAPTER THIRTY

Captain Hettrick sent First Sergeant Greer back to Fort Benton with twenty-five of his forty soldiers along with seven of the dozen pack mules and three of the five civilian packers. In addition, they took with them three carts full of buffalo hides and twenty-eight stolen horses. It was a tempting prize. Hettrick admonished Greer before he left, *if the Lakota attack you, it may be difficult to hang on to the horses while defending yourselves. Use your judgement, but if it is necessary to surrender the horses in order to gain defensive positions, I am alright with that.* It was this fear that dominated Hettrick's thoughts on the tedious three-day escort of Charbonneau and his people to the Medicine Line. Their pace was slow on account of the two-wheeled carts that they had been allowed to keep. But, at last they came to a broad expanse of yellow grass with a pile of sod that was surrounded by a knee-deep trench. From a distance, the sod pile looked like a round top teepee that was about six feet in height. It had been constructed there, on the 49th parallel, by the North American Boundary Commission. The mounds were easy to miss as they occurred at three-mile intervals. But for those committing depredations and murder on the American side, the location of the line, and the safe haven it provided, was well known.

Claude waited until his party had gone beyond the mound before reining his horse around to face Hettrick and his soldiers lined up on the south side of the line. He looked at the captain and shouted, "You will never do this to me again." He stopped short of verbalizing what his threat might mean.

Hettrick came back, "Mr. Charbonneau, you should heed the consequences of your actions, fore if you repeat them, I can almost guarantee there will be violence."

Claude gave Hettrick a hateful look and snorted, "I suspect you are right." And with that, he turned his horse northward.

Hettrick watched the Metis's departure until they were black specks on the horizon. In that time his mind's eye traveled across the Canadian prairie to Old Bear's village and the plight of Sarah Bellows. Visions of her treatment, none of them good, cascaded through his mind. Ever since he had downplayed the idea of ransoming her his conscience had been chastising him. He took some solace in there being no money for her rescue and government rules that forbade the Army from going past this hump of sod. This arbitrary line that men looking through a sexton at the sun had decreed, *build another mound here.* But now, that thinking, all of it, seemed flawed. It was a matter of what was right and what was wrong. The pendulum of uncertainty had just swung back to being all wrong when, to his left, a horse nickered. It was only then he became aware of how long they had sat on their horses looking north. He noted some of the men were looking at him, differently, he thought. Like they sensed the conflict within him. He said to Sergeant Hall, "Let's head back. Put a man on point."

The Sergeant saluted, "Yes, Sir," and then proceeded to form the men into a column of twos. He rode over to a soldier who had not ridden point since they had left Fort Benton almost two weeks ago. The man had a fearful look on his face as he knew what was likely coming. Hall, said, "Private Lucas, you're on point. Lead us by at least a half mile, understand?"

The Private nodded. His voice had a slight tremble to it, "Yes, Sergeant." He hesitated before exposing his concern, "You purty certain that gun we took off the Metis was the sharpshooter's that got Harkness?"

Hall said, "The Captain and First Sergeant is."

"Are you?"

"Lucas, I'm more worried about stumbling into an Indian ambush than some guy making a lucky shot from way hell and gone away. You just keep your eyes open, and we'll all be okay. Alright?"

Lucas, in a totally unconvincing voice, stammered a reply, "Yes, Sergeant." He then rode off on their back trail.

CHAPTER THIRTY-ONE

Hettrick was anxious to catch up to First Sergeant Greer with the carts and stolen horses. So it was, they covered close to twenty miles after leaving Claude at the border. They made camp in a big coulee alongside a little creek that afforded them good water with plenty of grass on either side of it. There were dense rose bushes and willows as tall as a man on horseback growing next to the creek. And scattered amongst them too were occasional cottonwood trees. After allowing the horses and mules to drink their fill, the soldiers and packers had picketed them close to a hundred yards out from the creek.

It may have been the grousing that he had overheard, or it could have been simply the existence of ample dead wood for cooking fires that trumped Hettrick's initial idea of a cold camp. That they would eat pemican and the last of their canned peaches and there would be no coffee. But, for whatever reason, he gave in to the temptation to have hot food and coffee. They had four cooking fires scattered over about seventy-five yards next to the meanderings of the creek. The collective blue smoke rose straight up, there being no wind to carry it away. It did not go very high before it pooled above the coulee. Hettrick thought this was good, rather than it drifting a mile or two away and being smelled by Indians that might otherwise not know of their presence.

There was the aroma too of coffee and bacon frying in the air. And at the packer's fire, if a person got real close, the smell of Dutch oven biscuits that were almost done could be had. It was a good camp, especially after their long day in the saddle.

Darkness had now pushed out all the light this side of the western horizon. They stood, the three of them, with tin cups of steaming hot coffee in their hands. For the most part they stared into the fire and the roily smoke, processing their thoughts. The fear of dying, and truth be told, the fear of living. It was the packer, Tom Egbert, that attempted to extract them from this melancholy that had descended upon them, he said, "Gonna be colder than a well digger's ass tonight, I fear."

Hettrick offered a polite smile as he looked across the fire to where it was reflected in the moisture of Egbert's eyes. He said, "Well, it is September."

"It is?"

Sergeant Hall and Hettrick laughed before the captain came back in a dry tone, "Been that way for three days now."

Straight-faced, the packer replied, "The hell you say."

Hettrick and the sergeant laughed again.

Away from the fires and the social bantering, Private Lucas, having survived his first-time riding point, now stood guard with another private over the stock. They were positioned on either side of the picketed horses and mules. Each animal was restrained by a fifty-foot rope attached to an iron picket pin driven about a foot into the ground. The two men were to continually walk one-half of the perimeter meeting in the middle on the west side and then reversing to walk around to the east side. To make the loop around the entire picket area would entail at least a quarter mile. It was, therefore, not overly alarming to Lucas when he arrived at the midpoint on the west side when his counterpart, Private Sherman, was not there. Lucas strained his eyes in the direction from which Sherman would come. The sickle shaped moon provided little light. It was involuntary and simultaneous, the hair on the back of his neck standing up and his heart racing. He spun around, certain that an Indian was sneaking up on him. And then fear took hold of his right hand as he levered a round into his Spencer repeater. He sighed deeply, looking to the front and side of him before spinning around to look behind him. He whimpered, barely a whisper, "Come on, Sherman, please be here."

It had taken time and stealth and patience, but finally the Lakota warrior emerged from behind a big sorrel horse barely five steps away. His buckskin moccasins came down light and silent upon the grass. Lucas never saw the heavy stone war club coming. It crushed a divot into the back of his skull the size of a goose egg. He was unconscious and near death as he fell forward to the ground. Nerves and muscles do odd things when dying. Just before Lucas hit the ground, his finger jerked the trigger of his rifle. The Lakota's plan to silently steal as many horses as they could without having to engage the soldiers was now compromised. The nighttime tranquility was shattered by the 56-50 cartridge exploding and sending its heavy bullet harmlessly out into the night and, at the same time, a terrifying warning to the soldiers clustered around their fires. It had them frantically scrambling into the shadows beyond the firelight to retrieve their rifles from where they'd left them with their saddles and bedrolls. In their haste, men tripped and fell in the dark. Spurred on by spontaneous shouts, fearful voices, "Indians. Damned Indians are after the horses. The sonsabitches are stealing the horses." They instantly sprang up desperate to reach their Spencer repeating rifles.

Hettrick, as well as the others at his fire, tossed their coffee cups to the ground. He shouted the obvious so all would hear, "They're after the horses. Save the horses." And then, in a lesser voice, he said to Sergeant Hall, "Take half the men and go around the north end of the picket area. Send the other half to me and I will do the same on the south end." He then turned to the civilian packer, "Tom, you and your man take up positions in the trees with your Winchesters." And then they moved quickly away from the light of the fire. Hettrick drew his Colt .45 pistol and thumbed back the hammer. He looked into the darkness towards the picket area. It was totally still. A few of the horses were distinguishable but most were not. Neither were the men guarding them. The thought of having to cross the expanse of open ground between the camp and the picket area caused his hands to shake. And then to his right a voice sounded, "Corporal Harris with five men, reporting as ordered Sir."

Hettrick willed himself to do what came next. He pushed his fear to the side as if it were a tangible thing like a gate that could be opened. He stepped through and said, in a steady voice, "Our objective, Corporal, is to secure the perimeter of the picket area and then bring the horses back into camp. Any questions?"

Corporal Harris, who was beginning his second five-year hitch in the Army and had tangled with Indians numerous times in the past, replied smartly, "No, Sir."

"Alright, follow me, single file."

Harris turned and parroted, barely above a whisper, Hettrick's order. They proceeded slowly, five feet between each man, into the quiet darkness. Their hearts in competition with the frenetic images in his mind of a bullet or arrow coming from the blackness and striking him in the chest. And not dying before some horribly painted savage set upon him and proceeded to cut away his scalp. Their fear caused them to breathe deeper, faster, trying to satisfy their pounding hearts. This, in spite of moving slowly, straining their eyes to see the enemy before he saw them.

By and by, they finally came to the animals. Hettrick could make out four horses close to them. He paused and stepped next to Harris before whispering, "Have two men pull those horses' pins and lead them back to camp. Have them tie those animals in the trees along the creek and take up positions there so they can protect them."

Harris nodded and then went about directing two privates to carry out Hettrick's order. Hettrick and the others watched as the men pulled the pins and gathered the picket ropes to lead the horses away. The fact that they were able to collect the four horses without incident gave the captain some solace. He motioned the men onward into the silence. With each uneventful step he allowed the naysayer in his mind to placate his fear. *They're afraid of a big fight. Must not be many of them.* But then, before he could absorb this reassurance, he saw a dark shape lying in the grass. Another step and he saw the yellow stripe. His legs immediately froze. Hettrick dropped to a crouch with his pistol trained on the area to his front. He, and the others behind him, searched the darkness lest they end up lying face down in the grass. After a reasonable time, brave men would stand up and move toward the dead man, so they did, still single file behind the captain. And then they were there, at least the captain and the corporal were, standing over Lucas's body. Although his face was in the dirt, there was little doubt it was him and not Sherman. Lucas was a skinny man with blonde hair. He'd been left enough along the sides to confirm its color. In spite of the obvious, Hettrick knelt and felt of Lucas's neck for signs that his heart had somehow survived this grotesque mutilation. Hettrick knew of a man that had survived scalping, but the back of his head hadn't been caved in. Momentarily, Hettrick drew back his hand from Lucas's neck. The tips of his fingers were wet with blood. He glanced at it and then pinched up some dirt before briefly working the bloody fingers against his thumb and then swiping them on the grass. He stood and whispered to Harris, "Let's move into the picket area and gather all the horses we can. Get 'em back to camp."

"What about Lucas?"

"We'll recover the Private's body at first light"

"Yes. Sir."

And then Hettrick seethed the words, "Those thieving bastards." He nodded beyond Harris. Less than fifty feet away, his own horse, a big Palamino that stood out in the darkness, was slowly walking toward the edge of the picket area. Hettrick said nothing more but started at a quick pace toward his horse. He was nearly to it when he saw under the horse's belly, on the far side, an Indian's legs. The horse began to move faster. On impulse, Hettrick shouted, "Stop or I'll shoot." In the next instant, the futility of his demand that the Indian stop struck him. His inner voice called out, *that was stupid. He knows you won't shoot the horse.* Now, he felt himself running, breathing hard. His pistol waving in the direction of his horse and the Indian. And then suddenly the horse stopped and from beneath its neck a pistol belched fire and smoke. The Palamino reared up and spun away leaving the Indian exposed. Had Hettrick not sagged to his knees trying desperately to not take his place, like Lucas and Sherman, lying face down in the grass, he would have shot the thief. That honor fell to Corporal Harris and the others. They launched a volley that pummeled the Indian's naked upper torso. The impact drove him backwards whereupon he ended up laying on the ground still clutching his old Colt .44 while his lifeless eyes looked up at the stars.

The smoke from the soldier's guns had not yet dissipated when Harris reached the captain who had toppled over on his side. He had been shot in the chest. It was a neat round hole that was difficult to see on account of the dark blue blouse and the night. But it was not difficult to find as each breath Hettrick took, his perforated lung struggled to take in air and with it came blood. Its wheezing was painful for the men to listen to. After a time, it stopped.

CHAPTER THIRTY-TWO

James was torn if he should go directly to Charlie's place and tell Otto what he had learned about his sweetheart or go on with his quest to find his Uncle Antoine. Just bury himself in the Metis culture. But finding his uncle while dodging the law, for who knows how long, would be no easy task. Another option, which had some appeal, was to simply vacate this Montana country all together. Actually go to Idaho and try his luck in the gold fields. Be himself and stop pretending to be someone else. He wrestled considerably with this dilemma that first night after leaving Claude's group. By sunup he had concluded that it might not be wise to return to Charlie's so soon after the deputy being there. And he was not equipped to set out for Idaho. He made another decision as well. The naysayer in his mind was persistent that someone in Claude's party might give up his identity to the Army if they thought it would get their carts and buffalo hides back. It was these nagging fears of running into either the deputy marshal or Captain Hettrick that motivated him to cross the Teton River. His roan horse that he had named Buck, was surefooted in navigating the water. He wore an old brand on his right flank that was haired over. James had been surprised that the Army had not questioned him about the horse. It had not occurred to them, apparently, that he was riding one of Claude's stolen animals. Had he not been so desperate to put distance between himself and the Army, he might have offered up this information as a demonstration of his honesty.

For two days, James followed the Teton River. He stayed to the south of it by close to a mile, so as to lessen his chances of encountering people and their animals coming to water that might be hostile to him. However, it was on that second day, riding as he was through the sagebrush and grass well out from the river, when he saw a lazy column of smoke rising up from a shallow coulee off to his right. *Makes sense,* he thought, *near suppertime.* He continued to study the smoke as Buck plodded along through the brush, his leather saddle squeaking in time to his steps. "Well, Buck, whaddaya reckon they're having for supper? I'll wager you it's not pemican." James laughed, but then said in a sympathetic tone, "Be nice if you had a pail a oats for supper." And then justification for the smoke appeared on a little flat mesa that butted up to the coulee's east side. James squinted his eyes some before declaring, "Buck, that's grain growing over there." He pulled back on Buck's reins even before he was certain as to why he did so. *Could be a hot meal and some company*, he thought. For a time, he sat there on Buck, weighing the risks and inwardly cursing the need to do so. Deer flies pestered both him and Buck. He swatted at them, always a little too slow. *Be nice to have a meal that I didn't have to share with the damned flies.* And then he saw it, an upright figure in the yellowness of the grain. He sighed, "Oh, what the hell, Buck. Let's go see what's for supper."

James started up the coulee with the smoke. He'd not gone far when he saw that the dark figure in the grain field was walking towards the smoke as well. After a few minutes of Buck walking up the coulee it jogged left revealing the source of the smoke. A sod house, not very big, stood in the middle of the coulee. A rusty stovepipe protruding from its roof was puffing away. A black and white mutt looking dog standing near the front door was barking at a steady pace. By and by, a woman, old enough to be James' mother, appeared in the doorway with a double-barreled shotgun. Her attire was brash. Brown cotton pants that showed dirt and a hole in the left knee. And a blue long-sleeved shirt with the sleeves rolled up to the elbows. In spite of her uneasiness, she said nothing. Just stared at James, sizing him up, he reckoned, until he was inside shouting distance and well within the effective range of the shotgun. She aimed the gun directly at him. He could see that both hammers were cocked. She said, "What's the nature of your business?"

James had surveyed the place as he rode up. A privy to the left of the house. To the right, a pole corral and a pine board barn. Its loft showed to be near full of grass hay. Beyond the house was a good-sized garden. A little further on was a string of chokecherry trees and willows that was part of a pasture that was ensnared by another pole fence. Within that was a milk cow and two mules. Taken as a whole, it made James envious. This feeling, however, was offset by the fact he couldn't help but look into the cavernous barrels of the scattergun instead of the woman's eyes. He said, "I'll be straight up with ya, Ma'am. I'm a little down on my luck. I saw your smoke from over yonder, and it being supper time, well, I was hopin' to wrangle an invite. Not for free, mind you. I can pay or do some chores for you."

Keeping the gun aimed as it was, she came back, "You appear to be traveling pretty light for being this far away from civilization. Why is that?"

Shame briefly pulsed within James as he conjured up another lie, "Indians stole my pack horse."

From behind James came a man's voice, "You're a liar, Mister."

Reflex caused James to instantly twist around in his saddle to see his accuser. A man wearing a flat brimmed gray Stetson and carrying a Henry repeater was walking quickly toward him. James continued the ruse, "Sir, I take exception to that."

The man stopped near his wife. He came back in a sarcastic tone, "Well, Sir, if anybody is going to be taking any exceptions here it's likely gonna be the man you stole that horse from."

James was taken aback such that he had no immediate response. He could tell by the conviction in the man's words that he was rock solid in his belief.

A contemptuous smile formed under the man's full black beard. He uttered a brief laugh like he'd read James' innermost thoughts. He then nodded to Buck, "That horse belongs to a fella by the name of Bill Monk. Lives a coupla miles on down the crik from here."

James said, "I ain't no horse thief."

The man stared at James while slowly shaking his head, "Well, something ain't right about you. I know you're a liar, so that ain't a good start with me."

James sighed. His inner voice pleaded, *just tell him who you are. Be done with this game.* He sighed again and shook his head in exasperation. He looked first into the woman's blue eyes and then her husband's. They were vacant pools of mistrust. To tell them that he was wanted for murder would only confirm their judgement of him. Nonetheless, James confessed to the events on the Destiny. The couple listened but did not act shocked. When he was finished telling how it was on the riverboat and with Claude Charbonneau, he said simply, "And that's how I came to be sitting on Bill Monk's horse in your front yard."

The woman made eye contact with her husband and then lowered her shotgun. She even eased the hammers down. Her husband said, "We came up the Missouri on a riverboat. We were deck passengers, so we know something of how things are on those boats."

James felt relief, "I'm telling you God's truth."

The man nodded, "You know, son, I suspect you are."

James drank in the man's words as he felt some of the tension leave his body. He offered, "By the way, my name's James Coumerilh."

James noted in their faces that the mention of his name piqued a recollection of some sort, but the man came back as if it hadn't, "I'm Simon Shaffer and this is my wife, Agnes."

Agnes added, "You're welcome to take supper with us."

James nodded, "I'm much obliged. Be alright if I step down from my horse and tend to him?"

The cordiality that seconds ago had been in Simon's demeanor now vanished as he said in a stern voice, "You know, Mr. Coumerilh, with respect to that horse, I expect you to make it right with Bill Monk."

It was just human nature that James felt insulted but, knowing he was in the wrong, he caught himself before responding in kind. He said, "That is my intention, Sir. I don't have much money, but I'd be more 'an willing to work off the price of the horse."

A ghost of a grin came to not only Simon's face but his wife's too, "I believe, Mr. Coumerilh, that I could accommodate your desire to work for the horse. I am in need of help harvesting my grain. We can talk to Mr. Monk tomorrow and see if he would be willing to sell the horse on that basis. Is that agreeable to you?"

James nodded, "It is, most definitely."

"Fine enough, then," said Simon as he walked over to Buck and extended his hand up to James, "We have a deal then?"

James grasped Simon's hand. It was rough and calloused with black dirt defining the folds of skin on his knuckles. His grip was strong, almost to the point of intimidation. James replied, "Yes, we do."

"Fine enough," replied Simon. "Follow me, I'll show you where you can pasture your horse."

James nudged Buck's sides and fell in behind Simon as he walked to the side of the house toward the barn some fifty yards away. Simon was wearing a badly faded red shirt. It showed sweat real good. Most of his back was covered with new, moist sweat mixed with old salty stains. *Gonna be labor on the order of wood hawkin'*, thought James. And then, in a few more steps, his inner voice pointed out, *here's a man that you just confessed to being wanted for murder and he's walking with his back to you.* James felt shame. Before he came to this country called Montana, such a thought would never have entered his mind.

Simon stepped through the barn's big open double doors. It was immediately shadowy and cooler inside. He pointed to a rough plank door with a white doorknob to his left. "You can hang your saddle in there," he paused and then added, "You can sleep in there too if you like."

"Much obliged," said James.

Simon revealed a little more of who he was, of why he would walk with his back to a killer, he offered, "There's oats in there too if you wanna grain your horse."

James looked on purpose at Simon and grinned, "Buck will appreciate that"

"That's what you call him?"

Enbarrassment showed in James' face, he nodded, "Yes, Sir. He seems to have taken to it."

Simon gave a brief laugh, "I believe I like Buck better than Rocky."

James got down from his saddle and began undoing the cinch. Without thinking, he said over the top of Buck's back, "So, is it just you and Agnes that work this place?"

Dead silence, save for a sparrow flitting from the top-most pole of one stall to another before flying out the big doors cropped up between them. The quiet was such that James looked away from the saddle toward Simon, thinking that he hadn't heard him. Simon said, his voice still edged with bitterness, "We had three boys. The war took 'em."

James instantly regretted probing the issue, "I'm sorry."

"Waste a life, that war. Were you in it?"

James nodded, "Yeah, I fought for the Confederacy."

"My boys too. Took all three of 'em inside a year. The grief nearly killed their ma. That's a lot of the reason we came out here." His voice trailed off before taking a deep breath and sighing, "One misery for another I reckon."

"How's that?"

Simon shook his head, "Indians, you never know when they might take a notion to kill you and take your valuables."

It may have been because James was part Indian that the words tumbled from his mouth, "All Indians ain't that way. In these parts I reckon it's mostly renegade Lakota that's causing the trouble."

"I'd wager the bunch that stole Buck is the biggest culprit."

"Well, I know they've got the Bellows girl."

Simon's eyes showed surprise, "You know that for a fact?"

"Yes, Sir, I do. Supposedly, for five hundred dollars they'll let her go."

Simon snorted, "No disrespect but you'd be getting damaged goods. I don't know that she would ever be able to fit in the white man's world again."

"I can't say," said James, "But I know a fella that would want her to try. At some point I intend to get word to him of her whereabouts, for all the good it will do him."

Simon's look became more serious, "Can it wait till after we've got the grain harvested? A fella never knows about the weather. One good hard rain or hailstorm and I'll lose it all."

James made eye contact with Simon, "Your crop and buying Buck will come first. You can count on that." He then pulled the saddle and blanket from Buck's back and started toward the door with the white knob.

CHAPTER THIRTY-THREE

It was at breakfast the next morning that Simon announced, *I believe first rattle outta the box we ought to ride on down to Bill Monk's and clear the air on his horse.* So here they were, James and Simon riding along the Teton River while the sun was barely peeking above the horizon. It was that time of day when it seemed extra quiet save for the birds singing. Even in the sage and grass where they were riding, James on Buck and Simon on one of his mules named Mabel, the birds were singing. When the terrain allowed they went at a trot with Simon admonishing James, *I'm hopin' we catch Bill at the house so we can settle this matter right there and not have to chase after him till noon or some such. We got oats to cut.* By and by they came to a good-sized bow in the river that was lined with trees. On the other side of it, James could see blue smoke hanging in the air and in the next little bit he could smell it. Simon turned his head slightly and called back to James, "Monk's place is just around this elbow of the crik."

James thought to holler back, *alright,* but his mind's preoccupation with the possibility Monk wouldn't sell him Buck precluded it. And then they rounded the elbow of trees. Dead ahead was a good-sized pine board house with a black tarpapered roof. Two rocking chairs separated by a little table with a white porcelain coffee cup sat on the covered front porch. There was plenty of other evidence to suggest Bill Monk was a man of means. His barn was twice the size of Simon's. And there was a shop, bunkhouse, chicken coop, root cellar, two privies, woodshed, sawmill and a set of corrals big enough that a man could get lost in them. A green Studebaker wagon was parked next to the barn and beyond it a mower, similar to the one James had helped Charlie load in Fort Benton. It was intimidating to James as his past experience with wealthy people was things generally went their way. Two dogs, one mostly brown, the other black and white, came running out of the barn. They were barking furiously and nearly to Simon and James when three men stepped from the shadows inside the barn to its big open doors. The older of the three, who was wearing a sharply peaked black Stetson, shouted, "Wolf, Brownie. Get the hell back here."

The dogs immediately stopped and started back to the men at the barn who were already pointing at Buck, or Rocky as they knew him and talking excitedly such that James picked up on it, "Pa, that sonovabitch is riding Rocky." The older man then said something that James couldn't hear but all three of them went silent and waited with near hateful looks on their faces.

Simon called out from a good way off, "Mornin', Bill."

Bill Monk allowed Mabel and Buck to take another half-dozen steps before he shouted, "I see you caught yourself a horse thief."

Without staring, James took in the men's appearance. All three of them were wearing six-shooters. A sick feeling immediately came over him. He'd hoped things wouldn't start out like this.

Simon shook his head and reined Mabel to a stop, "It's more like this young fella is returning your horse with an offer to buy it."

The man farthest away from his father yelled back, "And whose idea was that, Simon? A horse thief whose conscience got the better of him, or you making him do it?"

James blurted out, "I got this horse from the Metis. They traded with some Lakota for it. Yesterday, when I rode into Simon's place, he recognized the horse and insisted I make it right. So, yes, coming here is Simon's idea."

Simon cut in, "Bill, the boy would like to buy Rocky if you're willing."

Monk came back, "We lost thirteen horses the night Rocky came up missing. Did these Metis have any others? Mostly sorrels and one paint."

James nodded, "They did, but the Army confiscated them, and some carts loaded with buffalo hides. They're on their way to Fort Benton. I suspect they might not be too far from here, but north of the river."

The elder Monk studied James for any signs he might be lying until finally he said, "I'll tell ya what I'm gonna do. If the Army is like you say, close by, and they've got the rest of our horses, I'll let you keep Rocky. But if this turns out to be a wild goose chase and you were the thief all along." Monk paused and sighed, "Well, God help you."

James came back, "I'm much obliged, Sir."

The feisty son on the end spit tobacco juice in a defiant manner in the direction of James who was well beyond its reach, "I don't know, Pa. I ain't so sure we ain't being hoodwinked."

The middle son, seemingly a skinny shy kid up till now, threw in, "I say we keep Rocky till we see if the Army really does have our horses."

"I believe that's a damned fine idea," said the feisty son. "Won't hurt to keep Rocky here till we see if this fella is telling the truth. Hell, we don't even know his name."

In that instant, the emotion that flooded James' mind was exasperation with lying, of not being able to be himself.

So, he said, "James Coumerilh. I've got kin somewhere in these parts."

"You related to Antoine Coumerilh?" asked Bill.

"He's my uncle. Do you know him?" asked James in a hopeful voice.

Bill nodded, "Some years back he and his people cut timber for us. Bucked it up so they could haul it down from the mountains to our sawmill. They did a helluva job."

"Would you happen to know where they are?"

Bill shrugged, "They move around a lot. Fall's nearly here. They'll be looking to settle in for the winter somewhere soon, I reckon. But I don't know where. Could be across The Medicine Line or maybe over near the Blackfeet country."

James came back, "Well, I'm going to be helping Simon get his grain harvested. So, if you hear of anything concerning my uncle's whereabouts, I'd appreciate your letting me know."

Bill nodded, "I can do that." He glanced at his sons and then looked back at James, "I reckon you can hang onto Rocky till we figure out this situation with the Army."

"I'm obliged," said James. In his mind, however, he was envisioning the Monk's catching up to the Army and telling them that James Coumerilh, not Jack Doyle, had directed them their way.

CHAPTER THIRTY-FOUR

Simon called out, "Must be dinner time. Agnes is coming up the hill."

James paused in scything the oats and stood straight. The fatigue and pain in his back eased a little as he looked away to the wagon clattering along the edge of the ten-acre field. He shouted, his familiarity with Simon having grown over the past three days, "I'll tell ya, the dinner wagon is more than a welcome sight today as I am well north of being downright gaunt."

Simon had given James the choice of cutting the oats or gathering and tying it into bundles. The shocks, as he called them, were the diameter of a good-sized fence post. James recognized right off that staying bent over all day swinging the long-handled scythe would be the more physically demanding of the two tasks. Nonetheless, his pride or common decency would not allow a man 25 years his senior, whose roof he was sleeping under and food he was eating to assume the harder job. But now on the third day of scything, both of his hands had developed open blisters that bled. The closest thing the Shaffer's had for a salve was grease for the mower. James had daubed it on thick. It seemed to help ease the pain until the friction of his gloves wore it away, as was the case right now.

About twenty feet of downed oats separated Simon and James. Simon nodded to it, "James, you wanna give me a hand shockin' this up 'fore Agnes gets here?"

James allowed the scythe to drop to the ground and went to his knees. He began pulling the long stems of oats together to form a bundle. The pain in the palms of his hands was less now that he wasn't gripping the scythe, but it hadn't gone away entirely. Sweat streamed down his temples and occasionally escaped his black slouch hat in such quantities that it overwhelmed his eyebrows and flooded his eyes with its burning saltiness. His discomfort caused him to laugh sardonically and call out to Simon, "You ever regret coming here?"

There was silence coming from Simon's direction save for his labored breathing and the rustling of the grain being gathered across the stubble. It caused James to glance in his direction thinking that he had offended him. About then Simon said, while looking down at the shock he was tying, "Nope, too many bad memories back home."

James instantly regretted saying what he had. *I likely reminded him of his boys being killed in the war.* And then the naysayer, mean spirited as he sometimes was wont to be when it came to reality, reminded him, *if you'd lived up to your obligation as a soldier, you'd likely be a bad memory too.* James was still immersed in his guilt when Agnes drew up the wagon next to where the shocks, standing on end, began about 75 yards away. Simon said, "I'll help Agnes load the wagon if you want to finish the shocking here."

James looked Simon's way, purposely not making eye contact, "Yes, Sir, I'll finish up here and be along to help you load."

Agnes climbed down from the seat on the flatbed trailer and picked up the first shock she came to. She said as she carried the bundle to the wagon, "With this load you boys will be well ahead of me. I'm about half-done threshing yesterday afternoon's load."

Simon came back, his voice filtered through the stems of oats he held against his chest, "That's alright, Ma. Better it be in the barn, if need be, than driven into the mud by a hailstorm."

"If worrying about such catastrophes keeps them away, we should be good," replied Agnes as she laid the shock on the wagon bed.

Simon frowned, "Come winter, when we've got a dollar or two in our poke and beans to eat, you can thank me for taking up your slack on the worrying."

"Speaking of beans, that's what we're having for dinner."

Simon blurted out like he'd been stung by a bee, "Isn't that what we had for supper last night?"

Agnes said a little louder as she picked up another shock, "You know damned good and well it was. What we're having for dinner today is leftovers from last night." She paused to fine tune the sarcasm in her voice, "Take your pick, Simon, you can either have your oats threshed or a five-course noon time meal. Now come tonight, you'll get a supper that'll bloat a fat hog. But today at noon," she scoffed, "no sir, I can only go in so many directions at one time. If the boys were -"

Agnes abruptly went silent, save for a sniffle, as she toted the shock to the wagon. She placed it on the flatbed and turned to get another one when Simon intercepted her. He put his arms around her and pulled her into his chest. She began to quietly cry. He whispered, "I'm sorry. I miss the boys too."

James looked away, allowing the Shaffer's some privacy to grieve the absence of their sons. In so doing, however, he saw a rider coming to the house below. Even at this distance, he was certain that it was Bill Monk. Momentarily, Simon, who was still holding Agnes, saw too, beyond her, that their neighbor was coming. He whispered, "Bill Monk is headed our way."

Agnes instantly stepped back and began wiping the tears away before walking briskly toward the farthest shock. She had not yet come back to the wagon when Monk came within hollering distance. Simon was extra cordial shouting out to him, "Mornin', Bill."

Monk nodded a far less enthusiastic, "Mornin."

James met Monk's stern look, "Mornin', Mr. Monk."

Monk shook his head and turned back to Simon, "Did you know Mr. Coumerilh or Jack Doyle or whatever the hell his name is killed a man on a riverboat?"

Simon nodded, "I did."

"That don't bother you?"

"I've heard his story. I don't believe he had a choice."

Monk snorted and spit tobacco juice to the side, "Well, a liar is something I can't abide, but I did get back all the horses that the Indians stole."

James spoke up, "So, where does that leave me and Buck?"

Monk sighed and shook his head, "Our deal still stands, I reckon. But you should know my boys are less tolerant of a liar than I am. They advised the army of your whereabouts. It was my understanding the Army was going to pass that information on to the marshal when they reached Fort Benton."

A mix of fear and anger rose up in James' eyes. He said, "I'm much obliged for Buck. I'll take good care of him."

A ghost of a frown came to Monk's face, "You'd better. My boys are not in favor of you having him. They make some sense when they talk of what will happen to Buck when the law catches up to you?"

James placed his throbbing hands on his hips and looked up at Monk sitting on his horse, he said, "If that time comes, I will advise the marshal that Buck is to be returned to you.

In fact, if I am destined to dance with the hang man, I will direct all my possessions go to you."

Monk was a little taken aback, surprised even. He said, his voice now possessing some compassion, "So, I reckon you're gonna vacate this country?"

It was like James was stuck in the moment before Monk's arrival and he was watching Agnes mourn the absence of her sons. The words poured out of him like water out of an upended bucket, "No, Sir, not until we've got Simon's grain harvested."

Shock surfaced on Simon's face and Agnes' too. Simon cut in sharply, "You'd be foolish to stay here until John Law shows up."

James' mind went back to the war, always the war, the damned war and how he'd not gone back to it. And now here he was with a choice. He could do the work the Shaffer boys would have done had they not died, senselessly or not. Or he could do like when he went home on convalescent leave and dodge the possibility of dying. He came back, "No, Simon, we'll get your oats in before I go."

It was obvious in Simon's eyes that he wanted to argue. To insist that James leave, save himself from the gallows. But it was equally plain in his wife's demeanor that he was asking too much of her. That the bulk of their crop was still standing, That the chances a fall storm would take the oats before he and Agnes by themselves could. So, he closed the gate behind James' declaration. He said, "I'm obliged, Son."

CHAPTER THIRTY-FIVE

The blisters on James' hands never healed, not entirely anyway. It didn't help that he had taken to threshing oats after supper. There was no sleeping, wondering, worrying if tomorrow the marshal would come for him. So, he worked most nights by lantern light until all of the shocks Agnes had brought in that day, but had not had the time, were threshed. He would spread the shocks on a piece of white canvas, about 12 feet square, laying on the ground inside the barn. And then he flailed them with a short wooden club that was attached by a six-inch piece of leather to a longer club that served as the handle. He directed the blows again and again at the seed heads until they were reduced to individual seeds in a milieu of broken stems. With a pitchfork he then removed the seedless straw for use come winter as bedding for the animals. In the morning, Agnes had only to separate out the finer chaff and then fold the corners of the canvas inward so as to collect all of the seeds in its center. She then could easily scoop the oats up and pour it into canvas sacks that she stitched shut with a long sewing needle and string.

It was nearly ten o'clock. Pitch black outside. James had set a coal oil hand lamp on a three-legged stool next to the threshing canvas. Its yellow light cast a dull, weak shadow on the walls of the barn. He was down on his hands and knees picking chaff out of the seeds when, from the quiet, came Simon's voice, "You could have left that for tomorrow."

James spun around, quick as a cat, on the canvas to face Simon.

Simon came back, "Been 17 days since Monk was here. Kind of makes me think the marshal has got more important desperadoes than you to tend to."

James' heart had not yet settled itself when he said, "I don't know, Simon. I feel like everyday I'm edging a little farther out onto this frozen lake and ignoring the fact that spring is coming."

"You can leave whenever you've a mind too, James. Another coupla days and we'll be done with the oats."

And then James said, not to draw attention to it, but it did, "Tomorrow is likely to be a slack day with me being the only one here. You may want to tack on another day or so to your estimate."

James watched the shadow of Simon's head go side to side on the wall behind him before he said, "Agnes and I talked after supper. We know you want to get word to your friend about his sweetheart the Indians has got. You taking the oats to the stage relay station tomorrow makes more sense in that regard. It could be a chance for you to pass that information onto that fella you know that rides shotgun for them."

The day before, a man from the relay station had come and said they needed oats now. That they couldn't wait until the first of October as they had agreed. James had seen the way Agnes' face had lit up upon hearing this as the prospect of making the trip with Simon and a day away from the drudgery of threshing would be a treat. James came back, "Simon, my observation is that Agnes wants very much to get off the place for a spell. Even if it's just to the relay station and eating their chuck and talking with some new folks. I know she'll be genuinely disappointed not to go."

The shadow on the wall bobbed left and right again as Simon said, "She's in agreement. It's the least we can do for you."

James nodded his conscience having healed somewhat these past 17 days.

CHAPTER THIRTY-SIX

There was just light enough that they could see to not step into the prairie dog holes. There were lots of them between the house and the pasture where the animals were kept. James had walked it plenty of times. Nonetheless, Simon cautioned him, "Be mindful of where you step. A fella can bust an ankle if he plants a foot wrong."

Trailing behind Simon with a partial bucket of oats suspended from each arm, James spoke to Simon's back, "Oh, yes Sir. Got no need of a busted foot."

Simon came back like they'd been talking about the trip, "I have little doubt you can be back by supper time. Mabel and Ted pull good together. I think you know that."

James said, there being some concern in his voice, "You say the trail down there is marked clear enough that even a southern boy like me can find his way?"

Simon laughed, "Like I said at breakfast. You start out like you're going to Bill Monk's. About halfway there you'll come to that fork in the road that goes south. Be mindful of places where folks has drove off into the hoorahs for one reason or another, but don't you follow 'em. Just stay on the real worn-down wagon tracks. They'll take ya right to the Deer Creek relay station."

"It's kinda the way outta this country, is it?" said James.

Simon stopped at the pole fence and rested his hands, filled with the lead ropes for the mules, on the top rail. He looked over at James, "I suspect you'll be there by noon." Before James could respond, Simon looked out across the pasture to where the mules and Buck were standing near the creek. He laughed, "They know something is up. Rattle that oats."

James opened the wooden gate and went part way to the mules, who were staring at him, before shaking one of the buckets so they could hear the oats. He called out, "Come on, mules." At first, they did not move, but when Buck did, they came along too.

It took less than an hour to harness and hitch the mules and load the wagon with 25 sacks of oats. Worrisome clouds hung over the eastern horizon. They were dark and billowy and wreaked of anger. Such was their look that Agnes came from the house as Simon and James tied a canvas tarp over the load. Her voice was sharp, "Simon, this is foolhardy. Deliver the oats another day. We should all work today at harvesting what we can before this storm hits."

Simon did not pause in lashing the tarp to the wagon. "The stage line is paying top dollar. They'll go elsewhere for their oats if we don't get it to them when they say."

"And if we lose what we've got left standing in the field, where's the profit in that?"

Simon tugged on the knot to make certain of it and then turned in a deliberate, exasperated manner to look at Agnes. He spelled it out for her, "It's ten miles to the Deer Creek relay station. They'll give us $1.25 a bushel, delivered. It's 35 miles to Fort Benton where we might get $1.05 a bushel." Simon paused and frowned before adding, "I don't want to lose the stage company's business."

Agnes glared at Simon and shook her head in silence before turning away and walking toward the low mesa where their oat field was located.

Simon watched her go. There was hurt, but not regret, in his eyes. He came back to James and handed him a note, "Harvey Kaime is the station manager. Give him this so you can collect payment. Should be $62.50. I trust you'll not tarry."

James nodded, "No, Sir. I'll not linger."

Simon put his hand on James' shoulder, "Be wary of anyone you meet along the way. There are scoundrels aplenty hereabouts."

James came back, "I'll keep a sharp eye out." But even as he said it, he envisioned his demise if the Lakota or outlaws set upon him.

CHAPTER THIRTY-SEVEN

The road was as Simon had said it would be. So much so that the ease in following it caused the naysayer in James' mind to point out, *a route this well-traveled is likely known to thieves. Why hell, it is likely their source of plunder. It is akin to an old boar hog going to a trough to satisfy his hunger.* The naysayer's words, like a taunt they were of what lay ahead, hung in James' mind. They caused him to swivel his head left and right, peering up the myriad coulees that poured into the broad valley where the road now lay. The scenario of Indians rushing out of one of these brush-filled draws prompted James to check the readiness of his Winchester. It was lying on top of the load behind the Studebaker's seat. He scoffed at his naivete, "They'll shoot me down before I can ever bring it to bear." In that moment he shifted both reins to his left hand and drew his .36 Caliber Navy Colt from where it rode on his right hip. He studied it, recalling how long ago it had been that he had loaded it. It gave the doubt monger within him cause to recall that it was this gun's failure to fire the first time that had allowed him to live. It was only natural for him to think that today it would be someone else's turn for a second chance.

There were patches of gray clouds overhead. They were here and there, such that they allowed some blue sky and sunshine. Over the tops of the mule's ears, nestled in a sea of sagebrush, James could see up ahead several structures and a corral with horses. White smoke was pushing up at a steady rate from the only building with a stovepipe. James whispered, "Just in time for dinner, it appears." He then gently rippled the reins over the mule's backs, "Git up, mules."

In a short time they arrived at the relay station, which was located, as its name implied, on a shoestring of water called Deer Creek. Willow and alder mostly traced its existence through the sagebrush. James brought the wagon to a halt in front of the barn's open doors. A big yellow dog followed by a short fat man with gray hair came out of the building with the smoke. He called out as he wiped his hands on a white flannel shirt that James recognized as military issue, "You the fella with the grain?"

From the wagon seat, James shouted, "I am. Got a note here from Mr. Shaffer."

The fat man shot back, "I don't need any note. Just my oats."

James jumped down to the ground, "Where would you like it?"

The man and the dog walked past the mules toward the barn door, "In here. All the way to the back against the wall."

James nodded, "Alright."

The fat man watched as James began to untie the ropes that held the tarp in place. He said, "Damned good thing you showed up today. I'm down to a half sack of oats."

James started working a second knot. The palms of his hands still smarting from the blisters. Out of the corner of his eye he could see the fat man was content to watch. A frown came to James' face but not so the fat man could see it. He said, "We been workin' daybreak till the sun is long gone trying to get all of Mr. Shaffer's oats harvested. He sent me today even though we got oats still standing in the field and a storm is brewing."

The fat man came back, his tone near indifferent, "Well, I got a stage line to run." He wheezed while nodding toward the bags in the wagon, "You can stack these by that piddly half sack in there. Come inside when you're done, and I'll pay you."

James tossed the canvas back from the bags of oats saying as he did, "I won't be long. I'm trying to beat this storm that's coming so I can help the Shaffer's bring in the last of their crop."

Oblivious to what James had said, the fat man replied, "Got venison stew and sourdough biscuits just out of the oven for dinner."

A pulse of emotion ran through James that caused him to think better of the fat man until he followed up with, "Be four bits to ya."

James pretended to be straining with lifting the first bag of oats from the back of the wagon as reason for not looking at the fat man, while saying disingenuously, "I appreciate the hospitality, but I reckon I better head on back soon as I'm done unloading."

The fat man snorted and shot James a dirty look, but not before James had stepped through the open barn door into the heavy shadow.

From the wagon to where the sacks of oats were to be stacked was 47 steps. James had counted them when he was about halfway through the load. He was in the process of tallying in his mind how many steps he would have walked after he got the last three sacks in the wagon unloaded when he heard, on the other side of the barn, hoofbeats and the squeak and rattle of the stage. A good feeling instantly came over him. *What luck it would be if Frank is riding shotgun.* He paused at the rear of the wagon waiting for the stage to come into view. And then it was there, stopping in front of the station where everybody on board would get the four-bit stew. Right off, James recognized Frank Murphy. He was sitting to the left of the driver holding, not a shotgun as his job title suggested, but a yellow boy Winchester. James immediately allowed the sack of oats he was about to heft from the back of the wagon to topple over. He started at a quick pace toward the stage calling out, "Frank."

Frank Murphy was wearing a tan, wide brimmed, high crowned hat that sometimes prevented a person from gauging the look in his eyes. His head jerked around like he had been shot at, only to say nothing. There was no mistaking that he had recognized James. At first, it was hurtful to James that Frank hadn't acknowledged him, but then all that had happened on the Destiny flooded his mind with the reality of what his life would always be. He rounded the horses and the young man unhitching them and was about to continue to where Frank was helping passengers from the coach when his legs locked up on him. A woman was just stepping out of the stage with Frank's help. James instantly knew her. She was wearing a blue and white paisley dress with a matching bonnet. The smooth brown skin of her face was framed by the bonnet. It was exactly as James had remembered it from that day on the levee in Fort Benton. He went toward her in such a way that it caught her eye. She smiled and turned toward him. James removed his hat and said, "Jack Doyle, Ma'am. From Fort Benton, if you recall."

Nettie Bell, having heard the talk concerning the murderer, James Coumerilh, played along, "Oh, yes, Mr. Doyle. I had hoped to see you again so that we could make arrangements for you to escort me to my brother's grave."

James nodded, "Yes, Ma'am. I haven't forgotten." James paused with a quizzical look on his face and then said, "If I may ask, where are you bound for today?"

A sudden pall of sadness came over Nettie's face, "My employer, Captain Hattrick was killed by the Indians. Mrs. Hettrick left yesterday by steamboat to take his body to Ohio for burial. Obviously, she will not be returning and without the captain's salary she cannot afford to keep me on. So, I am going to my sister's place in Helena."

Beyond Nettie, James could see that the last of the passengers were off the stage and going inside the station to partake of the four-bit stew and biscuits. Frank, on the other hand, was feigning a need to check the luggage boot at the rear of the coach. James could see in Nettie's eyes an attraction beyond the agreement they had for him to take her to her brother's grave. He could not deny that it was a mutual feeling, he said, "And when I am free to take you to Eloy's grave should I contact you at your sister's?"

Nettie smiled, not broadly but enough that James knew it would please her, even being wanted by the law as he was, if he were to call on her, she said, "My sister and her husband own the Parker House in Helena. That is where I will be."

A shiver pulsed through James. He was fearful that it would show through to Nettie as he said, "I will call on you as soon as my affairs here are completed."

Sensing they were alone, Nettie looked around. It was just the two of them now. The stable man had led the team off. Everybody else but Frank, who was leaning against the back of the stage, had gone inside to eat or to the privy out back. Nettie caught James' eye in a piercing way, she said, "and when do you think your business here will be concluded? In another month there will be no more boats going down river."

James sighed. His thoughts went to the Shaffer's, his Uncle Antoine and to Otto and his sweetheart that Old Bear held captive. And looming over all of this and his feelings for Nettie Bell was the possibility that he could run into Deputy Marshal Jim Hays and then none of it would matter. He said, "I hope to be free of my obligations here within the month."

Nettie flashed a purposeful look of concern for his well-being as she reached out and touched James' forearm, she whispered, "Be careful. There are wanted posters in Fort Benton."

Fear abruptly consumed James' face, he nodded, "That is good to know."

Nettie looked at him like she had more to say but instead, turned and went inside.

James watched her walk away, pouring his eyes over her shapeliness until she disappeared through the open door of the relay station. There was no doubt in his mind that he felt more for her than just an obligation to take her to her brother's grave. However, equally certain to him was the fact that his past was going to complicate his acting on these feelings.

Frank, who had stepped from behind the stage, had a smile that struggled to show itself amongst his dark whiskers, he said, "She's a fine lookin' woman."

James countered, almost as if he was diffusing any potential school yard banter of him liking a girl, "She's Eloy's sister."

Frank's smile disappeared, James added, "She wants me to take her downriver to his grave."

Frank shook his head, "I'm of the belief that would not be in your best interest, James. You've become somewhat of a notorious celebrity in Fort Benton."

James sighed as the events of that day on the Destiny played in his mind, he muttered, "Damn those people."

Frank moved on, "So, how you farin'?"

"Been workin' on a farm for some time, but I believe the law will soon be after me there."

"What are your intentions?"

James snorted and shook his head, "I don't know. Some days I think I would be better off turning myself in and hope for a fair trial."

Frank's hesitation to comment on James' proposal belied the veracity of his words, "In the end that might be best."

Anger welled up in James that his friend would agree to his impetuous idea that was fueled by his fatigue of dodging the law, he said, "I've got a favor to ask of you, Frank."

Uneasiness instantly showed in Frank's face, "What is it?"

"You recall, Otto Weiss, the man working for Charlie Reed?"

Frank nodded, "I do."

"I want you to get word to him that his sweetheart, Sarah Bellows, that was taken by the Lakota is in Canada. A chief by the name of Old Bear has claimed her as his wife. But, and I cannot guarantee this to be true, he might be willing to give her up for five hundred dollars."

Frank scoffed, "Well, if that boy finds his self a gold mine, he'll be in a position to do business with that savage but otherwise, I reckon he'll just be spittin' in the wind."

Undeterred, James double-downed with intensity. He said, looking Frank hard in the eyes, "A Metis fella by the name of Claude Charbonneau, who is likely camped across the Medicine Line to the west of Paradise, will know where Old Bear's village is located. If anybody can palaver with the Lakota, it will be him."

Frank sighed and shook his head saying, "Since that day the Sioux nearly killed us when we was woodhawkin' for old man Crawford, I've had a powerful mistrust of them. But I will pass on this information. It'll have to wait, though, until I come back from Helena."

James nodded, "I'm obliged, Frank."

Frank's words were wrapped in doubt, "Least I can do if it frees that poor girl of her misery." He paused and then went away from what his eyes said was a mission of folly, he said, "You gonna eat?"

James shook his head, "No, I need to get back soon as I can."

Frank extended his hand, "My advice to you, James, is to quit this country all together 'fore the law catches up to you."

James shook Frank's hand, "Appreciate the advice." They then went their separate ways, Frank to partake of the four-bit stew and James to unload the rest of the wagon. And too, unbeknownst to the fat man, James filled his hat with oats from the half sack in the barn and allowed the mules to share it before starting back.

Save for the fifty-cent paper bill with a picture of Abraham Lincoln on it, the money James collected for the oats rode hard in his pocket. The heavy lump of three twenty-dollar gold pieces and two silver dollars along with the constant rubbing of the reins on his blistered hands were a constant reminder of what the last 17 days had been about. A little over an hour north of the relay station an ankle-deep trickle of water crossed the road. James stopped at it so Mabel and Ted could quench their thirst and him too. He'd walked a dozen steps or so upstream from where the mules were drinking and dropped down on his belly. The water, which surfaced in a willow thicket just up the coulee a short way, was as clear as fresh air. A potpourri of colorful rocks, the equal of a rainbow, lay beneath it. James was in the process of slurping up a cold drink when he heard what sounded like a far-away gunshot. So far in fact, it caused him to look east. The dark clouds that had been recruiting help since sunup now appeared to be no false threat. James cocked his right ear towards them thinking he'd heard thunder. It was dead quiet save for a gust of wind that screamed loneliness. And then, as he was about to suck up another drink, there were more gunshots. Four, five, maybe more. Barely audible. James whispered, "Ain't no doubt that's shootin'." He got to his feet and instinctively stared off in the direction of Helena. He strained to hear. A meadow lark called, chipper and melodic. It being unfettered with the emotion of what rapid gunshots likely meant. James took a deep breath to quell his racing heart as he tried to deny the images in his mind of the Helena stage being attacked. He had visions of Nettie and Frank, and the others being killed. And then his mind's eye ratcheted up his helpless guilt with images of the Lakota capturing Nettie. In that instant, he knew Otto's anguish. It caused his thoughts to become irrational. *I could unhitch one of the mules. Be there in less than an hour.* The voice of common sense then scolded him. *You fool. You'll ride off to confront God only knows how many Lakota and get yourself killed. And in the process lose the Shaffer's mules, wagon and money. And do nothing for Nettie or Frank.* James was drowning in this frustration when thunder sounded behind him. It was sharp, rumbling away and away across the wall of near black clouds to the northeast. The wind, colder now, was suddenly noticeably steady, like it was a messenger from the storm clouds of what was coming. James looked into the wind pondering what to do. Even as he stood there, he knew it was mostly to appease his conscience so that he could tell people later, *I was sorely tempted to go to their aid.* To which they would respond, *why that would have been a damned fool thing to do.* And so, he did what he knew all along was the right thing. He climbed onto the Studebaker's seat and took up the reins. "Giddup mules." Off they went into the storm, the big wagon bouncing over rocks and in badger holes. By and by the rain began. Light at first. Then, it was like God filled his bucket and poured it out directly over James and the mules. They were drenched. The rain came down hard and cold, so cold James questioned how it hadn't been ice. Clayey mud began to form in the wagon tracks running through the sage that defined the road. It clung to the wheels of the wagon and the mules' hooves. James felt sorry for the mules as their freedom from the burden of the load of oats going was now replaced with the clay temporarily capturing their feet with every step they took. At times, the wind was so strong it brought the rain sideways. The mules squinted their eyes and leaned hard into their harnesses. The wagon tracks, any depressions, were full of water. James came close to cursing God for inflicting so much misery on him and the mules and the Shaffer's. It played over and over in his mind, *their oats in the field will be ruined. Maybe Agnes was right. No, no, the fat man would've taken his business elsewhere just for spite.* Lost on James, however, was the storm's one redeeming quality. It had sucked under, like so much rain-soaked clay, images of the Helena stage in his mind.

At last, beneath the quilt of black clouds and unrelenting rain a speck of light appeared in the distance. The mules' recognition of it caused their pace to quicken. On they went, into the near darkness with the expectation of shedding their harnesses and an oats reward.

James drove the wagon across the open space between the house and the barn splashing through puddles of water. As he came to a stop next to the barn, he looked over at the sod shanty and the white smoke coming from its stovepipe. His mind's eye spun a pleasant vision, *Agnes has likely got hot coffee and vittles on the stove.* His spirits lifted, he jumped down from the wagon and started unhitching the mules. From behind him he heard a pistol being cocked and a voice commanding, "James Coumerilh, raise your hands. You are under arrest."

Anger, contempt for what was happening to him and maybe being bone shivering cold caused James to leave his arms at his sides.

The voice came again, "Do as I say, son, or I'll be obliged to shoot you. Make no mistake, I'll not allow you to pander about here until you pull your weapon. Now, this is your last chance, raise your hands."

From the darkness behind the deputy, Simon called out, "You better do as he says, James. This one fancies his self a tough customer."

James sighed and shook his head as he slowly raised his hands. He thought to blurt out, *Marshal, I had no choice. It was kill or be killed.* But he knew this man would not have persisted this long or come this far to capture him only to be deterred with an excuse he'd likely heard many times before.

The deputy now ordered, "Turn around."

Reluctantly, James did as he was told. The deputy stood just inside the barn door out of the rain. He looked at James standing there. He was soaked. His hat had taken on so much water it had lost its shape. His appearance caused the lawman to snort a laugh. "You look like you swam up a river to get here." James said nothing but instead stared at the deputy as he laughed some more.

Simon shouted angrily, "For hell sakes, Mr. Hays, let the boy come in where it's dry."

Hays nodded towards James' pistol, "With your left hand, reach across and pull that six-shooter out with two fingers and drop it on the ground right where you're standing. Then you can come inside."

James slowly pulled the pistol from its holster with his index finger and thumb before dropping it in a puddle of water at his side. He said in a bitter tone, "Mister, these mules have had a long day. They need to be unhitched and grained."

The deputy shook his head with indifference, "Maybe so, but you ain't doing it."

Simon came around Hays and out into the rain, "They're my mules. I'll do it."

Hays motioned to James with the barrel of his pistol, "Step inside here."

James had barely cleared the barn door when Hays produced a set of manacles from his coat pocket and tossed them to him, "Put these on."

James looked down at the brass restraints, absorbing how they functioned. Straightaway, he was consumed with a feeling that was akin to claustrophobia. To lose the freedom to do with his hands as he liked was a feeling that terrified him. His hesitation caused Hays to shout, so as to be heard above the rain pelting the barn's roof, "You're trying my patience, son. Put 'em on."

James glanced over at the deputy. In that instant a tremendous crack of lightning lit up the inside of the barn. It enabled him to see clearly the ominous features of Hays' Colt .45. Most importantly, he could see that Hays' finger was curled around the trigger. Brilliant lightning flashed again, seemingly accentuating the wrongness of him having to give up his freedom. He sequestered first his left hand and then, with more difficulty, his right. Hays stepped close to him, the barrel of his Colt not six inches from James' heart. He took hold of the chain separating the manacles and raised James' hands for inspection. A smug look came to his face, he said, "I been lookin' for you for some time now."

James stared back at Hays and said, "I ain't had nuthin' to eat since breakfast."

Hays snorted, "Well, I ain't got nuthin' for you."

"I reckon Mrs. Shaffer does."

Hays nodded his head in a mocking gesture, "I'll bet she does too since her and her husband been hiding you out for who knows how long. I bet you've gotten real fond of her grub."

Seeing that Hays was toying with him, that he could care less about his hunger, James went silent. Hays noted it and motioned with his pistol towards the pile of straw next to the threshing canvas, "Go on over there and sit down. That's where you're sleeping."

James countered like he had a right to, "Got my bedroll across the way there."

Hays glanced in the direction James indicated. He shook his head, "I reckon you can have a blanket but you're sleepin' in the straw." He added, absent any wrongness in his voice, "There's a good rail above that manger that'll be handy to tie you to."

James glared at Hays, "You got me trussed up in these brass bracelets and you think you need to tie me up as well. Just how bad do you think I am?"

Hays came back, stone cold indifferent, "When it comes to avoiding the hangman even the meekest of men will do desperate, stupid things."

"Is that how you see me, already halfway up the steps to the gallows?"

"I just carry out the law."

"The law ain't always right."

Hays shook his head with the calmness that it wouldn't be him getting his neck broken, "It's been my experience that the men I arrest are most always guilty. In fact, I can't recollect any of them that wasn't."

"So, I'm as good as hanged then?"

"Ain't my call, but I wouldn't bet against it."

James went quiet owing to the sheet of fear that had just been dropped over him. It gave rise to one of those odd things in life that, out of nowhere, a thought pops into a person's mind. A thought that has little to do with the conscious world. At first James considered this to be true, but the longer he pondered this random thought the more it made sense. His regret became such that he verbalized in his mind, *hell, I should of gone back. Died in the war. Been a hero to some. Would have been a whole lot better than dying a scoundrel on the gallows.* The fear James now felt caused him to feel quivery weak. He dropped down in the pile of straw that Hays had directed him too.

Hays took up a coiled rope that was lying near the threshing canvas. James had never seen the rope before, which suggested to him that it had been Hays' plan all along to wait in the dry comfort of the barn and ambush him, so to speak. Hays finally lowered the hammer on his pistol and holstered it. He said, "Hold out your hands."

From a sitting position, James held his hands up. Hays ran the rope around the chain between the manacles and tied multiple knots before taking the tag end of the rope and throwing it over a beam above James' head. He then stood on the leading edge of the manger so he could reach the beam above and again, tied multiple knots in the rope. He left just enough slack so James could lay down. When he was done, he jumped down from the manger and looked at James, "If in the night you try to untie these knots you'll likely not succeed in doing that, but you will in pissing me off as that's what will happen if you wake me up."

James allowed a purposeful smirk to come over his face as he looked up at Hays, "Maybe you shouldn't go to sleep, that way I won't wake you."

"Your being flippant, Mr. Coumerilh, is not the way to gain favor with me."

Resigned to his fate, regardless of what he said or did, James scoffed, "You do what you're going to, Deputy, and I'll do the same."

James' words came across as cryptic, almost threatening to Hays. He came back, "Be aware, Mr. Coumerilh, I will shoot you without hesitation should you attempt to escape."

"I'm a peaceful man, Deputy, except when I'm hungry."

Hays looked down at James. His face was smug in the satisfaction that he had captured his quarry and at ease with his chances of escape or retribution. He said, "I'll ask Mr. Shaffer if his wife can fix you a plate. That way, maybe we can both sleep the night through."

James came back in a humble tone, "I'd be much obliged."

It was some time after Simon had finished tending to the mules that the rain stopped. From where he lay on the straw, James could see stars out the open barn door. Sleep would not come due to his hunger and fear. He sensed in the darkness that, across the barn floor, Hays was still awake, but he did not talk to him. He was certain that nothing good would come of it. And then he heard voices and sucking footfalls in the mud. Simon and Agnes paused in the open door to focus their eyes before coming in, Simon to Hays and Agnes to James.

James smelled the hot food and coffee even before Agnes set it down. She took silverware, a fork and steak knife from the pocket of her apron. She'd no sooner handed them to James when Hays was standing over her. He snarled, "Give me the knife, Ma'am."

Agnes took the knife back from James and handed it up to Hays. "I wasn't thinking, I guess."

Hays came back, curt in his tone, "Go back to your house."

James called out, "Much obliged, Agnes."

Agnes said over her shoulder, in spite of Hays and how it looked for her and Simon, "You're most welcome James."

CHAPTER THIRTY-EIGHT

For some time, James had watched it get light outside. Birds had begun to sing into the rain cleansed air. Agnes' rooster, named Wilbur, was crowing his approval of the orange glow on the horizon. It would have been soothing to James had it not been for what lay ahead of him. That Deputy Marshal Jim Hays was now the keeper of his fate and there wasn't a thing he could do about it. He had turned the hourglass of James' life upside down and the sands were running out way too fast. And, unlike most people who knew death was inevitable but so far into the future they could savor this morning, James could not. For James, it was a tease of what he would be missing once Hays got him to the gallows.

The mumbled cursing and splashing steps from the direction of the privy grew louder until they materialized in the form of Hays coming through the barn door. He headed straight for James saying, "Get up, Coumerilh, if you want breakfast."

James pulled himself up by the rope attached to his manacles and waited for Hays to untie the knots.

Hays looked James in the eyes like he wasn't certain of what he was about to do. It was obvious that he was conflicted hence his words that followed, "I'm gonna allow you to go in the house and eat breakfast. Betray my good will and I'll kill you on the spot, savvy?"

James held up his hands, "Can you take these off? I need to visit the privy."

Hays frowned and shook his head as he reached for the key to unlock the manacles. He said, holding the manacles by the chain that coupled them in his left hand and his pistol in his right, "Let's go."

James walked ahead of Hays, meandering this way and that to avoid the numerous puddles of water. As they neared an obvious juncture to the privy he called out, "I'll make for the outhouse now."

Hays came back, "I'll be waiting right here, so be quick about it."

In that moment, James could see Mrs. Peterson, his grade school teacher, responding to his request to visit the privy, *yes, James, you may go but do not tarry. You don't want to miss out on today's lesson.* She had been hardnosed about enforcing her belief in promptness to the point of knocking on the privy door. James recalled when she had knocked on his door. She shrieked, *James Coumerilh finish your business right now.* The thought of it brought a smile to James' face. The kids lived in fear of Mrs. Peterson rousting them out of the privy and she didn't even have a .45 Caliber Colt.

James did not tarry, lest he incur the wrath of Jim Hays. As he stepped inside the Shaffer's sod house, he could see right off that Agnes had gone all out, like it was a condemned man's last meal. There was bacon, which he knew they had little of, and fried eggs from their few chickens that vermin had not gotten, sourdough hotcakes with chokecherry syrup, and coffee. Agnes looked at the pistol in Hays' hand and gave him a dirty look. She said, "I believe you can put that away, Marshal. James is an honorable man."

Although it had been on his mind throughout the night, James seized this moment to give Simon the money he had collected for the oats, and more. He dug into both of his pants' pockets and laid the money on the table next to a plate of hotcakes. He said, "Here's your money from the stage company."

Simon could see there was more than $62.50. He said, "There is way too much here, James."

James mustered a wry smile, "I ain't gonna need my money where I'm going."

Tears came to Agnes' eyes. In 17 days, James had become like a son to her. He had taken the place of her own boys who had died because it was expected of them. She said, "When you come home, it will be here waiting for you."

James caught the look in Hays' eyes. It suggested he had just confirmed how much, *aiding and abetting a fugitive from the law*, the Shaffer's were guilty of. James' inner voice called out, *I hope this fool has got better sense than to arrest these folks for helping me.*

Simon said simply, "Thank you, James. You've been a blessing to us." He then picked up the money and put it in a mason jar that he took down from a cupboard behind him. He set the jar on the table and said, looking at Hays, "I reckon we better eat so the marshal can be on his way."

It was not necessarily a concerted effort to shame Jim Hays, it just turned out that way. Him sitting next to the Mason jar full of the money James could have run off with if he was truly some kind of immoral reprobate as the marshal believed. Not even asking for God's intervention during the saying of grace to save the life of an innocent man swayed Hays to leave the manacles off for the ride to Fort Benton.

CHAPTER THIRTY-NINE

James was certain of it, that Buck sensed the pall of doom hanging over them. That things would be different for him once they reached Fort Benton. It all depended upon Hays keeping his word to stop at Charlie Reed's place so James could ask Charlie if he would come to town and fetch Buck. *Git him back to Bill Monk up on the Teton River.* But it was still three days ride to Charlie's.

Not quite an hour ago they had passed by Bill Monk's ranch. As luck would have it, they encountered Teddy Monk on the road. He was the meaner of the Monk boys. The one who didn't like James on account of him consorting with horse thieves and being a wanted killer. He had stopped his horse on the side of the road like he intended to watch a parade coming his way. He sneered at James, *Well, looky here. Bout time you got your comeuppance.* He paused to laugh while looking James in the eyes and then added, *Won't be long now an' they'll have you doing a jig at the end of a rope.* James made no reply, mostly out of respect for the fact Bill Monk had allowed him to keep Buck. To his credit, or maybe not, Hays had said, *now Teddy, don't be badgering my prisoner. It's a long way to Fort Benton.*

So, here they were now riding along in the bright sunshine that was having little effect on the mud. It clung to their horses' hooves. From time to time, a chunk of it would flip up to where it was visible by the riders who had not spoken a word since their encounter with Teddy Monk. It was peculiar, therefore, when Hays launched a prodigious stream of tobacco juice off the right side of his horse and said, "Has the cat got your tongue?"

A rush of emotions flooded James' mind. Foremost in them was how could Hays, the man taking him to the gallows, want to engage in friendly banter? He came back, "Is it boredom or curiosity as to what a condemned man has to say that motivates you to engage me in conversation?"

"Hell, son, you ain't been condemned till a judge says it."

James scoffed, "You yourself said you wouldn't bet against me not getting hung."

Hays paused to spit again before saying in a carefree tone, "Well, I reckon you got a point there."

James came back, his tone angry, "Time, words, it don't mean a thing to you cause far as you know you got lots of both ahead of you. Me, on the other hand, I've not got a lot of either to spare."

Hays looked right at James, "So, pretty much you don't want to waste your time or words on me."

"What would we talk about? Striking it rich in the gold fields. Getting married and having kids. Carving a ranch out of this country. Dreams. The future?" James paused and snorted while staring hard at Hays. "It don't bother you that I'm a walking dead man, but because you're bored you expect me to shoot the shit with you like there is no difference between us." James then held up his hands and said hatefully, "You take these manacles off, Mr. Hays, and I'll talk to you. Otherwise, I reckon you'll just have to be bored until we get to Fort Benton."

Hays was about to reply when his eyes suddenly grew big with fear. Instinct had his right hand sweeping back his light coat to reach for his Colt when the masked man standing in the road shouted, "Don't do it or you'll die."

Hays' gun hand froze as he studied the dark eyes showing in the holes of the flour sack that hooded the road agent's head. Within a few seconds he decided the man's moxie was genuine and brought his gun hand to rest on his saddle horn. He called out in a voice that was struggling to be respectful of the Spencer repeater aimed at his chest, "Alright, Mister, I'll do as you say, but you should know, I'm a Deputy United States Marshal. Persisting in what you're doing here will bring a whole peck a trouble on yourself."

The gunman was unphased by Hays' warning, he ordered, "Get down, both of you."

Hays shook his head and scowled in James' direction, "I reckon you better do like he says."

It gave James some satisfaction to see that there was a mix of fear and anger in Hays' face. His inner voice was already spinning a plea for the bandit to set him free and not Hays as he got down from Buck. But it was unnecessary. The bandit gestured to Hays with the barrel of the Spencer, "Take those things off him."

Hays came back, quick, "This man's a killer."

The bandit immediately parried, "In these times lots of men are killers. I'm of the belief it'll be up to God to decide who needs punishing. Now, free his hands."

James held out his hands as Hays fished the key from his vest pocket and unlocked the right and then the left manacle. Unencumbered by the restraints, he flexed his fingers and gently rubbed the red and raw abrasions on his wrists. He said to the bandit, "I'm much obliged, Sir."

The bandit said, "Take his gun."

James pulled the deputy's pistol from its holster and stepped back.

The hooded man pointed with the Spencer, "Let's take a walk back into the trees."

Hays' face was instantly contorted by fear and then anger. He lashed out, "You sonovabitch, if you want to kill me, you'll do it right here and not where it accommodates hiding your cowardly deed."

"No Deputy, one peck of trouble will be enough. But, if I have to tell you again to go into the trees, I'll have no choice but to take on a second peck."

Behind Hays, James said, his tone mocking, "You can do this, Marshal. It ain't like there is a gallows at the end of it."

Before Hays could respond to James, the voice inside the flour sack growled, "Move, now."

Reluctantly, Hays began walking into a stand of box-elder trees. James, still in possession of the deputy's pistol, followed close behind with the bandit leading Hays' horse next. When they had gone far enough that the road was not visible, the bandit called a halt. He looked around for a moment like he was searching for a place to spread his bedroll before he finally pointed, with the barrel of the Spencer again, at a young boxelder tree. He said to Hays who had followed his actions like he was a schoolmarm or something, "Go sit down facing that tree and hug it."

It was clear to Hays what was about to happen, he whimpered, "No, no, you don't need to do this."

The bandit came back, "Well, are you willing to swear on the good book that if you're not cuffed to that tree, you won't come after us?"

Hays stood silent as two ravens spying the movement in the trees began to circle overhead and cackle. They were on their third orbit when Hays sighed deeply, shook his head and went to the tree without speaking.

The bandit said to James, "put the manacles on him". James knelt at the tree, which was about a foot in diameter, and locked the cuffs onto Hays wrists. It was impossible to not feel the anger coming from Hays' eyes. He whispered, "There'll come a day when justice will be served."

James did not respond to Hays' threat. Instead, he stood and held out the manacles' key to which the bandit responded, "Put it in his vest pocket."

Although James' curiosity was piqued in no small way as to who was saving him from the gallows, he sensed that he should remain silent until they were well away from Hays. He did as the bandit asked and tucked the key in the deputy's vest pocket. As he did, he could smell the chewing tobacco on his breath and feel his heart hammering like a woodpecker.

It was not until they had picketed Hays' horse near where he was cuffed to the tree and walked down the road to where the bandit had left his horse, that he removed the flour sack. James looked at the man. He'd never met his Uncle Antoine, but he had seen old family pictures. Antoine and his father looked a lot alike. And so did this man. Before he could ask, the bandit held out his hand, "I'm your Uncle Antoine, son."

James took his uncle's hand briefly before they hugged one another saying, "I been looking for you in between running from the law."

Antoine laughed, "And none too late, I reckon."

"No indeed, you've saved my life. But how is it you found me?"

Antoine tossed the flour sack on the ground and kicked leaves and dirt over it before looking back at James, "Your Aunt Angelique was thrown from a horse and broke her arm. I took her to the doctor in Fort Benton. Between him and what soldier talk I overheard in town I headed this way." He paused and nodded to the bluffs above the river, "I had my spy glass on you and the marshal for some time before I concluded it was you he had in custody."

James uttered a weak laugh, "I guess my prayers were answered." Foremost in his mind, though, was why God hadn't answered his prayers yesterday to stop the rain and wind to save the Shaffer's crop. God perplexed him more times than not. And then, seeing Antoine gather the reins of his big gray horse and step up into the saddle, he left his frustration with the God of yesterday to savor the present, he said, "How long you reckon 'fore that deputy gets free?"

Antoine looked in the direction of where they'd left Hays. His dark whiskers hid his emotions, but his voice was as calm as still water, "Might be an hour from now or, it might be sunset. This road gets traveled so we need to get shed of it." He touched his heels to the sides of the gray and started through the trees.

James got on Buck and fell in behind his uncle. Momentarily, they came to the road and crossed it in the direction of the Teton River. They had gone only a short way when they could hear, but not see, the river on account of the trees. James' aversion to water, or maybe his common sense warning him about crossing rain swollen rivers, caused his heart to kick up. He had crossed the Teton several weeks ago when it had been tame, barely reaching Buck's belly. But now, he could not see it yet and it scared him. He sensed that Buck was scared too. And then Antoine and the big gray veered to the left of a willow thicket and there it was. Muddy, roily, running fast. Foamy dirty curls showed here and there where a big rock or a log lay hidden beneath the surface. Antoine shouted, "Is your horse a swimmer?"

James' heart had climbed up into his throat such that it was difficult for him to keep the fear from his voice, he said, "I don't know. Ain't had him but a few weeks."

Antoine frowned slightly as he studied Buck's features and then the raging river.

James interrupted his uncle's evaluation of he and Buck's chances of surviving the river with the improbable, "There ain't no bridges hereabouts?"

Antoine looked at his nephew and laughed, "We got no choice, James."

James nodded, "I reckon not."

Antoine reined the gray around, "This ain't a good spot. We'll go downstream till we find a place where buffalo have come to water. Those are always good fords for our carts."

James felt some relief. Like he had just avoided certain death. Off they went, working their way through the box-elder trees and willows but staying next to the river. They'd gone about a half mile when over on the road they heard the snicker of a horse. It caused Antoine and James to stop and listen. By and by they heard men's voices. Casual banter. Straining to hear, Antoine suddenly held up his hand and whispered, "Did you catch that? He called him sergeant. Gotta be an army patrol."

James said what they both instantly feared, "They'll come to the deputy in no time. He'll surely be able to alert them. They will be on us before we can get across the river."

Antoine, again, held his hand up for James to be quiet as the patrol was still filing by. They could hear the soldiers when he looked at James and then the river and then back to James, he said, "Jump your horse in. Once he's swimming, slide off his back. Lighten his load. You hang onto the saddle horn and paddle with one arm as best you can. Alright?"

James nodded even though as he did an entire tree came bobbing down the river.

Antoine came back, "I'll go first so do as I do." And with that Antoine turned the gray to the river and kicked its sides giving it no choice but to plunge into the raging muddy water. The whites of the horse's eyes showed, and its nostrils flared in response to the fear of drowning. At first the current caught it and Antoine, taking them more downstream than across. James was certain that they would be unable to get past the center of the river where the current was strongest but finally the gray, a strong swimmer, pulled out of it with Antoine hanging at his side. God, or maybe random luck, presented a stretch of riverbank that was not vertical like so much of it was. The big gray lunged up out of the water with

Antoine falling on the bank. The gray continued into the trees away from the terror of the water. Somewhat stunned by the hard fall from his horse, Antoine lay on the riverbank for a moment before getting to his feet and looking for James, expecting him to be swimming Buck across. When he saw that they were still standing on the other side of the river he silently stabbed at the rushing water and angrily motioned for James to cross.

James could feel Buck's fear of the water. It was no less than his own that was manifesting itself in his trembling hands. His inner voice shouted, *just do it.* But at the same time, he saw he and Buck being swept away by the current and then going under and taking in more and more water. He could feel the pain in his lungs. The absolute helplessness to escape it until he had to take a deep breath and look away from the river. When he came back to it, Antoine made eye contact before jabbing his index finger at him and then dragging it back across the river. The anger in his body language was not lost on James. Maybe it was shame, or simply the fact his uncle was risking a lot to help him, that he abruptly dug his heels into Buck's sides causing him to leap into the river. James could feel the power of the water and Buck, struggling to keep his head above it. It was just a glimpse, Antoine frantically gesturing for him to slide off Buck's back and hang onto the saddle horn. He reacted to it as if it was a guarantee to him surviving the power of the river. But he no sooner left the relative security of Buck when he was struck with the coldness of the water. At the same time, however, Buck seemed to be now holding his own against the current. It came to James, floating to the side of Buck, *we're gonna make it,* and then a piece of a boxelder, about the size they had cuffed Hays to, struck the saddle horn. His fingers recoiled to the collision and in an instant, his optimism turned to abject fear of dying as he was swept away from Buck. He began windmilling his arms in a desperate effort to stay afloat and make it to the far shore. His boots, being full of water, made it impossible to kick his legs in sync with his arms. The current took him into a boiling cauldron of white frothy water. He felt himself being tossed into its center and sucked under. In a heartbeat, he went from being able to hear the roar of the river and seeing the sky to a world of darkness and a gurgling, dull noise within his head. Frantically, he pawed and kicked at the water unable to reach the surface. His inner voice screamed, *God please help me. I don't want to die.* His lungs were on fire, begging for air. But the God of yesterday had seemingly returned. On impulse, he lay over on his side and began pulling his arms through the water. He started to move downstream. The darkness was giving way to light. A hint of jubilation flashed in the chaos of his mind. He was going to live. And then, when he was nearly free of it, his lungs betrayed him to the river. Pandemonium erupted in his psyche. *This is what it's like to die.* For a few seconds it was a certainty that he would cross over. That he would meet this fickle entity that was one day his protector and the next, not. But just like that, God gave him a reprieve. It seemed he had no part in coming to the surface. He drew in huge gulps of air in deference to the muddy water he'd been forced to swallow. Straight away he began coughing and wheezing while flailing the water with his arms. He was beyond panic, but somehow his inner voice got through to him, *don't cry out. The soldiers will surely hear you.* He could see his uncle wading out to help him. He was chest deep before he was able to grab James' hand and tow him back to shore. James fell to his knees in the mud and threw up river water and all of Agnes' breakfast. His relief was short lived as Antoine took hold of his right arm and pulled him to his feet, "Come on, son, we've got to get under cover."

James said, still breathing heavy like he was fearful of losing access to air again, "Buck, where's Buck?"

"He's alright. He's with my horse."

They went inside the tree line and worked their way back upriver to where the horses were tied. Both them and their horses were completely soaked. The early morning September sun was doing little to warm their thoroughly chilled bodies. Nonetheless, Antoine whispered, "Are you good to ride?"

James knew that he had no choice. He nodded and mouthed, "Yeah."

CHAPTER FORTY

For a good way, on either side of Goose Creek, the Lakota horses had eaten the grass down to ground level. From afar, it looked like someone had laid a yellow rug beneath the specks of gray sagebrush. The choke cherries and currents within reasonable walking distance had all been picked. And the firewood and buffalo chips had been gleaned from the land. Even the fish in the creek near camp were now scarce. Goose Creek had been good to Old Bear and his people, but it was time to move. Before Louis Coumerilh, who had been given the honor of leading a raiding party south of the Medicine line had left, it was agreed that the camp would be moved to Buffalo Jump Creek. It would take most of the day to get there towing travois with all their belongings as they were.

A big bay horse with a US brand on its right flank had been selected by Shield Woman, who was one of Old Bear's two Lakota wives, to pull the travois loaded with the poles from his lodge. Although she could have ridden the bay, Shield Woman would not allow Sarah Bellows to do so. She insisted that she walk and lead the horse. Even though most nights Sarah was Old Bear's pick to share his blanket, he would not stand up for her. It would have been the prudent thing to do if he wanted to keep any semblance of peace in his lodge.

There were very few people in Old Bear's band who understood English. Doe Eyes, who was Louis Coumerilh's wife, was among them. But her hatred of white people caused her to have little to do with Sarah. As a consequence, Sarah had almost no opportunity to talk to anyone in her tongue. Old Bear knew some English and French, but his conversations with her were mostly about getting her to accept this new life. And at night, under his blanket, there was little talk. He smelled of sweat and smoke. His hands were rough and calloused as was his physical exploitation of her. It was going on three months now. Sarah had concluded that no one was coming for her.

From where the sun was in the sky, Sarah judged it to be about noon. She had thrown up that morning before they left and now, she was feeling the urge again. There was no place to hide her shame. They were in knee high sagebrush. She stopped and bent over, still clutching the reins of the bay horse. She began to vomit, bile mostly. But it was enough to attract Shield Woman who rode up alongside her and struck her across the back with a leather quirt. Sarah's involuntary shriek in response to the pain while spewing her stomach contents, made her choke. Shield Woman laughed. She knew all too well why Sarah was throwing up. She seethed one of the few English words she knew, "Whore," and then she hit Sarah again. The blow knocked Sarah to her knees. Shield Woman glared at her and said in Lakota, "One day I will kill you." She then rode on.

Still on her knees, Sarah began to quietly cry. Others rode by her. Some pulling travois, some not. Most, disgusted with her weakness, said nothing. Some young men, knowing that Old Bear was at the head of the column, laughed and made crude gestures as to Sarah's condition.

A horse paused near Sarah. In broken English, she heard, "Get up. You bring shame to yourself and Old Bear."

Sarah looked up. Doe Eyes was staring down at her. She was indifferent to Sarah's misery. Sarah did as she was told lest she get hit again. But then she said defiantly, "Maybe it is Old Bear who should be ashamed. He kills my family and brings me here against my will into his lodge when he already has two wives. It's not right."

Some years ago, Doe Eyes had been an attractive woman. Not beautiful, but worth five good horses and a Sharps rifle. Then she bore Louis Coumerilh's daughter and worked daylight to dark taking care of her and Louis, picking berries for making pemican, skinning buffalo and working hides. And that had been when they had been part of Antoine Coumerilh's band of Metis. Since coming to live with her people, her life had gotten harder. It was no wonder that she had crow's feet at the corners of her eyes. Her skin appeared leathery. Her hands had open sores from being nicked with a skinning knife. And she had gotten fat, something that Louis did not let her forget. So, it was natural for her to say, "Maybe it is not right for Old Bear to have another wife, but it is our custom. He must kill enough game to feed all of you. Has he not done this?"

Sarah looked at Doe Eyes and shook her head. "This isn't about food. I don't want to be here. I don't want to have Old Bear's baby."

A glimmer of compassion showed in Doe Eyes' expression, but she said, almost with resignation, "You are no longer in the white man's world. You belong to Old Bear now. He will never give you up."

Sarah's eyes begged for understanding, for Doe Eyes of all people to help her, but she looked away and nudged the sides of her pinto horse. The poles of her travois scratched two lines in the dirt as she rode away.

Sarah looked around her. She was at the tail end of the procession now. She picked up the reins of her horse and began walking. She could not help crying. Her vision was blurry from the tears that pooled before spilling down her cheeks. Some joined at the corners of her mouth with the snot that ran from her nose and over her lips. At one point her pace had become so slow, perhaps troublesome, to the horse she was leading that he nudged her in the back. It occurred to her that she had no more freedom than he did. She knew when they got to where they were going, pregnant or not, she would be working until dark or later setting up camp. And come tonight when all the work was done and Old Bear and the other men were finished smoking their pipes and recounting their deeds in battle, he would come to his lodge and crawl under the blanket with her and she would be expected to give of herself.

On they went hour after hour, the travois poles grating over the ground uprooting small wildflowers and grasses and breaking down sagebrush. The September sun was just touching the western horizon when in the distance Sarah could see the buffalo jump. It comprised most of the north end of a small mesa that was located east of the creek where the new camp was going to be. Way in the distance, at the head of the column, Sarah could see Old Bear's sorrel horse starting up the east side of the mesa. It was a relatively gentle climb that was conducive to buffalo walking up it to get the good grass on top. The mesa, and the creek on the other side of it, owed their name to the fact Indians chased buffalo off the north end of the mesa. Buffalo, in their blind, fear-induced rush to escape, jumped off the cliffs about two hundred feet high to their deaths. But that had been back when there were lots of buffalo. Today, there was just good yellow grass on the mesa for the Lakota horses.

The route that Old Bear had taken going up the side of the mesa and across its top followed what others had done in the past. It paralleled the cliffs, keeping about a hundred yards away from them. Sarah and the big bay horse were now straight out from the highest part. She had been thinking

about it, seriously thinking about it from the time she realized she was pregnant a few weeks ago. At about this time
too, she had concluded, *Otto won't want me now anyway.*
She had stopped her crying over an hour ago. Her mind was
clear. She dropped the reins of her horse and began walking
towards the cliffs. She was a little more than halfway there
when she heard her name called. "Sarah." She turned around.
A pulse of feel-good, like someone cared, went through her.

Doe Eyes was off her horse, standing in the sagebrush
next to it and the travois it pulled. She said, "Where are you
going?"

Sarah said, her voice calm and confident, "I'm going
home."

Doe Eyes stood quiet, spinning the meaning of Sarah's
words before finally nodding, "Maybe it is for the best."

Sarah came back, "I think so." And then she started to
walk off but stopped and said, like it had been the first kind-
ness shown her in a long time, "Thank you for talking to me."

Doe Eyes raised her right hand to wave, but Sarah did
not see it. She had now begun to run toward the cliffs and
her freedom. Her buckskin dress raked against the sage as
she tried little to avoid the brush. She was intent on gaining
her freedom. At last, she reached the flat granite rock. One
step, two steps, three steps, and then she was gone, without
a sound.

CHAPTER FORTY-ONE

To his credit, Old Bear prepared a burial platform for Sarah on a rise near Buffalo Jump Creek. Shield Woman had insisted that he take Sarah far up the creek where she would be less likely to see her. And there were those too that said she wasn't deserving of such a burial. That maybe some rocks piled on her was enough. The controversy had generated lively talk and disharmony in the camp. It had been three sleeps and the rancor from it had not yet died away.

The wind was not strong but enough to cause a shower of yellow leaves from the cottonwood trees along the creek to flutter down to the ground. Doe Eyes, who had a small reed basket nearly full of choke cherries, took note of the falling leaves. She said to her twelve year old daughter, Arielle, who was pulling cherries from the same tree as her, "Winter will soon be upon us."

Arielle came back, like there was a logical nexus for her saying, "I miss Uncle Antoine."

Doe Eyes frowned and looked at her daughter, "We are with my people now. Your people, your grandparents."

"It is because of Papa, isn't it?"

Does Eyes shook her head, "It is what we both want. Your Uncle Antoine has taken on too many of the white man ways. Here is who you are."

"But, Mama, I am part white."

Doe Eyes became more stern, "The white man is destroying my people, our people's way of life."

"But Mama, I don't like it here. It will snow soon. When it does, I'd rather be with Uncle Antoine and the Metis in their winter cabins."

Doe Eyes snapped, "We can't go back there."

"It's because Papa disobeyed Uncle Antoine, isn't it?"

Before Doe Eyes could respond to her daughter, a commotion erupted in camp. She knew right away what it was likely about, "Come, Arielle, your father is back."

Arielle said nothing, but purposely left her face a blank slate as she fell in beside her mother on the way to camp.

They drove before them stolen horses. Some of them clearly displayed the brand of the stage line company. There were random war cries and shouts to individuals as they paraded into the camp. Many of the people, however, had gathered around Louis' horse and the horse he was leading with a pretty black woman on it. A bloody dark-haired scalp hung from his waist. He had proven himself worthy of being appointed leader of this raiding party.

Arielle, standing beside her mother looked on. She was not particularly impressed. She knew well Sarah's plight and how it ended, she said to her mother, "Is Papa taking another wife?"

Doe Eyes looked at the black woman. In that moment her mind's eye took hold, commanded her almost to watch again Sarah taking those final steps at the buffalo jump. She then looked at Louis, basking in the attention. Finally, she replied to her daughter, "I don't know."

Louis saw his wife and daughter. His look was uneasy, peculiar even. He raised his hand in greeting before sliding off the side of his horse and pulling the black woman, whose hands were tied, from her horse. He was leading his captive through the crowd when Doe Eyes blocked his path, she said, "Are you taking up the ways of Old Bear now?"

Louis frowned, "She is mine. I am allowed to do with her as I like."

Before Doe Eyes could respond, loud screams broke out when the two riderless horses of those braves killed in the stagecoach attack came into view. Louis looked at the dead braves horses and then back at his wife and daughter. He grasped the scalp hanging from his belt and held it out, he said in a haughty tone, "I have avenged their deaths. The stagecoach guard was a good shot. He almost killed me before I did him."

Doe Eyes acted indifferent to Louis' deed. Her anger at seeing the black woman and the threat she posed to what happiness she had in life overrode all else. Doe Eyes glared at him, she said, "We will talk later." She then walked away. Arielle, who had listened to what her parents had said, flashed a look of disappointment at her father before following after her mother.

CHAPTER FORTY-TWO

On the third day after they had crossed the Teton River, Antoine and James came to the Medicine Line. It was invisible. Just more yellow grass prairie except to those whose life depended on knowing where the American Army or law had to stop. Antoine broke the silence that had existed between them for the last half hour or so, "Well, we are safe now."

James came back, "We're in Canada?"

Antoine nodded, "You're still set on palavering with Old Bear for that Bellows girl, broke as you are?"

"It's the least I can do for Otto. He could have turned me into the law in Fort Benton."

"And if Charbonneau won't break the ice for you?"

James was slow to surface what he and his uncle had wrestled over to no good conclusion on the ride up here, he said as if the words caused him pain, "I reckon I'll need to impose on your good will or go it alone."

Antoine snorted before launching a dark mass of tobacco juice off the far side of the big gray. He turned back to James dabbing his fingers at the juice his moustache had intercepted and said, "Like we talked, son, they'll likely kill you if you go out there by yourself. And me, I chased off my nephew, so I suspect he's soured Old Bear on me."

"So, what do you propose?"

"Let it be. They ain't gonna give that girl back."

James sighed, "I've tried to convince myself of that more times than you got whiskers, but so far I'm not having any luck."

Antoine spit again and shook his head, "Well, I wrote your pa a long time back that I'd look out for you, so I guess this is living up to that."

James grinned, "I reckon he'd make an allowance for dumb things."

Antoine shook his head again, "No, this speaks well of you, son. It's the right thing to do."

CHAPTER FORTY-THREE

When she thought about it, Doe Eyes did not hate Nettie Bell even though the very sight of the woman made her mad. Louis, on the other hand, she was learning to hate. Her anger was such that, so far, he had not taken Nettie Bell under his blanket despite the fact she slept in their lodge. It was after their morning meal that Doe Eyes and Arielle had prepared, without any help from Nettie, that Louis ordered, "I want you to take Nettie and gather firewood."

Doe Eyes response was immediate and defiant, "No, you take her. Gather your own wood or do with her what you want out of my sight."

The back of his hand came so quick she could not defend herself. The shock of it hurt more than the blow. In all their years together, he had never hit her. She refused to cry. Instead, she glared at him and pursed her lips to spit in his face when he raised a closed fist and shook his head. He said, "Take her and gather the wood."

Doe Eyes looked around. To either side of their cooking fire and lodge, people were standing and watching. The sharpness of their words had carried through the cool morning air. Their venomous tone soiled the tranquility of the gurgling little creek bottom. She felt shame as she abruptly turned away from Louis and said curtly, without looking Nettie in the eyes, "Come." And then she began walking, not along the gauntlet of probing, judging eyes in the front of their teepees but rather she went behind and away from where they were aligned. Nettie, knowing there was no option to refuse, or escape, followed after her.

It wasn't until they were well into the trees that Nettie sensed Doe Eyes was quietly crying. She vacillated for a few more steps but finally said to her back, "I'm sorry."

Sarah's words, *thank you for talking to me*, echoed in Doe Eyes' mind. Their pitiful desperation had haunted her ever since she had heard them. She stopped and spun around, "You should hate me."

"I'm not prone to hating people."

"Not even my husband?"

Nettie hesitated, being the Christian that she was, before saying, "Hopefully, God will forgive me, but yes, I hate your husband."

Doe Eyes could see in Nettie's face that she had just answered the question that gripped her mind. Nonetheless, she had to know for sure. She looked Nettie in the eyes like she might lie to her and said, "Did my husband rape you?"

Tears now came to Nettie's eyes as she nodded her head before looking down at the carpet of yellow and brown leaves covering the ground.

Doe Eyes stood still for a moment and then she stepped next to Nettie and put her arms around her. While embracing her she whispered, "I promise you, as long as you are in this village and I am alive, he will not do that to you again."

CHAPTER FORTY-FOUR

It was Running Elk's job to alert the village to any danger from the east. Around mid-afternoon of the day that Doe Eyes had made her promise to Nettie, he saw them coming. He was sitting with his back against a big rock not far from where Sarah had gained her freedom. Three men on horseback, one of whom was leading a saddled horse with no rider. They appeared to be in a hurry with the intention of coming up the mesa where he was. His common sense told him that the men were either unaware of the village on the other side of the mesa or it was their destination. Regardless, at fourteen years of age, he had no desire to challenge them as to their intentions. He knew full well what he was going to do, but for a moment he lingered, fantasizing how he would kill the men. He aimed the Spencer repeater that his brother had taken from a soldier he had killed, at the lead rider. The man was way beyond the rifle's capability but, for a few seconds, pretending to pull its trigger and watching him tumble from his horse made Running Elk feel good. Reality then came back, and he crawled a short way before coming to a low crouch and running toward the bluff above the village. He weaved in and out of the sagebrush and past the horse herd guarded by two boys about his age until he finally came to the danger rock above their camp. The cream-colored rock was about a foot high, irregularly shaped and just big enough for one person to stand on. Running Elk stepped up on the rock and with his right hand, pumped his rifle three times above his head. It was the sign for friendly visitors coming.

And so it was, it didn't come as a total surprise to anyone in the village except Louis and his wife and daughter, when Antoine, James and Claude Charbonneau came riding down the ridge. Even from a distance, Louis recognized Antoine and Claude but not the third man. It struck him as no co-incidence that they would be visiting so soon after the stage attack. Especially Antoine and the stranger. Sensing something was amiss, he turned to Doe Eyes and Nettie, "Go to the lodge. Stay there until I come for you."

Doe Eyes glared at her husband. It was an emotion that had become increasingly easier to muster. She said, "But it is Antoine."

He said angrily pointing to their lodge, "Go now."

It was at this point that Nettie recognized the last rider and cried out, "James, James."

At first, James did not see her in the crowd that had gathered but then Nettie waved in desperation. Surprise, if not relief, registered on his face to see that she had survived the gunshots he had heard that day but was helpless to respond to. Now, however, he waved back.

Louis saw the communication between them and instantly stepped in front of Nettie to block her view of James, whereupon he then slapped her across the face. The blow was such that Nettie's head twisted to the side, but she stood where she was.

James seethed the words, "Why that sonovabitch."

Antoine quickly whispered, "Mind your manners, son. The odds are not in our favor."

Enraged, Louis' breathing became slightly exaggerated to accommodate his anger, he said, "If you ever show another man attention like that again, I will kill you. Now, the both of you go to my teepee."

She was about to refuse when Doe Eyes touched her shoulder and said, "We should go."

For a moment Nettie stood still, staring up into Louis' black eyes searching for compassion that wasn't there. Beyond him and the crowd, she could see to his left the procession of riders. First came Claude Charbonneau, then Antoine and finally James, who was looking her way. It caused her to entertain the idea of bolting around Louis and running to James.

But then Louis said, his words floating down to her on his foul breath, "I'm not going to tell you again."

Reluctantly, Nettie turned away from James' gaze. She and Doe Eyes then walked side by side to Louis' lodge and went inside. Doe Eyes said, "How well do you know this man you call James?"

Nettie scoffed slightly and shook her head, "Hardly at all, but I would trust him with my life."

Doe Eyes said, "The man riding the gray horse is Louis' uncle. Maybe he can talk Louis into letting you go."

Nettie shook her head, "He has told me that he will never give me up. So, what does it matter?"

Doe Eyes said, exasperated with how her life had been turned upside down, "I don't know this man I'm married to anymore. But he is not going to do as he has to you or me ever again."

It was the usual pandemonium with dogs barking and people hurrying toward the visitors to see who it was, especially since they were Metis. Louis looked hatefully at his uncle, who acted as if he hadn't seen him. James noted the exchange and whispered to Antoine, "I do not like that man."

Antoine replied, "He is your cousin."

James was taken aback such that he had no response.

Antoine shook his head slightly as if what he was about to say was justification for why Louis was so hateful, "He changed two winters ago when his parents died of the pox.

Lots of Lakota died then too. Your Uncle Paul was married to a Lakota woman. Louis blames the pox on white settlers bringing it here."

James came back, "That's no excuse to take a black woman against her will and treat her like I just saw."

Antoine replied, "There's lots a things in life that ain't right."

Old Bear, who was flanked by young men on either side, called out to Claude as if all that had occurred over the stolen branded horses had been forgotten, "Monsieur, Charbonneau, mon amie. It is good you have come."

Claude had come not because he believed in their mission, but rather it was the assurance from Antoine that he would help him get established south of the Medicine Line. That together they would break out ground in the Judith Basin, but only if he would do this for Antoine's nephew, the good one. Claude continued the façade, "It is good to see you as well. I have brought my friend gifts."

Claude got down from his horse and went to the horse he had been leading and removed two crocks of whiskey that had been tied to the saddle. He handed them to one of the young braves that Old Bear had directed to receive the gifts. He then opened the whiskey horse's saddlebag and took out two boxes of cartridges for the Winchester yellow boys that he had traded to the Lakota. He handed the ammunition, which he knew Old Bear would value the most, directly to him, saying, "May you have good hunting."

James' mind's eye instantly went back to that day when Old Bear and his raiding party had come to Claude's camp with their stolen horses and fresh scalps. The Naysayer did not spare his sarcasm, *more likely shooting down near helpless pilgrims.*

Old Bear took the cartridges with a stern look in his eyes that went beyond Claude to Antoine and then James, as he knew this was no social call. Nonetheless, he motioned for them to follow him and said, "Come, we will smoke the pipe of friendship."

James fell in beside Antoine and Claude in following the chief to his lodge. As he walked by the cooking fires, teepees and hides stretched and being scraped of any bits of fat and meat it gave him pause to think that he was Metis. A lifestyle not much different than what he was seeing now, but very different from how he had grown up on a southern farm.

Old Bear loaded the long pipe with tobacco, a precious commodity, and with a burning twig that he took from the fire in the center of the lodge brought the pipe to life. He took several puffs, expelled the sweet smoke into the room and passed the pipe to Claude who did the same. Claude was about to pass the pipe to Antoine when the opening of the lodge was darkened by Louis. He said in a hostile tone. "Why is it a warrior such as myself is not invited to smoke, especially when it is my uncle who has come calling?"

Old Bear, who was unphased by Louis' hostility looked directly at him and said, "These men have brought me gifts, not you. This is not your concern."

Louis shot back, "Gifts, that is their only reason for coming?"

Old Bear paused to allow the white elephant in the room time to draw out the tongues of the Metis and then said, "When my guests are ready, they will tell me."

Louis looked at his uncle and the others before snorting derisively, "They are like sheep, afraid their throats will be cut."

Claude looked at Old Bear, "We have come to palaver for the white girl you have."

Impetuously, James threw in, "And the black girl, Nettie Bell."

A sad look abruptly gripped Old Bear's face that left him speechless. Louis, on the other hand, was quick to fill the void, he said in a haughty voice, "The girl you call Sarah is dead. She was weak and worthless and threw herself off the buffalo jump." Louis paused and looked at James through the lingering smoke of the friendship pipe and the flickering fire in the center of the room, he said, "The black one, she is mine."

James came back, "How much do you want for her?"

"Nothing, she is not for sale. She is going to be my wife."

Antoine interjected, "You already have a wife, Louis."

"And now I will have two."

"Doe Eyes, Arielle too, they will not like this."

Louis scowled with indifference, "It is not for them to decide."

Antoine said rhetorically, "So, no amount of money or goods can buy this woman from you."

"I've already gave you my answer."

"And if I were to let you and your family come back and be Metis? Winter with us on the Milk River and in the spring go to the Judith Basin and break out land. Give up your warring ways. Would you allow the girl her freedom then?"

Louis laughed, "You want me to give you the girl in exchange for becoming a pig farmer among the whites?" Louis then laughed some more while looking his uncle straight in the eyes. His laughter had not died away when James blurted out, "Then I will fight you for her."

Louis was briefly taken aback by James' challenge. He stared at him through the heavy shadows and smokey haze of the lodge wondering if he was a man to be feared when it came to him that James was much smaller than he was. He was quick to laugh. He said in a mocking tone, "You? You are no man. I will kill you as if you were a bug that crawls on the ground."

The naysayer in James' mind was frantically shouting, *No, look at his size. You cannot beat him. No.* Pride, however, is a powerful thing. James' tongue had already betrayed him. There was no going back, he said, "I saw that you are good at hitting women. Maybe hitting a man, if you are fortunate enough to do so, will get you a response different from Nettie's."

Louis snorted and tossed his head back in an arrogant way before saying, "The guard on the stagecoach tried to stop me from taking this black woman. Now, his scalp hangs in my lodge. I will put yours' next to his."

Sadness and anger instantly competed for space within James. He said, his words laced in bravado that he was uncertain of, "You give me even more reason to kill you. That man was my friend."

"Your friend was a fool."

Old Bear shouted, "Enough. You are like bull elk in the time of yellow leaves. You paw the ground and rub your antlers on trees and whistle and grunt. Enough. It is time to fight or be quiet."

Courage is a fickle thing. Moments ago, it had surged within James. Now, his inner voice pleaded, *Oh, God, please help me.* The naysayer interrupted; *you want God to help you kill a man so that you can have this woman for yourself?*

Louis sensed the fear in James, he said, "Since I am the one being challenged, I will choose the weapon."

Up to this point, James had assumed the fight would be with fists. His eyes reflected shock such that Louis laughed and added, "I choose knives."

Antoine jumped in, "Louis, you are fighting your cousin. This does not need to be a fight to the death."

There was a brief glimmer of recognition of what his uncle had said before Louis came back with total indifference, "No one insults me the way this one has." And with that, Louis got to his feet and said, "I will be waiting by the creek." He then ducked his head and went out the lodge's doorway into the crowd that had gathered. In Lakota, he began making his case. Soon there were shouts of support and an appetite to see him kill this Metis outsider.

Inside Old Bear's lodge there were looks of bewilderment at how, in a few minutes, the tranquility of smoking the pipe had gone to an aura of certain death that everybody assumed would be James'. Antoine looked at him and said, "Son, you don't have to do this. He's a good head taller and thirty pounds heavier than you, and meaner."

James was trembling inside, knowing that he likely had only minutes to live. Not since the battle at Chickamauga had he felt this way. It caused him to touch the red welt of scar tissue on his stomach left by the Yankee bayonet. And then the naysayer in his mind told it like it was, *your cowardice in not going back to the war has allowed you to live this long. You've cheated the Grim Reaper out of his due and now it's time to pay up. Just like the Shaffer boys, except they paid their tab on time.* With great difficulty, James willed himself to say, "I reckon I'll need to borrow a knife."

Antoine closed his eyes and shook his head as Claude withdrew a knife from an elk skin sheath on his hip and handed it to James. "It's scary sharp."

James nodded and took the knife into his shaking hand, a condition that everybody in the lodge observed. He looked down at the knife's ten-inch blade. He knew nothing about knife fighting. As if Claude had read his mind, he added, "A trick I saw a fella pull one time was to yank his hat off in one fell swoop and catch this other fella's knife with it and at the same time stick 'im with his knife. But you gotta be quick as lightning."

James' desperation caused him to seek immediate validation of what Claude had just said, he came back, "Did it work?"

Claude hesitated before saying, "It would have if he wudda stuck the guy better. He didn't give the guy but a pin prick that pissed him off and he come back and killed him. But that hat trick wudda worked if he hadn't been squeamish about stickin' the guy good. There's no do-overs in knife fightin', boy."

Once again, Old Bear cut in. He looked at James. The Crow's feet at the corners of his eyes were relaxed in the poor light. His face was calm like death and violence were as ordinary to him as watching the sun go down. He said, "It is time. Either take the knife and go fight or get on your horse and leave my village, but do not ever come back."

It had occurred to James over the last minute or so that, if he did not fight Louis, his nighttime self-chastisement for not returning to the war would have company. And then, in his mind's eye, he saw Nettie watching him ride out as Old Bear had offered. She was crying. He sighed, angry at the demons that plagued him, and got to his feet.

The Metis, Old Bear, and a mob of voyeurs consisting of most everyone in the village walked the short way to the creek where Louis was sitting on a stump. Upon seeing them coming he got to his feet and sneered at James. "I see the mouse has found its courage."

James said nothing, fearing that it would only add to Louis' anger. His silence abruptly became moot as Louis' eyes shifted beyond James. They grew big, radiating hate like red hot coals. James turned in the direction of Louis' angry stare. There stood Nettie, Doe Eyes and Arielle. Nettie cried out, "No, James, don't do this on my account. He is a killer."

Louis shouted at James, "You should listen to her. Maybe it will allow you to see the sun come up tomorrow." He then laughed, "No, I have decided. I am going to kill you."

Old Bear stopped in front of Louis and then motioned for James to come closer. James gripped his borrowed knife tighter and willed his legs to move next to Old Bear. He looked at Louis and said, "Your right to possess this woman you took in battle is being challenged. You have accepted this challenge rather than give her up. Is this not true?"

Louis seethed the words while staring intently into James' eyes, "Yes, I will kill this fool."

Old Bear nodded and said like his voice was tired, "Then fight." He had barely turned to step away when Louis lashed out at James who sprang backwards, but not before a thin red line about two inches long appeared on his chest. The contrast of the blood on his blue shirt defined the wound very well. An outburst of guttural groans and shouts of approval from the crowd fueled Louis' confidence that he could kill James.

Antoine shouted, "Watch his eyes. Watch his eyes."

In the fog of noise around him, James heard his uncle but was unable to take his eyes from Louis' knife hand. His knife was bigger than James'. Its deer antler handle fit his hand as if it had grown from it.

Above the din of the hostile crowd, Claude called out, "Remember what I told you."

But it got that man killed, thought James.

And then, while smiling and looking James in the eyes, Louis suddenly parried forward two quick steps and slashed at James' stomach. James jumped backwards, and at the same time, brought to bear the adrenaline speed of his knife hand. His blade sliced across Louis' right bicep. A rivulet of dark red blood began to run down his arm. If he was concerned by it, he did not let on that he was. Instead, he yelled a war cry and lunged at James causing him to recoil backwards. For a few seconds it appeared his retreat would be successful, but then his left foot went into a badger hole and down he went. The uncontrolled fall caused his knife hand to be dragged through a lone sagebrush plant. In the process it raked the knife from his grasp. James landed hard. The back of his head hit a big rock that barely protruded above the surface of the ground. It was enough, however, that the torrent of adrenaline in his system could not prevent him from seeing a flash of lightning, then darkness, and then Louis crashing down upon him with his knife ready to stab him. Fortunately for James, his senses recovered in time to thrust his left hand up and intercept Louis' knife hand. Instantly, he was aware of the futility in holding the knife back. Within seconds he would be dead. He could see himself back at Chickamauga and the Yankee bayonet coming down. It was time to pay his dues. And then, it was like God intervened and he hadn't even asked. Louis grunted and abruptly collapsed on top of him. He was limp and heavy and unresponsive as James pushed him off. Standing over him was Doe Eyes. She was holding Louis' own war club. A faint smear of blood showed on the dull nose of the river cobble lashed to its head. Silence had fallen over the crowd. In the distance, ravens, always the irreverent ones, called out. Louis was and wasn't Lakota. Just as he was and wasn't Metis.

Before the sun had set, the Metis and the black woman rode out of the Lakota village, never to return.

EPILOGUE

It was two days before Christmas that a letter addressed to Otto arrived at Charlie Reed's ranch. It read:

December 2, 1874
Pierce, Idaho

Dear Otto & Charlie,

Hope you are doing good and Santa Claus finds your place. By now, I suspect you have received the news regarding Sarah. I was saddened by it as I know you surely are. Sometimes God just doesn't get things right.

Life for us here is good as can be expected. We're scraping by in the gold fields. Will write again someday.

Your friends,
Jack Doyle & Nettie Bell